OUT LAWED

SHERWOOD OUTLAWS

BOOK ONE

HAYLEY OSBORN

LEXITY INK
PUBLISHING

Lexity Ink Publishing
Christchurch, New Zealand

Publisher's Note: This is a work of fiction. Names, characters, places, and incidents are a product of the author's imagination. Locales and public names are sometimes used for atmospheric purposes. Any resemblance to actual people, living or dead, or to businesses, companies, events, institutions, or locales is completely coincidental.

Book Layout ©2019 BookDesignTemplates.com
Cover Design by Covers by Combs
Editing by Melissa A Craven

ISBN 978-0-473-49039-3
also available as an ebook

For Hayden

ONE

SIX months after my seventeenth birthday, in the darkness that came right before dawn, I stood unwillingly at the foot of the largest tree in Sherwood Forest. According to Dad, this was where the magic gathered. My older sister Carrie stood quietly by my side. Her stick-thin body was shaking, but whether from cold or fear, I couldn't tell.

It was difficult to properly see the huge and ancient tree Dad had dragged us to. The Major Oak, its massive gnarled limbs supported by poles, had stood for over a thousand years. It was the oldest tree in Sherwood Forest, and the final stop on our once-in-a-lifetime vacation to the other side of the world. Tomorrow we were supposed to get on a plane back home to New Zealand, but apparently Dad had other plans for one of us.

Instead of staring at the enormous oak with the awe it deserved, all I could think about were Dad's words as he'd gripped each of our wrists and pulled us along the forest trail by the fading light of the full moon. *One of you needs to go back in time to save Robin Hood's life and legend.*

God. It sounded insane. It *was* insane.

"I'm not doing it." I shook my head, attempting to yank my wrist from Dad's hand. Time travel ran in our family. We got to do it only once, and when I went, I wanted to choose where I would go. The same as he'd done. The same as his mother had done. I did not want to go to a place chosen by him.

"You better, Maryanne." Carrie's voice carried through the crisp morning air. "Because I'm not."

Dad dropped our wrists and stepped up to the tree. Raising one hand, he tapped out a staccato beat on the rough bark. Like I said. Insane.

I jerked my head, trying to get Carrie's attention, but her eyes were fixed firmly on our father. She'd managed to pick her way over the uneven trail in a pair of cork wedges, Dad's grip on her wrist probably the only thing keeping her upright. She'd need to run in them if she didn't want to be Dad's science experiment.

"Shhhh." Dad threw us an angry glance. "I need to concentrate."

I folded my arms across my chest, still not believing he meant to go through with this. "Last night you told us to be ready early this morning for, what was it? *Unimaginable fun* on the final day of our vacation? Then you drag us out here in the dark, without Mom or Josh, and announce you're sending one of us back eight-hundred-years into the past to save some dude whose father you killed. Sorry, Dad, but that's not going to happen. Not to me. And," I glanced protectively at Carrie. "I'm pretty sure, not to her, either."

Dad tapped once more on the tree. "I didn't kill him," he murmured. "I ran when we were attacked in the forest. If I'd stayed and fought, Avery Woodhurst might have lived, and eighteen years later his son would not have felt the need to seek revenge."

I huffed out a breath. *That* was what he chose to hear? "Are you even listening?"

"We're at the tipping point, Maryanne. If we don't step into Robin of Woodhurst's life now, he'll spend the rest of his days as a thief rather than a hero. And since this is the last time the portal will open before he seeks his revenge, it's now or never." Dad turned slowly, a shaft of weak moonlight falling on his graying beard. There was a sigh in his voice. "I can hear how scared you are—"

"I'm not scared. I'm annoyed. You're taking away my choice and forcing me to go somewhere I don't want to go, to deal with a problem that has nothing to do with me!" When I was younger, I'd talked to Dad for hours about where I might choose to go when my chance to time travel came. He'd sat and listened, smiling softly. That was back when the two of us would spend hours in each other's company, back when I would tell him everything that was happening in my life. Lately though, we'd barely spoken to each other about anything.

He sighed again, his words slow as if I were a child struggling to understand. "If *you* travel today, you'll be going exactly where you're meant to be." He shrugged. "But it could be that Carrie is our traveler."

I shook my head, glancing again at Carrie. Her face seemed overly pale in the weak light, and she was definitely shaking. There wasn't enough fat on her body to keep her warm in the sundress she was wearing. "We're not going." My desperation to talk him out of this nonsense ramped up a notch as he showed no signs of stopping. I grasped at anything that might change his mind. "What about Josh? He needs me. I'm the only one who can comfort him when he's upset, the only one he'll let read his bedtime story."

My little brother was the most important person in my life. He'd been lying on the couch of our hotel room, sick with the stomach flu when we left in the dark this morning. He'd kicked his thin blanket back revealing his bare stomach, his pajamas rucked up to his chin. As I'd kissed him goodbye, he'd stared at me with those big unseeing eyes—his blindness pushing a familiar surge of guilt through my veins—and reached out for me. I'd known what he wanted. Crouching on the soft carpet beside his makeshift bed, I'd taken his hand and whispered the lines from his favorite storybook into his ear until his eyes fluttered and he fell back asleep. He'd be beside himself if I didn't come home today.

Carrie put her hands on her hips, her glare focused on me. "Don't you think you've done enough damage to that boy? If I were him, I'd be happy the person who hurt me was out of my life. For a while, at least."

"Carrie." Dad's voice was laced with a warning.

I was used to the way Carrie lashed out, trying to make herself feel better by hurting me. Still, her words pierced a hole in my heart. I couldn't argue with her because she was right. I often wondered why Josh put up with me; he had every right to refuse to speak to me ever again.

For all her bluster, I doubted Carrie's twig-like frame was due to her high metabolism as she insisted, but rather from her refusal to eat anything other than a few leaves of lettuce or a slice of cucumber, which had started about the time everything went wrong with Josh. She was in a worse mental state than me, and that was saying something. There was no way either of us would survive what Dad was proposing.

I caught her eye. "Run," I mouthed. She stared at me, unmoving. "Carrie," I whispered, then motioned with my head in the direction we'd come.

She glanced at Dad. He was whispering to himself, taking no notice of us. If we were going to get away, now was the time.

"Run!"

Carrie was already moving. I raced down the trail behind her, jumping the barrier rail around the Major Oak then picking her up as she tripped. Should have made her take those shoes off.

"Stop!" Dad's footsteps were heavy on the leaf-strewn dirt behind us.

I pulled at Carrie's hand, urging her on; I doubted we'd have another chance to escape. "Come on," I tugged on her hand again.

Carrie was slow, puffing even though we'd barely run a hundred meters and Dad was nearly on us, his heavy breathing almost drowning out Carrie's. I should let her go, sprint down the trail and away from them both. I could go back to our hotel, to Mom, who would never force me to go anywhere I didn't want to. And to Josh, whose face would break into a huge smile when I returned.

"Carrie! Maryanne!" Dad was so close. Another five steps and he'd have us. Five more steps and he'd take our choices away from one of us.

I grabbed Carrie's upper arm, holding her upright as she tripped yet again. My thumb and middle fingers reached each other as I held her. I drew in a shocked breath. She was sicker than I'd realized. She needed the sort of support she couldn't get where Dad wanted her to go. If he'd been a better parent, he would have seen his oldest daughter was crying out for help, and that his youngest daughter could have done with some, too. But he was too focused on this foolish mission.

I pushed Carrie ahead of me. "Go! And don't stop until you get back to the hotel."

Her eyes met mine in a shaft of moonlight falling between the trees. She paused, and I thought she might refuse. Then she gave a single nod, slipped off her shoes and sprinted.

"Tell Josh I love him," I called, wishing I was braver. I could outrun her without breaking a sweat, and I desperately wanted to. A better person wouldn't have thought like that. A better person would have been pleased one of us was free.

Dad's hand clamped around my elbow. "Maryanne. What are you doing?" His breath came in heavy bursts.

I sighed. "Nothing."

He looked at the trail behind me, and probably at Carrie's receding back. I braced myself to prevent him going after her, but Dad didn't seem to care for chasing her. He tightened his grip and dragged me back toward the tree. "This is important, Maryanne. I owe a debt to the boy's father. Saving the boy's life and helping him live to his potential will clear that."

"Perhaps you should go back and do it yourself?" I spat, knowing it wasn't possible. I was angry at myself for staying. Angrier at him for forcing this on me.

Dad shook his head. "That's not the way it works, Maryanne. There and back one time. That's all the time travel anyone gets."

I jerked my arm, but his grip was tight. "The *boy* you seem to love so much was nothing more than a common thief. He stole from people. I say let him hang." Dad's opinion of Robin Hood was the opposite of mine. Legend said he was a bandit whose skill with a bow was unmatched, and who took lives the way he took gold. He terrorized the innocent and everything he did was solely to benefit himself. But Dad knew a different version, one where Robin Hood passed that gold to the poor rather than keeping it. A version where Robin Hood was a hero.

Dad's eyes focused somewhere in the distance. "When I was younger, before I went back in time and before I left the boy's father to die, people loved Robin Hood's legend. There were movies about him. Books and comics, too. Now, people don't care, or call him a villain and I can't help but think that's my fault." He shook his head. "History has changed, Maryanne. Robin of Woodhurst's need to avenge his father's death is about to cause him to set fire to a manor house, killing the owner and forcing him to steal just to survive. This is the last chance we have to return his legend to what it was before I traveled. The last chance we have to bring the hope that surrounds his rightful legend back to our world."

Dad stopped in front of the tree, drew a deep breath and knocked against the rough bark, slowly this time. Tap, tap-tap, tap, tap.

"It's not because his legend is dying that I consider him a thief. It's because he *was* one, no matter what version of the story I listen to."

A blast of icy wind blew through the forest, kicking up leaves and dust. I closed my eyes against it, the cold reaching right into my bones. When I opened them again, a young woman stood beside my father.

I took a step back, pulling against Dad's hold on my arm. He hadn't explained the how, only the why. And I hadn't expected anyone else to turn up.

Dad's mouth opened in mild surprise. "You're not who I expected."

The young woman nodded serenely and folded her hands into the wide sleeves of her russet-colored gown. "I am Tabitha. The Keeper of the Portal." She looked my father over. "And you've already used your travel passage, sir." Her voice was soft but strong and she held herself like a queen, her head high, her movements considered. Jewels sparkled in her black hair that was pulled into an elegant knot. She might be the most beautiful woman I'd ever seen.

Dad drew himself up tall. "Not me." He nodded in my direction. "My daughter."

I pulled against Dad's hold. He was not doing this to me. I wasn't going to fix a problem he'd created.

Tabitha's eyes moved to me and I realized she was glowing. Or something around her was glowing, lighting up the forest like daylight. Her bright blue eyes roamed over me, drinking me in. "She doesn't want to."

Dad swallowed. "She's...meant to do this. She just doesn't know it yet. You'll see."

"*She's* not going anywhere." I raised my chin, daring them to disagree.

Tabitha turned to Dad, ignoring me. "Do you have the tithe?"

Dad licked his lips, suddenly nervous. He put his empty hand into the pocket of his sweatshirt and pulled out a brown pouch. It jingled as he passed it to her. "Gold. To pay for her journey both ways."

Tabitha's hand shot out, closing around the pouch and returning to the folds of her dress before I could blink. "Yes. That will do fine."

Dad's shoulders sagged in relief. Mine did the opposite. He was handing over his hard-earned cash to a stranger, so I could go and fix his mistake. If I hadn't quite believed him before, I did now.

I pulled from Dad's grasp and started to run. But instead of moving away, my feet took me forward. Toward the tree. Toward Tabitha. I couldn't stop.

"Please, Dad. Don't make me do this." My voice broke as the words rushed out. He didn't care that he was sending me back to a time when just surviving the day was a battle. He didn't care that I might die alone with a sword through my neck because I happened to be in the wrong place at the wrong time. He didn't care, so long as I fixed his damn mistake. I had no interest in his stupid mistake. I just wanted to stay with my family. I wanted to be in a place I was loved, even if I wasn't loved by him.

Tabitha ran a long-nailed finger down my cheek. She smiled. "Her tether?"

Fumbling in the pocket of his jeans, Dad pulled out a tarnished copper coin. It had a hole in the middle, through which a piece of leather hung. A breath caught in my throat. I'd seen the coin once before. At Nana's house. That day, much to my disappointment, Dad hadn't let me touch it. Today, he held it toward me like an offering, and I didn't want to be anywhere near it.

"Keep this safe, Maryanne. This coin was forged in 1196 and it wants to find its way back there. It'll help Tabitha send you to the right place. It belongs to me, which also tethers it to the current year so Tabitha can return you home once you've saved Robin Hood's legend. After your task is complete, come to this tree, call

Tabitha and she'll bring you back. If you ever find yourself in trouble, go to Lord Robert Fitzwalter in Nottingham. He's your many times great-grandfather, and I knew him when I was there. Tell him I sent you."

I glared at my father, hating him. And hating the big tear that raced down my cheek. I didn't want him to see me cry. "Please don't make me do this," I whispered. Pleaded.

"I have to." A tear rolled down Dad's face, too. I wanted to slap it away. He was doing this to me. He didn't get to be sad about it.

Dad slipped the leather bracelet with the coin dangling from it over my wrist.

"Please. I don't want to die." I didn't want to leave my family, either. Didn't understand how he could do this to me.

He didn't hear, watching Tabitha instead.

Tabitha touched my shoulder with her out-stretched forefinger. A jolt of electricity jumped between us and I closed my eyes tight, waiting for whatever would happen next.

But there was nothing.

I opened my eyes. They were staring at me, waiting. I was still here.

Still here.

A hysteric laugh bubbled from my chest. "It didn't work. I can't travel through time." I felt suddenly light. Safe. They couldn't force me to go to a dangerous place on a fool's errand.

The cold wind whipped up around me, dragging up leaves, dust and twigs. Dad's eyes brightened and he shoved a hessian bag into my hands and gave my cheek a fleeting kiss.

It was happening. I was going.

I reached out to hold onto him, but my hand was shaking too much. He was too far away. It was too late. His lips moved like he was speaking, but I couldn't hear him.

"Tell Josh I love him," I yelled. He didn't answer.

Everything around me slowly faded to white, and I was alone.

And as good as dead.

Two

Voices echoed inside my head. Dad's voice. Tabitha's voice. In unison and alone.

I stretched for them, reaching out to the familiar and begging to stay. Their voices wrapped around my body like a cloak. Warming me. Giving me courage.

But opening my eyes was like waking from a dream. As the world drifted into focus, their voices floated away. Try as I might, I couldn't catch their words.

Chilled air smacked against my skin like I was holding my head out the window of a moving car in a winter storm. I could barely breathe for it, let alone think in a straight line. Maybe I had stopped breathing.

No. If I was dead, my teeth wouldn't be rattling hard enough they might crack. I was still very much alive. Though with the cold, I was starting to wish I wasn't.

It felt like hours before the chill began to recede, and I could feel the tips of my fingers again. It could have been minutes. Slowly, I noticed the forest around me; a bird chirping in the distance, the rustling of leaves beneath me on the ground.

The massive tree above me was a younger version of the one I'd just left. It stood alone, as if the rest of the forest sensed it was special and wanted to give it space. Around its base was barren, nothing but dry, dusty dirt. Farther out where light filtered through the masses of leaves, the tree was surrounded by thick bracken, wild grass, and tree ferns. Despite the heavy grey fog that hid the highest branches and leached all color from the lower ones, the forest was beautiful.

At my feet lay the hessian bag Dad had thrust into my hands. I pulled open the ties, hoping he'd thought to bring me a sweater. Nope. Why would he have thought of something so practical? Inside was an old-fashioned blue dress made from rough wool that would scratch my arms and body. I threw it aside. He should have known better. I never wore dresses in my own time. Black t-shirt, black jean shorts, black Converse on my feet, black leather bracelets and black nail polish to match, that was my current attire. My usual attire. I didn't care that I'd stand out like a sore thumb if I remained in my modern clothing, I wasn't about to start wearing dresses now I'd rather freeze than put that thing on.

And with the current temperature, freeze I probably would.

I put my hand inside the bag again, fishing around to see what else Dad had deemed worthy of a trip to the past. I found a loaf of bread and a chunk of cheese, a bar of soap and a tiny dagger. I tucked the dagger into my sock, not because it would be in easy reach——I had no clue how to use it—but so it didn't stab me while I was carrying the bag on my back. A map might have been a more useful inclusion than the soap. Even better, a map showing where to search for the boy.

"Hello? Anyone?" I yelled into the greyness, wondering if it was foolish to hope someone who knew Robin of Woodhurst might hear me. The fog muffled my words, eating them up as they left my mouth. No one answered. Even the birds were quiet.

Closing my eyes, I tried to ignore the tightness in my gut. I could not allow myself to give in to fear or panic. Find people, see if they could tell me where to find the boy, then tell the boy to forget about revenge and become a thief instead—but keep none of the spoils—that was my plan. Easy, hopefully. I needed to get it done and return home to my little brother.

I got to my feet. A narrow trail led through the bracken and tree ferns. Throwing my bag over my shoulder, I started down it, picking between low hanging branches along the rough path, while I considered the task Dad had set. Robin of Woodhurst was the boy's name. I should probably start referring to him by it. His name and the fact he was about eighteen, were the only things I knew. I had no idea what he looked like, what his current occupation might be or where he lived. Dad hadn't been able to source that information. He didn't think it would matter; he was certain the magic from the portal would bring us together. Even if that proved to be true, the tightness in my gut would have eased a little if I at least knew where to start searching for him.

A high-pitched clanging drifted through the trees, rhythmical and probably human. I started toward it.

As the noise grew, voices—shouting—accompanied the sound. People. Exactly what I needed. I pushed through low hanging branches heavy with leaves, stopping at the top of a small rise where the fog cleared and the forest thinned. Down below was a large field with a cluster of wooden huts in the center. Smoke spiraled from most of them. It took me a moment to realize the smoke wasn't from chimneys, but from the burning thatch of the roofs. It took another moment to realize the shouting—screaming, now I was this close—came from people running for their lives. Not in terror of the fires, but from men on horseback racing through the muddy and rutted village streets slashing their swords at anything that moved.

The riders were organized, part of a team, all wearing chainmail beneath their long burgundy and gold riding cloaks. They chased down villagers who scrambled for the forest. Men, women or children, the riders didn't make any distinction. They killed as people fled. Everywhere I looked, there was a rider with his sword raised, ready to sever an arm, or leg, or head. Or there was a rider pulling a ruby-red blade from a newly lifeless body. Or a child with a tear-stained face alone and screaming in fear.

A kick of adrenalin shot through me. I had to hide. Get away from this place, keep myself safe. As I thought it, my eyes caught on a woman sprinting up the slope toward me. Her face contorted in terror. One hand was wrapped in her faded grey skirt, lifting it high so she didn't trip. The other was wound tightly around the child clinging to her hip. Behind her, a man on horseback chased her down, his sword raised ready to strike.

The hoof beats pounding against the ground were hypnotic, a rhythmic instruction speaking to me above the din of the massacre. *Run-hide, run-hide, run-hide.*

I should have.

Instead, I bent and picked up a rock from the ground, took three steps forward and hurled it as hard as I could.

I was too slow. The rock hit the rider's thigh just as he brought his sword down into the woman's shoulder. She dropped to her knees with a grunt, placing the child delicately on the ground as she went down.

The rider's dark eyes zoned in on me. He lifted his sword, streams of ruby red flowing over the decorative etchings of his blade and down his fingers. If I didn't move, I would be next.

I turned and sprinted, the foggy edge of the forest close enough I could feel the dampness on my skin, but too far to outrun the edge of a sword.

Before I got to the tree line, something flew from the forest, whistling over my head. The rider screamed in pain and I twisted around to see him fall headfirst from his horse, an arrow protruding from the center of his chest.

Time slowed as I stared at him, mesmerized. Blood, dark red and slick, pooled around the arrow and dripped over his burgundy and gold riding cloak. Dead. Or about to be, judging by the speed his blood was exiting his body. Not that I could muster any sympathy. After terrorizing that woman, he deserved to end his day exactly this way.

A crying child pulled me from my stupor.

The woman's baby had balled her little hands into fists and was screaming at the top of her lungs. I couldn't blame her when I felt like doing pretty much the same thing. I glanced at the soldiers in the village, unsure if I was brave enough to go to the girl. None of the riders seemed to have any interest in me at this moment—they had other targets. Whoever had sent the arrow from the forest hadn't shot at me yet, and there'd been plenty of opportunity, so I had to assume they'd moved onto another target as well. I couldn't possibly leave a helpless child alone amongst the carnage while I ran to safety. I forced myself to jog back down the hill to the little girl.

As I bent to scoop her up, the woman groaned. I crouched beside her and touched her shoulder lightly. Her eyelids fluttered, then quickly closed again, the way Josh's eyes had done as I kissed him goodbye this morning.

There was so much blood flowing from the deep wound in the woman's shoulder, I couldn't believe she was still alive.

Her good hand shot out and gripped my wrist so tightly it pinched. "Run...get away from...here. My sister, Edwina, is...on her way...from Blyth. Take my Ellie to her."

"I'll get help for you. You're going to be all right." My lie was hollow. The woman's face was so white, she was the same pallor my grandfather had been in his casket.

She didn't answer. But her hand on my wrist loosened then fell heavily to the ground.

She was dead.

Dead.

I squeezed my eyes shut, hoping when I opened them I'd be back in my own time at the Major Oak, with Carrie shivering beside me. Hoping this was just a nightmare.

Wish as I might, I couldn't blank out the metallic smell of blood. This was no dream. I was here, and people were dying around me.

If I didn't move, I'd end up like the woman. Scooping the little girl into my arms, I sprinted for the forest. The twenty steps or so felt more like five hundred.

As I reached the trees, someone grabbed me roughly around the shoulders and pulled me onto the ground. Before I could scream, a big dirty hand clamped over my mouth.

THREE

"QUIET!" A boy a year or two older than me held me down. His grip across my mouth was tight, fingers digging into my cheek. His sandy blond hair fell forward, hiding his entire face except for one green and very angry eye. How had I run from one life-threatening situation straight into another? Despite his warning, I squealed and wriggled, desperate to loosen his grasp. But he was too big. Too strong.

The child began to cry again.

"And keep her quiet too. Unless you want to end up like your friend down there." He removed his hand and rose swiftly to his feet. A bow rested over one shoulder, and a sword was suspended at his waist. His eyes rolled quickly over me, stopping, not on my revealing-for-this-time-period clothing, but on my face. He stilled, his mouth slightly open and a frown creasing his forehead. For a moment, it seemed like he might turn and run. Or perhaps drag me down to the village and hand me over to those riders. Then he squared his shoulders and met my eyes, some sort of challenge flaring in them.

I scooped up the baby, his gaze making me uneasy. "She wasn't..." It suddenly seemed important I tell him I didn't know that woman, but before I could, the boy huffed out a breath and strode toward the edge of the forest.

"If you want to live, don't move." He set his mouth in a thin straight line, speaking just louder than a whisper.

With a shaky sigh, I tightened my grip on Ellie, cuddling her close. The hug was as much for my benefit as hers. My hands shook. My whole body shook. There was a large possibility there would be more than one person crying any moment, and the other set of tears wasn't going to come from the boy at the edge of the forest. I'd just traveled eight-hundred years through time to watch people die. Killed in cold blood. I'd almost been killed myself. Part of me was desperate to run away; the rest of me was too scared to move.

Ellie shifted in my arms and began to cry again. She wanted her mom, not some stranger from a different time. The boy turned toward us, his eyes hard. He didn't need to speak for me to understand. We were all dead if I didn't shut her up.

I murmured meaningless words in Ellie's ear trying to convince her my rigid posture didn't mean I was terrified. The boy turned back to the battle below and I relaxed a fraction. It was hard enough keeping Ellie quiet without him watching while I did it.

I flicked one of the many leather bracelets off my wrist—making sure it wasn't my tether—and held it out to her, twisting it between my finger and thumb before dropping it over her wrist. Immediately, she set about figuring how to get it off. Without crying. The slightest tremor of relief rolled through me.

The screams in the village were growing less, the clashing of swords almost gone and the smell of smoke heavy. Although that undoubtedly meant bad things for the villagers, for me, the baby and the boy, it might mean freedom was close. With any luck, the riders would tire of their one-sided fight and disappear back to wherever they'd come from.

Stretching my neck above the bracken, I watched the boy, because looking at him didn't create a knot of terror in my stomach the way watching the riders did. He stood beside a birch tree, his dark brown fur-lined cloak making him almost invisible against the undergrowth; it was only his blond hair that made him visible.

Now that his angry eyes weren't on me, I took him in properly. He was tall, almost a head taller than me, with broad shoulders and strong legs, the lines of his quads visible through his dark green pants. His shoulder length hair was partially tied at the back of his neck, the front portion having come loose. Good looking, with those high cheekbones and full lips. But only if I ignored the angry eyes.

His bow was raised, the string pulled taut against his cheek while he lined up his target. His form was so perfect, the local archery range could have posted a picture of him on their wall as a lesson. Moving slightly, he readjusted his aim then loosed the arrow. The distance was long and the chances of the arrow hitting the rider were slim. But it flew straight and lodged into the shoulder of a rider who was holding his bloody sword high in the air. By the time I looked back at the boy, he had another arrow nocked and stood, muscles tensed, waiting to take his next shot. With the fog swirling around his feet, he seemed more like a mythical warrior than a teenage boy. More like the legend I was here to find.

A loud whistle sounded from the village and as one, the riders turned their horses around and thundered up the narrow trail and into the forest. Suddenly the air was thick with silence. There wasn't a person left standing down there.

I waited, hoping none of them would ride this way, searching for us.

The boy watched their backs, too, as if waiting for the same thing. Only once the last rider had disappeared did he turn and walk toward us, his bow hanging loosely between his fingers. He stopped beside me, watching Ellie play with my leather bracelet.

I wondered if I should fear him. He was as much a killer as the riders had been, yet I didn't think he was going to kill me.

When he didn't speak, I filled the silence, voicing the thought I'd been trying to push from my head. "She was killed. This little girl's mother is dead." I'm not sure why I said it. The boy knew already. Perhaps I was simply trying to make sense of it in my mind. "Was it you who shot the rider who killed her? The one who was about to kill me?"

He nodded.

I drew my lips up into an almost-smile, the best I could manage right now, and blinked slowly. I was alive because of him. "Thank you," I said, quietly.

His eyebrows rose, surprised, and his gaze shifted to me. As he searched my face, I found myself glued to the spot, unsure whether his stare made me uncomfortable or breathless. Even once he'd broken his gaze to look back at the village below, and I'd gulped down a breath of air to steady my racing heart, I still didn't know.

The village was quiet and still, and the fog was beginning to creep slowly out of the forest toward the burning huts. Nausea rose in my chest as I realized what that meant.

"The rest of your friends didn't fare so well."

I shook my head. "They're not my friends. I...I don't know them."

His eyes rested on me for a second, like something in that statement made him curious. But he didn't ask, and a moment later, he turned back to the scene below.

I ran my hands through my long hair, wishing I could rub out the image of Ellie's mother's dead eyes, which appeared every time I blinked. "They just...killed them all. Those people didn't stand a chance."

Still gazing at the village, he nodded.

"Why?" My voice wobbled. Now we weren't in imminent danger, the enormity of what I'd witnessed was beginning to hit me. People were dead. Lots of people. And I'd watched it happen. "Why did they do it?"

He swallowed, lifting one shoulder. "Because they can." He met my eyes. "Although I guess you'd know more about that than I do."

It was too much effort to explain again that I didn't know these people, so I let his comment slide, looking from the village to the boy, then back again. "What do we do now? Should we go down there and check whether anyone is alive?" My voice was about an octave higher than usual. I didn't want to go down to the village—if those riders came back, we would die. Yet, I couldn't leave without first checking for survivors.

He nodded, holding his bow in his left hand and scooping the baby up with his right before starting down the hill. For the second time in as many hours, I forced myself to ignore the absolute terror that was unraveling in my gut. Curling up in a ball and sobbing seemed like a better option than following him down to the site of the massacre. Except.

Except I was here for as long as it took to complete Dad's task, and this, it seemed, was what life was like eight hundred years ago. The sooner I put on my big girl pants and dealt with it, the sooner I'd be able to ask the boy if he knew Robin Hood. I followed him down the hill.

"What's your name?" I called quietly, as we picked our way down one side of a rutted trail. "I'm Maryanne."

He turned slowly to face me. This time, when I met his eyes, there was something hard there, something angry, something that made me step back.

"You think that will fool people?"

I frowned. "Fool people?"

He huffed out a breath and turned away.

He was kind of rude, but maybe that's how people were in this time, too. I tried again. "I have no idea what you're talking about, but it would make things easier if I knew what to call you.'

He paused, his back to me and shoulders hunched. I looked at the bow slung over his shoulder, the quiver on his back. At the dark green of his tunic and the sword at his waist, and wondered. Could it be that easy? Could this be the Robin of Woodhurst I was here to find?

Without looking at me, he spoke over his shoulder. "Henry. My name's Henry."

I let out a breath. Not Robin Hood. Good. This boy was prickly. I didn't like the idea of having to work with someone like him to get back home.

"Nice to meet you," I mumbled.

It was even quieter down beside the burning huts than it had seemed in the forest. All but three homes were reduced to ashes, the fires burned almost out. I followed a few steps behind Henry as he moved between each person on the ground, checking if they were alive, then closing their eyes when they weren't. Which was everyone.

"Is there someone we should call for? Like the——" I nearly said police but stopped myself. "Someone who can help?" My voice wobbled again. I felt useless. I *was* useless. I knew nothing about survival in the twelfth century.

Henry put the baby on the ground in the open leaving her to play in the dirt and crouched over the body of a little girl younger than Josh, his lips still set in that grim line. As I spoke, he slowly raised his head, eyes narrowed. "And who, exactly, were you planning to call for?" Everything, from the set of his shoulders to the curl of his fingers, looked relaxed, yet I couldn't get past the feeling he was prepared to spring up and sprint, or perhaps fight, should I utter the wrong words.

"I don't know. But there must be someone. A healer?"

Henry sighed. "You can call to whoever you like, but it won't stop any of these people being dead."

I clenched my teeth together to stop my jaw from trembling, and the tears that were so close from spilling. I knew that. "What about those riders? The people who did this? We need to tell someone about them, make sure they don't get away with it."

"Grand idea, my lady. But since they're the King's men, I think it's safe to assume they *have* gotten away with it."

Great, he'd forgotten my name already. As much as I wanted to call him on it, I had more important questions. "What makes you so sure it was the King's men?"

"Burgundy and gold. Nottingham's colors. And since King Richard has left his cousin, the Sheriff, in charge in his absence, they are the King's men." He rolled an old woman onto her back. The bodice of her brown dress was drenched in blood. He leaned over her and listened for her breathing, then closed her eyes and moved onto the next one, a little boy.

These had been people half an hour ago, now they were bodies.

A couple of chickens pecked for food on the straw-covered floor of one of the remaining huts. Outside, two earthen pots lay broken in half, the dirt around them wet with water or whatever had been stored in them. These simple huts had been homes; not long ago they'd been lived in.

I swallowed deeply. Perhaps helping would make me feel better. "Can I do anything?"

He blinked warily, searching my face again. Whatever anger he'd been holding onto slipped away. "All I'm concerned with is checking for survivors then getting out of here in case the soldiers return, or before someone else comes along and blames us for this." He waved his hand around the village. "If you want to do the same, I'd be most grateful. If not, kindly keep quiet and let me finish."

He turned back to the fallen people, pushing his cloak aside to keep from dirtying it.

With clammy hands, I walked over to the person nearest me—the body. The only other dead person I'd ever seen was Grandad. This person, this man, was most definitely dead. His arm had been completely severed and lay on the dirt nearby, blood making the ground around him sticky. I put my hand over my mouth, swallowing down my nausea and crouched beside him, gently closing his eyes. "Do you know where I might find Robin of Woodhurst?" I called to Henry, hoping a conversation would remove the sick feeling in my gut.

His head shot up. His eyes were again hard, and I was pinned to the spot, unable to move, unable to look away, but knowing I'd somehow said the wrong thing.

"Is this some kind of joke?" He kept his voice quiet, but there was something menacing behind it.

I shook my head. "No. I just...I need to find him. It...doesn't matter." It did. But if asking Henry that question elicited a response so angry, I'd find out from someone else.

"He's dead." Henry spoke so quietly, I almost missed it.

"Pardon me?"

"Dead. Robin of Woodhurst is dead. Has been for six years."

All the air in my lungs left me in a rush. "Dead?" How could that be? Why hadn't Dad known? He'd said the boy, Robin, would be hanged within the next few weeks for burning down a manor house with the owner inside. He'd said Robin's need for revenge had driven him to do it. Robin was supposed to be alive for me to find. He was supposed to turn into a thief with a conscience so I could go home.

Henry's eyes narrowed. "Yes, dead. An arrow shot into his unsuspecting back." He glanced around at the devastated village. "I'm sure you understand the concept."

I shook my head. This wasn't right. I couldn't help him if he was in the ground already. "Are you sure?"

He blinked so slowly I didn't think he was ever going to open his eyes again. "More than sure. Saw it happen with my own eyes."

No. Dad would have known. Perhaps...perhaps I hadn't come to the right time. That had to be it. My racing heart slowed a little. Maybe Tabitha had screwed up and I was ten years too late. "Who is your King?"

"I'm sure you know the answer to that question, even if you've been gone a while."

I pulled my lips into a tight smile, trying to keep my growing impatience, and annoyance at his tone, in check. This was important. "Humor me."

Henry set his jaw and gave a measured nod. "Richard."

"So, this year is 1196?" I cringed as I spoke. Asking something like that could lead to questions from Henry that I didn't want to answer; everyone should know what year it is.

"Don't be ridiculous." The narrowed eyes and irritated glare returned to his face.

I couldn't breathe, felt like I was going to be sick. I'd been sent to the wrong time. And I didn't know how to get out of here.

Henry shook his head and climbed to his feet. "As if anyone could live that long. It's the seventh year."

The confusion must have shown on my face, because he sighed loudly. "Of King Richard's reign."

When I was much younger, before Dad started hating me and long before he'd started seeing me as a way to right his wrongs, we'd spent many happy hours together every summer down in Nana's little study, learning about our ancestors. Robert Fitzwalter—our most famous relative—had a childhood friend who had awed me so much, I'd done a little extra research. Prince Richard, later to become King Richard the First. The seventh year of his reign was the year I knew as 1196.

I laughed aloud, a jagged, crazy sound. I was exactly where I was supposed to be, but the person I was supposed to help was no longer alive. I had no clue what to do next.

Henry bent over another blood-soaked body. "I think you might be in shock, my lady."

Quite possibly.

I wrapped my arms around myself, the coldness I'd felt at the Major Oak beginning to seep into my bones again. I didn't want to be here.

Henry took a long look at me, then disappeared into one of the remaining huts, returning a moment later with a pile of clothing in his arms.

"Here." He held the pile out to me.

The moment I took it from him, I wished I could hand it all back. It stank like manure and body odor. "What am I supposed to do with this?"

"Dress yourself." Henry went to check on another villager, not looking up as he spoke. "You're in your underwear. And you're shivering."

I climbed to my feet, feeling like I was watching myself from above. I had a headache and I wasn't sure if it came from the trip through time, or the magic—or whatever it was—that helped me understand what Henry was saying. Each time I spoke, the words that came from my lips were not how I wanted to say them—same meaning, different words. Likewise, when he spoke to me, if I concentrated hard enough, I heard something other than what he was saying. It was subtle, and the longer I was here, the less I was noticing it. But the version of English these people spoke was most definitely different to mine. The adjustments I was hearing were helping us understand each other, but it was also hurting my head.

I walked into a hut, bringing the pile of clothing with me. Henry had found a brown dress of a similar coarse material to the one Dad had sent for me. I held it up against me. It was ankle-length with long wide sleeves. It would probably fit, and along with the cloak he'd found, would keep me warmer than my current attire. But I wasn't wearing a dress.

Feeling like a thief, I picked up a pair of pants from the end of a straw mattress and pulled them on. They fit nicely around my waist, even if they were a little tight in the leg. I slipped on an undershirt and tunic—all of which smelled better than the dress—then wrapped the cloak Henry had found around my shoulders. Henry hadn't given me shoes, but there was nothing wrong with my Converse, so I left them on.

I was already warmer, which meant I could think properly again. Form a plan, because I couldn't stay here, in this time. There was no point with Robin of Woodhurst dead already. I needed to get back to the Major Oak, call Tabitha and ask her to take me home.

Stepping out of the hut, I called to Henry. "Will those soldiers be gone by now?"

Henry looked up. He raised his eyebrows, but if he was surprised to see me in men's clothing, he didn't say so. Instead, he dropped his head to concentrate on the body beside him.

I took a deep breath, carefully ignoring his snub in my eagerness to leave. "It was nice to meet you, Henry. I'll be on my way now."

Henry's head shot up. "You're leaving?"

I gave him a tight smile, surprised he cared one way or the other. "Is that a problem?"

He opened his mouth to speak, closed it, then opened it again. Grimacing, he asked, "Do you have somewhere to go? A safe place to stay?"

"I think so." Hoped so.

He let out a breath, which I could only assume was relief at not having to help me find a bed for the night.

I narrowed my eyes. He might be having a bad day, but I was pretty sure mine trumped whatever was going on in his. "Why bother asking when you clearly don't want to help?"

His face clouded as he stared at me, then he blinked and shook his head, and the confusion was gone. "I'm sorry if I seemed insincere. It wasn't my intention." He pressed two fingers to the bridge of his nose. "I've...got somewhere else I'm supposed to be. Something else I'm supposed to be doing. But if you need a place to sleep tonight, I can help you."

I could feel his need to be gone from here, to finish whatever business he'd been doing before the soldiers interrupted. I understood it. Felt exactly the same way.

I shook my head. "I'm fine. Thank you." He was still hovering over a body as I started up the hill toward the forest. I'd seen how Dad had knocked on the tree to summon Tabitha. I could do that, too. I'd explain why I couldn't complete Dad's task and I'd be back in our hotel in time to read Josh his bedtime story. Tears pricked my eyes as I imagined the pout on his lips as he implored me to read it again.

This place, the twelfth century, was dangerous and dirty. All anyone wanted to do was shove a sword through their enemy's gut or fire an arrow through their back. Since the day I turned five and learned I would get one chance to time travel, I'd been dreaming about the place and time I'd choose to visit. That place was not twelfth century England. I wanted to go back and meet Princess Diana, or Amelia Earhart. Or maybe someone from my own country like Kate Sheppard or Dame Whina Cooper. I certainly wouldn't have come somewhere as dangerous as this. Now I knew I couldn't complete Dad's task, I was out of here.

I didn't hear Henry's footsteps until he was beside me on the rutted trail. "Running out on your responsibilities again, my lady?" His voice was like a honey-covered blade, and he jumped from one mood to another faster than I could change my clothes.

I glared at him. I had plenty of faults, but irresponsibility wasn't one of them. "You don't know me. You have no idea how responsible I am."

"You were about to leave a helpless child to fend for herself. I'd say I do have an idea on your definition of responsible." He held the squirming baby in his outstretched arms. "Damned if I'm going to be left with a baby."

How could I have forgotten her? I hadn't saved her just to leave her to die alone in that village. I wasn't thinking straight and wasn't sure whether to blame the time travel, or the massacre. I snatched Ellie from his arms, covering my embarrassment with snark. "It's a little early in our relationship to be having this conversation, don't you think?" I smiled tightly.

Something I couldn't decipher sparked in his eyes, something that made my heart stall. "No matter how long we've known each other, it will still be too early for that particular conversation." His tone was too soft for him to be truly offended and he was hiding a smile.

I lifted my chin, matching his tone as I walked away. "Likewise."

Maybe Ellie could come home with me. Josh would love a baby sister. And having someone else to focus on might be the distraction Carrie needed to consider getting herself well again since she'd struggled almost as much as me since Josh's accident. Or maybe I could go home via Blyth and find Ellie's aunt before going back to the tree.

I hugged Ellie to my chest, murmuring in her ear. She had to stay quiet once we reached the forest, which meant I had to convince her she was safe with me.

"Keep off the wide trails. They're dangerous." Henry's voice floated up on the foggy air. When I turned back to thank him, he was shaking his head slowly as if he was surprised. The strength of his gaze made my words dry in my mouth, so I left without speaking.

I pushed through the thick bracken at the edge of the forest and into even denser undergrowth. It was dark among the trees, like the last few minutes before dusk turns to night. Nothing looked familiar. The trees seemed taller, the undergrowth thicker and the fog heavier. I squeezed Ellie tight and pushed on, hoping there were no soldiers nearby to hear us.

A branch broke behind me.

My heart dropped deep into my stomach. I spun around, expecting to find a man in a burgundy and gold cloak. Instead, there was a young woman wearing a murky brown dress.

The bodice was stained red with blood, but not her own.

She raised her chin, her voice wobbling as she spoke. "You have my niece. I'd like her back." She took a step forward.

I gripped Ellie tighter as I tried to remember what instructions her ma had given me in the moments before she died.

"Her name is Ellie. Her ma, my sister, died today." The girl's voice shook, but there were no tears. "I arrived from Blyth about the same time the soldiers got here."

My eyebrows rose. "Edwina?"

A tear rolled down her cheek. "I tried to get to her, but you were quicker. I watched you from the forest when you went down to the village. I was too scared to come out. But I'd like her back. She's...she's my only family now."

"Ellie's mother said you'd look after her."

Another tear rolled down her cheek. "She's all I have left." She reached out her hand toward the little girl. Ellie took hold of her finger and smiled. It was the first smile I'd seen. I guessed Josh wouldn't be getting a little sister after all. I passed the baby to Edwina.

"Thank you for saving her." Her lips quivered. "I don't know how I can repay you."

I shook my head. "You don't have to. I'd have wanted someone to do the same thing if my little brother was in trouble."

Her lips wavered again, and she hugged the baby tight. Then she nodded and turned, disappearing into the forest.

I drew a deep breath, far less confident of my ability to find the tree now I was alone. Not that Ellie could have helped, but she at least kept me calm. I drew my cloak tightly around myself and started walking, pushing past branches that scratched at my face. I could do this. I would. Even if every damn tree looked exactly like every other bloody tree in this forest.

"Where are you heading?" There was a sigh in Henry's voice as he appeared suddenly beside me. "I'll take you."

"I thought you had someplace better to be." As much as I wanted to be angry for his comments before I left, I was tired and hungry, and my snark lacked substance. He was trying to help. The least I could do was be pleasant.

"I..." He shrugged. "It can wait." His lips stretched into a tentative smile. Perhaps I wasn't the only one who'd decided to play nice. "The forest can be a dangerous place."

With another deep breath, I swallowed my pride. I couldn't find my way to the tree without help. "To the Major Oak."

Henry frowned.

"The biggest tree in the forest?" At least, I hoped it was.

"Ah." He nodded. "Well, you're going the wrong way." He straightened the bow over his left shoulder, and beckoning with his head, turned left and pushed through the thick undergrowth.

I followed, images of bloodstained people running through my head, their screams for mercy loud in my ears. It didn't take much to imagine what would happen if the soldiers found us.

But Henry kept us on the narrowest of trails, and we saw no one else. In less time than I expected, he nodded to a huge tree. My shoulders sagged. It was the same place I'd woken up; the dress Dad had given me was lying in the long grass where I'd tossed it.

"Thank you for your help, Henry. Good luck with...wherever you're heading next." I waited for him to excuse himself, to leave me here. When he didn't, I shrugged and walked over to the tree. If he wanted to watch, what did it matter?

The clearing felt different than earlier. The chill was gone, and the air no longer alive.

"Does the tree have a name?" My words fell almost on top of each other in my rush to get them out, to cover the fear rising inside me. The fear that said because I was unable to find Robin of

Woodhurst, I might be stuck here until...until forever.

Henry shrugged. "Not officially. I've always called it Big Tree. This isn't where you wanted to go?" Henry's forehead creased. He seemed more relaxed than he had earlier. Perhaps because there were no soldiers here.

"It is." So long as Tabitha turned up. Going around the back of the tree, away from his always-watching eyes, I tapped on the trunk using the same rhythm Dad had used. *Tap, tap-tap, tap, tap.*

Nothing happened.

I moved to the front, tapping again. Henry watched silently, walking toward the tree and slipping his bow and quiver from his shoulders. He set them to rest against the trunk and stretched out his back before untying the piece of leather that bound his hair, quickly capturing the loose strands and retying it, while I tapped again. "Everything all right?" His raised eyebrow glance suggest he thought I was totally nuts. I probably would have felt the same in his shoes.

"I thought...someone was supposed to meet me here." Not quite true, but close enough to avoid unanswerable questions.

I was suddenly short of breath. She wasn't here. Tabitha wasn't here.

Henry's eyebrow's rose. "Are you sure they were meeting you *here*? Not down in Edwinstowe?" When I didn't answer, he clarified. "The village? Where the soldiers were?"

I shook my head again. "She wasn't meeting me there. I thought...she'd be here. My mistake, I guess."

Henry rolled his eyes over me, lips pursed. Finally, he said, "If you need to wait for her, I can stay a little longer. Or...you can travel with me. I have a safe place we can sleep tonight."

As much as I didn't want to admit it, I already knew she wasn't coming. The magic that had been in the air this morning was gone. "She'd be here by now if she was coming." I took a deep breath. I had to trust someone; it might as well be him. "A safe place sounds good."

Suddenly Henry put a finger in the air, his body going still. He turned slowly away from me. "Stay right there," he whispered.

My heart rate tripled. Visions of soldiers and swords filled my mind. I sank back against the Big Tree, wrapping my arms around my waist to keep from shaking.

Henry crept toward the trail, his hand resting loosely on the hilt of his sword, his shoulders tight with tension. Whatever he'd seen or heard, I hadn't. I squinted into the forest, searching between trees, undergrowth and fog, trying to find whatever had put him on edge. Then the fog shifted, and I saw.

A soldier.

Striding down the trail toward us.

Four

THE soldier wore a neatly clipped full-face beard, and his long black hair was pulled in at the back of his neck. Now I'd seen him, I could hear the slight jingling of his chainmail as he moved.

Like Henry's, the soldier's hand rested on his sword. He almost certainly knew we were here. I pushed myself farther back against the oak, the bark rough against my back.

A movement among the trees and fog caught my eye—another soldier. I glanced quickly at Henry, then peered into the forest again. Henry's full attention was on the first soldier. I didn't think he'd seen the second one.

"Everything all right?" The soldier stopped just short of stepping beneath the large canopy the Major Oak provided and looked between Henry and myself. His hand flexed on the grip of his sword.

Henry inclined his head, smiling at the man. "Of course. It's a beautiful day for a walk in the forest."

The soldier's eyes narrowed, then fell on the bow leaning against the tree. "You know it's against the law to carry a bow in this part of the forest."

"Well then, it's lucky neither of us are carrying one. Henry nodded over his shoulder. "That was there when we got here." He took a casual step toward the soldier, his head high. Nothing about his posture said he was frightened by the man. Unlike me.

"Don't get smart with me, boy. I could arrest you right now."

Henry twisted his head. "Under arrest, but alive. Better than many who've met you today, I think." His tone was light even though his words were heavy.

Irritation flashed in the soldier's eyes. "Those people were little better than animals. Animals who hadn't paid their taxes. They'd been warned and knew what would happen if they didn't."

Henry clenched his teeth and balled his empty hand into a fist. "Those people had families. It's been a hard year. They deserved leniency."

The soldier's face hardened. "That is not your concern, boy. You're under arrest for carrying a bow in the forest. You're coming to Nottingham with me."

Henry shook his head. "No. I'm not."

The soldier moved in the trees again and I stiffened. Whether there was one more out there, or twenty more, we were in serious trouble.

"Henry!" I whispered loudly. Somehow, I had to alert him, but not the soldier.

Henry's eyes remained on the soldier, as if he hadn't even heard me. Perhaps he hadn't.

I crouched and reluctantly pulled an arrow from the quiver resting beside me against the tree. The wood was cool between my fingers. The simple act of touching it made my heart quicken, and the all-too-familiar guilt pressed heavily on my shoulders. I hated the feeling, but I wasn't about to die today.

Swallowing down the nausea in my throat, I glanced at Henry's bow. I didn't want to touch it, but from the edge of my vision, I saw the movement again. I'd used a bow hundreds of times before—maybe even thousands. I could make myself do it now. The soldier was still arguing with

Henry, his burgundy and gold cloak a reminder of the killing the soldiers had done today. Of how they killed swiftly and without mercy, killed defenseless women and children, too.

A reminder that I had no choice.

Ignoring my shaking hand, I picked up the bow and nocked the arrow. All I had to do was aim.

"Henry." No response. I drew the string back beside my cheek.

Trying to put off the inevitable, I called to him again, louder this time. "Robin!" I blinked. Dad, with all his talk of Robin Hood, was to blame for that little slip up. Henry's gaze flicked in my direction, then returned to the soldier. There was nothing he could do while that man stood in front of him.

Memories of the last time I'd held a bow came flooding back. Before I could blink them away, I saw the yellow center ring of the target, and my arrow leaving my bow. This was nothing like that day. This was a matter of life or death. I forced myself to focus on the shot that would save two lives, dragging in huge gasps of air until a familiar calmness washed over me.

As the second soldier moved again, I let my arrow go. It flew into the trees at the exact moment Henry and the soldier drew their swords, the metallic hiss ringing around the forest. There was movement in the trees followed by the cracking of branches as my soldier fell. A hit. At least I wouldn't have to force myself to fire off another arrow. Now Henry just needed to get rid of his soldier, and so long as there were no others lurking out there, we'd be fine.

Henry's soldier swung his sword, but Henry parried the blow. Taking the briefest moment to balance himself, Henry swung at him. Within seconds, he'd disarmed the man, the soldier's weapon falling onto the ground with a thud. Henry placed the tip of his sword on the man's throat.

The soldier put his hands up by his ears, his voice shaking as he spoke. "Don't kill me, please. I have a family."

"I have no intention of killing you. *I'm* not that sort of person." Henry tilted his head to the side. "I believe you were saying something about how we should be careful on the rest of our journey?"

The soldier nodded enthusiastically, sensing a reprieve.

"Thought so." Henry pulled his sword away.

The soldier didn't wait another second, turning and sprinting in the direction he'd come from.

Henry watched him go, then looked at me with the shadow of a grin. "Well, that was fun." He bent and picked up the soldier's sword. "I see you've learned how to use a bow."

It was almost a question, asked with a raised eyebrow, but he didn't give me the chance to answer. "Fire an arrow into that patch of scrub out to his right. Don't hit him, just scare him so he doesn't go back and tell his friends where to find us." He followed the soldier's path with his eyes.

I glanced down at the bow hanging loosely between my fingertips, then at the retreating soldier. The burgundy and gold of his cape made him an easy target through the foggy and colorless forest. But he was running away, not attacking us. Suddenly, my hands began to shake and instead of seeing the soldier, I saw a pair of huge blue eyes looking up at me. They were full of pain and begging me to do something.

Henry mumbled a soft curse as the bow slipped from my fingers and clattered to the ground. The sound pulled me back to the present, back to what I'd just done. "I think there's more of them. Soldiers." I nodded in the direction I'd seen someone. "Out there."

Henry retied the loose strands of his hair again, then bent and picked up the bow and quiver, sliding both over his shoulder. "I'm quite sure there are." His movements were casual, but his jaw was tight.

"No. You don't understand. I saw someone, out there." None of his weapons were in his hands ready to use like they should have been.

He watched me a moment, something I couldn't decipher flickering in his eyes. "We need to go."

I followed Henry down the narrow trail, stopping when he did a moment later. He peered into the undergrowth. "More soldiers, you say?" He beckoned me to follow, stepping off the trail and pushing through the thick bracken. We'd gone less than five steps before he let out a low whistle.

I couldn't make myself move out from behind him. If I did, I'd have to see the damage I'd inflicted on another human being. I forced myself not to compare this to a different day—what I'd done here wasn't the same. If I hadn't shot the soldier, he would have killed us.

Henry stepped aside. "It would appear you've just killed the most dangerous thing in the forest." If the situation hadn't been so serious, I might have thought there was a hint of laughter in his voice. It must have been my imagination because his face was solemn.

I followed his gaze. Lying on her side, flattening the bracken beneath her, was a deer. She was a beautiful tawny color with a sweet face. Her eyes were open but unseeing, and the arrow I'd shot was buried deep in her body just behind her shoulder.

She was dead.

I looked at Henry. *This* was what I'd mistaken for a soldier? How could I have done something so stupid?

"Wild deer can be extremely dangerous." His lips twitched.

Something shifted inside me. "You're laughing at me? I just killed something by accident, and you think it's a joke?" My day had gone from bad to worse and I was close to losing it.

His features shifted back to neutral and his gaze dropped to the ground. "Sorry, my lady. It was a bad joke; it's just I've never seen a girl shoot so well." He bent and pulled his arrow from the deer, wiped it on a wide leaf, then placed it back into his quiver. He pulled a knife from his belt and made some deft cuts around the animal's legs and body. "This *is* the most dangerous animal in the forest when it's dead, though."

I frowned. I was too tired to follow that line of reasoning.

He continued with his work, slightly breathless from the effort. "That soldier will be back. And if he finds us with this deer, we'll be hanged without a trial. The King doesn't take kindly to people killing his game, and the Sheriff is more than happy to seek justice on the King's behalf."

I glanced around, expecting to see the soldier standing nearby. With his friends. "Why aren't we leaving then?"

"We have to eat." He made a few quick cuts and removed a chunk of meat from the animal's rump, placing it into his bag. "If that soldier sees either of us again anywhere near this area, he's going to drag us back to Nottingham to be hanged. If I wasn't so hungry, I'd leave the deer without touching her and get out of here. But..." He shrugged. "I have friends who are even hungrier than I am, and I'm hoping this will fill their stomachs tonight." He climbed to his feet. "Come on. We have a very long walk."

I followed him down the narrow trail, stepping over a fallen log. "Why didn't you take more? You know, if you're so hungry."

"Too much will slow us down, my lady. What we've got now is better than what I had a few hours ago." He grinned at me, but my mind was already elsewhere.

He kept referring to me in that formal manner and it made me uncomfortable. I was no one's lady. "Maryanne. Just call me Maryanne."

Henry stopped and faced me with a frown creasing his forehead.

"Not my lady. I'm not..." I shook my head and let my voice peter out, hoping that would be all the explanation he needed to stop referring to me with a title.

His eyes made a slow journey across my face. The strength of his gaze sent a flush to my cheeks

that made me drop my eyes. As I chastised myself for reacting to him, he took a step toward
me.

"Very well, I'll play your game and call you
Maryanne. But I have a request, too. Let's keep
this between the two of us." He indicated back
toward the deer. "No one should find out how we
came by the meat. All right?"

I nodded, feeling a little like I'd been
admonished.

He watched me a second longer. "Let's go.
When the soldier returns, he'll bring his friends."

His pace was brisk, too fast for me as I struggled over the rough trail and tried not to twist an
ankle on exposed tree roots. He seemed to know
exactly where he was going, changing trails
amongst the dense undergrowth without seeming
to check where we were. To me, the entire forest
looked the same as every other part.

"Can I carry something?" I felt like I should
offer. He had his bow, quiver, sword and the bag
on his back with the venison and goodness knows
what else inside, while all I had was the little bag
Dad had given me.

He slowed to walk beside me. "You're already
louder than a team of horses and slower than a
snail. But sure, why not add more to your load
and you can lead the Sheriff's soldier's straight to

us." There was an accusation in his voice, one I didn't understand.

I was tired, hungry and only just keeping it together. Being blamed for goodness-knew-what pushed me over the edge. "You can be a jerk sometimes." The moment the words spilled from my mouth, I knew I shouldn't have spoken them. Without Henry, I'd be fending for myself tonight. I'd have no food, fire or companionship while the forest grew dark and loud and frightening. I also knew those same words should be said to another male in my life, and would be, the moment I figured out how to get back home to Dad. In the meantime, I had to stop taking my anger out on Henry.

As I started to apologize, Henry shrugged. "Better a jerk who's alive than a trusting fool who's dead."

His tone made my hackles rise. "What's that supposed to mean?"

"It's not *supposed* to mean anything." He held a branch back so I could pass and snapped his lips shut.

Leaves crunched beneath my feet as I considered not giving him the satisfaction of biting. But I couldn't help myself. "Fine. What *does* it mean?"

He turned to me. "It means, *my lady*, if you're trying to get the attention of your soldier friends, it won't work. We're so far off the main trail they won't hear you, no matter how hard you stomp your little feet." He raised his chin, daring me to tell him he was wrong.

I hadn't asked him to come back and help me. He'd done that all on his own. If there was some reason he didn't trust me, that was all on him. "Now you've offered to help me, you wish you hadn't in case I'm working for your enemies and trying to have you killed?"

"The thought has crossed my mind. It does seem rather odd that you're out here on your own.'

"Obviously, I must want to kill you," I said, dryly.

Henry stared at me, then his lips flickered like he'd seen the ludicrousness in his suggestion. He dropped his gaze to the ground. "Obviously."

I couldn't believe I needed to spell this out. "My father is possibly the only person I want to see less than those soldiers right now. If I'm too noisy for your liking, perhaps asking me to walk quieter might be a better option, rather than coming up with a conspiracy theory inside your head. Don't you think?" I smiled tightly.

His mouth dropped open. "Since when did you...stand up for yourself?"

"Since always." Why was he speaking like he knew me?

Henry nodded. "Well, I like it."

"I'm so glad to meet your approval," I drawled.

The edges of Henry's lips flickered again. He knew exactly how to push my buttons. As if sensing my unhappiness, Henry's grin retreated. "I apologize if I offended you." He gestured to the track in front of him as if nothing had happened. "Shall we?"

My grip on my temper loosened with his apology, but I was still upset by his assumption. "Are you going to accuse me of trying to have you killed again?"

He pressed his lips together but couldn't hide his grin. "I believe I've been sufficiently told off to ever suggest it again."

I started down the trail ahead of him, his grin softening something in me. "At least you're learning."

Behind me, he barked out a laugh. After a moment filled with only our footfalls, he threw another question at me. "Did you really not know the child or her family when you rescued her?" His voice was wary.

I shook my head. "I already told you."

"So, why did you? Save her?"

I turned, walking backwards as I spoke, branches brushing against my arms and legs. "She would have died if I left her there. I couldn't have lived with myself if I'd walked away."

He searched my face, perhaps trying to see if I had another motive for saving her—though what he thought that might be, I didn't know. Finally, he let out a quiet, "Huh."

I was caught off guard by his reaction. "I don't know why you're so surprised. You would have done the same."

His eyes narrowed—green like the leaves of the forest—that intense stare gluing me to the spot. "You have no idea. You don't know me." His voice was hard and sent a shiver up my back. I didn't understand how Henry was able to elicit such intense reactions from opposite ends of the spectrum from me. Or why. What's more, I wasn't sure I liked it.

Get it together. He's just a guy. I forced myself to turn away and walk down the trail, speaking over my shoulder. "You chose to save me, didn't you? I did the same for the child."

"I don't know about that." There was something I couldn't decipher in his voice. "Why do you call yourself Maryanne? A change of name can't hide what everyone can clearly see."

"I'm not sure what you mean."

He pushed past me, stopping in the middle of the trail so I couldn't pass, not mad exactly, but something else. "I'm not blind, *Maryanne*. And neither is anyone else who sees you."

I bit down on my lip. When he called me Maryanne it sounded as if the name was forced from this throat, like he didn't want to say it. "Who, exactly, do you think I am?"

"I don't think. I know."

He met my eyes and I waited, unspeaking.

He gave a low and mocking bow, his eyes never leaving mine. "So very humbled to make your acquaintance, Lady Maud Fitzwalter."

Five

MY eyebrows shot up into my hairline. "You think I'm the daughter of Lord Robert Fitzwalter?" My many-times great grandfather.

Henry raised his chin, then nodded. "*Missing* daughter of Lord Fitzwalter. No one's seen you since you wandered into the forest alone one summer night two years ago."

"Are you out of your mind?"

"I could ask the same of you, gallivanting around in the forest. Alone. It's dangerous. You could be killed."

Was it really possible for him to mistake me so badly? "Do you even know her?"

His smile was humorless. "Not at all. And extremely well."

I stared at him. He couldn't have it both ways. Perhaps he was just picking up on some vague family resemblance. "I'm not her."

He narrowed his eyes and blew a breath out his nose. His look said he didn't believe me, but his tone said otherwise. "If you say so." He gave a shrug. "Come on. We've still got a way to walk."

It was many hours later and full dark when we finally pushed between two bushes and were suddenly in front of a small fire surrounded by three people. The delicious smell of cooking meat wafted our way and my stomach clenched with hunger.

The clearing was tiny, enclosed with thick bushes and tall trees on every side. At some point that I hadn't noticed, the fog had cleared and now the light of the fire glowed on the undersides of branches high in the air.

One of the men around the fire looked up. He was older than Henry, maybe mid-twenties, though it was difficult to tell in the dull light. "Ah. Here he is." He got to his feet, pulling his long brown robe down from riding up to his calves.

I turned to Henry, too scared to step any closer to the light. "Won't the soldiers find us here? See the light from the fire?"

He made a noise that might have been a laugh and shook his head, a lock of blond hair falling across his face. "They don't come near the forest at night, if they can help it. Scared of the ghosts that live here."

"Ghosts?" He must be kidding.

This time he gave a proper laugh then placed his hand on the small of my back, gently urging me forward. Any tension he'd been feeling because of me, or the deer, or the soldiers, seemed to have disappeared the moment he stepped into this clearing. At the touch of his hand on my back, my shoulders sagged, that small connection dialing back the terror sitting in my gut.

"No such thing, my lady. Not in this part of the forest, anyway." He looked at the man who'd stood. "Evening, Michael."

The other two stood as well, the taller of them striding over to us, his brown hair sticking out in all directions. "Well?" he said to Henry.

Henry shook his head. "Not today. I'll get him at the tournament." With the hand that still rested on my back, he pushed me into the light. "Miller, Michael, John, we have a guest."

The guy with the messy hair stepped closer to us. He looked to be the same age as Henry and wore a similar style of tunic and pants, but in a dark shade of brown. Wrapped around his shoulders was a heavy brown cloak. He bent, putting his face right next to mine and squinting. "Well, I never." He glanced back at the fire, then at Henry. "It's not often we get to dine with royalty. Where on earth did you find Lady Maud Fitzwalter?"

"I'm not a lady." Because that's exactly what needed clarifying from that comment.

"So, you're Sir Maud now, are you?" The boy grinned and ran a hand through his messy hair.

I smiled back. I was already fairly sure I was going to like him. I couldn't say the same about Henry.

"She's hardly royalty. Nobility perhaps, but not royalty. And *she* found *me*." Henry pushed me closer to the fire, indicating with a hand to the tall boy with the messy hair, the one who had spoken. "My lady, this is John." He pointed to the older one. "That's Michael." Then to the third, who was a few years younger than me and scrawny looking compared to his friends. "And Miller. Sit down. Hopefully there's food enough for two more?" He threw John the bag with the venison inside. "If not, you can add some meat to that meal."

"Rabbit?" John asked, peering inside the bag.

"Venison. Don't ask," said Henry.

I fished in my own bag and handed over my cheese and bread to add to the meal, before sitting beside Henry. I'd thought Henry calling me Maud Fitzwalter was a mistake, but now John had done the same. Our likeness must be strong. Perhaps I could use it to my advantage.

Michael lowered himself heavily onto the bare dirt, resting his arms on his knees. "Yes, do sit down. I'm guessing you have plenty to tell us." His tone was clipped, and he watched Henry's every move.

When Henry didn't answer, Michael fumbled in his robes and pulled out a rolled piece of parchment, throwing it to Henry. "Fine, then. I'll start. Thought you might like to see this."

Henry let it fall at his feet, then faced Michael with narrowed eyes.

"Read it." Michael pressed his lips tightly together and a thin sheen of sweat formed on his forehead. "Quickly, before it's burnt up by the fire."

The way Henry's jaw jutted out stubbornly made me think he already knew what was written on that parchment and didn't care to read it, which made me more than a little curious.

Henry warmed his hands on the fire. His movements were casual, but something told me he wasn't relaxed. "Or...you could tell us what it says."

"Ha." Michael rubbed a hand across his sweaty forehead. "Not bloody likely."

Henry continued the staring contest with Michael for another minute before he gave in and slowly picked the parchment up between his thumb and forefinger, as if it were a dirty rag.

Pressing his lips together, he rested it on his knee, slowly and deliberately unrolling it. John and Miller leaned forward, watching silently. I was as eager as everyone else to know what the note contained.

With it almost unfurled, Henry stared pointedly at Michael as if he was waiting, or maybe hoping, to somehow get out of opening it further. Michael rolled his shoulders then lifted his eyebrows, saying nothing.

"Well?" John leaned closer to the fire, his eyes glued on the page.

"What does it say?" Miller's voice was eager and excited.

Something about the set of Henry's shoulders made me think this wasn't going to be the good news Miller seemed to be expecting. If anything, based on the paleness of Henry's face and his reluctance to unfurl the page, it contained something very bad.

Henry held the parchment out toward John and Miller.

John shook his head, grinning playfully. "You know full well there ain't no point showing me or

Miller that. We didn't have the privilege of learning to read that scrawl."

Henry turned slightly and held the page out to Michael, who also shook his head. "I'm not reading it to them."

"What's going on?" John's smile faltered. Perhaps he was starting to get the same vibe as me.

Henry threw John an angry glare then turned my way. For a second, he was silent, the intensity in his eyes making my heart jump. "What about you? Do you want to read it?' He thrust the parchment toward my chest, letting go at the last moment.

I reached out, plucking it from the air as it fluttered toward the fire, and concentrated on opening it out flat. His stare had done something crazy to my stomach and I needed a moment to compose myself. I didn't know why I was reacting this way each time he looked at me. I really needed to chill.

I squinted to make out the ornate writing. Maybe Henry couldn't read either but was too proud to say so.

"Well?" Miller's smile was gone, although he continued to lean forward. "Can you read it, Lady Maud?"

I could. But I'd already read the first line and suddenly understood Henry's reluctance. I looked to him, unsure what to do. He shrugged one shoulder, his voice resigned. "Go on."

Licking my lips, I stared at the page, hoping my voice would work. The writing was suddenly all too easy to read. And the words on the page brought questions to my lips. Swallowing them down, I read aloud. "Have you seen this man?" Turning the page around, I showed it to John and Miller. As one, they sucked in a breath.

The drawing below the words was crude, just thin lines drawn with ink. But the full lips and creased forehead bore a strong resemblance to Henry. "Wanted for killing the King's deer in the heart of Sherwood Forest, near Edwinstowe village. Thought to go by the name of Robert or Robin." I glanced at Henry. The poster should have my picture on it, not his.

He shook his head, his solemn face and serious eyes warning me to keep quiet about that. Perhaps he wanted to be the one to tell his friends.

I looked back to the page in front of me.

Robert or Robin.

Not Henry.

I shot a glance at Henry. He stared at the ground, a muscle working in his jaw.

Could he have given me the wrong name? He'd looked up briefly after I'd called him Robin as he fought the soldier. Was there a chance that Henry was the person I was searching for? I swallowed. "Highly dangerous. Traveling with a female companion dressed as a man, possibly Lady Maud Fitzwalter. Reward offered."

There it was again.

Lady Maud Fitzwalter.

Michael's eyes were hard as he glared at Henry. "What the hell were you thinking? This ruins everything you've worked for. Everything!"

Henry shrugged, never once looking in my direction. Instead, his purposeful stare remained firmly on the fire dancing in front of him. Before I could question him about his name, a muscle in his jaw moved, and he said, "The poster's wrong."

Michael let out a breath, his entire body relaxing.

I stiffened. Suddenly, it didn't matter what his name was, because it was over for me. He was going to tell them I had killed the deer. I hardly dared to think what it would mean. They'd probably hand me over to the soldiers first thing tomorrow to keep themselves from taking the blame.

But that wasn't what Henry said.

"I shot at least two soldiers as well."

"You did what?" Michael balled his hands into fists and shook his head.

Beside me, there was a steady thud as Henry jammed a stick into the hard dirt over and over, looking at no one.

I owed him—he was the only reason I wasn't dead right now. I couldn't let him take the blame for my stupidity. I'd agreed not to tell anyone what had happened with the deer, but I would never have agreed had I known Henry would take all the blame. As far as I was concerned, that deal was off. "He didn't kill the deer. I did."

Henry blew a breath out his nose. A frown line appeared between his eyes that hadn't been there a moment ago.

"Don't be silly, my lady." Henry's smile was empty. And the frown was still there.

"I'm not..."

John broke into a smile. "You expect us to believe a girl could shoot a deer with an arrow?" He waggled his eyebrows suggestively. "Our Rob must be a mighty fine kisser if you're willing to take the blame on something like this."

Rob.

"Appreciate your support, Maud. But I'm quite capable of claiming my own mistakes." His eyes remained on the fire, that muscle in his jaw working.

"Wait. Your name's Rob?"

Rob...Henry, whatever his name was, swallowed. "Maybe."

"It either is or it isn't. There's no in between," I snapped at him, rubbing my temples and already knowing I was right. He'd said he was Henry. He'd let me call him that for half a day. Somehow, I was certain Henry wasn't his name.

As if I'd flicked a switch, he glared at me, his eyes asking things I didn't understand. Then he lifted his chin. "Yes. My name is Rob. Robin of Woodhurst."

"Robin? Of Woodhurst?" Okay, now he was toying with me.

His lips tightened. "The one and only."

"But...you said you were dead." I wasn't sure I believed him. Why would anyone pretend to be dead?

"Self-preservation. Long story." He spoke with a sign in his voice and watched me closely.

"I have all night."

Henry...Rob shook his head. "Sorry, my lady. That's a story you don't ever need to hear."

I looked at the others. "Is this true? Is he Robin of Woodhurst?" The three of them nodded and a weight lifted off my shoulders. Robin of Woodhurst was alive. I'd be able to complete Dad's task. And I'd be able to return home once I was done. Still, even relief didn't mean I wasn't annoyed at him for lying.

Rob flourished a hand, his voice dripping with sarcasm. "Nice to meet you Lady Maud. Or is it Lady Maryanne these days?"

His tone sparked something in my gut. "Oh, you're all pissy because you're not sure what to call me? I'd say we're even on that count, wouldn't you?" Except he had the added bonus of claiming to be dead.

"You have no idea what would make us even." His voice was level, but there was something slightly menacing behind those words and though I had no clue what he meant, I itched to throw back a response.

Before I could, Michael jumped to his feet. "Perhaps you two could have this lovers' quarrel at a more appropriate time. Like when we don't have life-changing details to discuss." He looked at Rob. "So, it's true? You *did* kill a deer? *And* you got caught?"

"If I'd been caught, I wouldn't be sitting here right now, would I?" Henry's...no, Rob's stare was defiant, and his fists were clenched tight. I had the feeling both Michael and I could claim a share in the credit for that. "Anyway, I had my reasons and I'm not sorry."

"Impressing a girl is not a reason." Michael shifted his gaze, his eyes rolling over me from head to foot, his mouth twisting with disgust. "She'll bring you nothing but trouble, that one."

Rob stood, moving as far in front of me as the fire would allow. "*She* is our guest and I'll ask you to treat her with the same respect we give all our guests."

Michael glared at Rob, his lips set in a hard, thin line. "Oh, you mean the same respect you showed last time I brought a guest home?" There was a pause before he added, "Seen Lizzie lately?"

John placed a hand on Michael's arm. "Now's not the time."

Michael stared at Rob a moment longer, then his shoulders dropped and he turned to me. "Sorry, my lady. My comments were uncalled for."

I nodded, not caring his apology was hollow. I was still trying to wrap my head around the news that I'd spent most of the day with the person I was looking for. And rather than save him from the gallows, my arrow caused him to become a wanted man. At this rate, I'd never finish my task and get back home.

Rob sat, all the tension draining from his body. His moods shifted so quickly, I could barely keep up. "Where'd you get it from?" He nodded at the page on my lap then looked across the bright embers of the fire to where Michael had also sat back on the ground.

"Brother Thomas was working on it when I called on him in Mansfield late this afternoon. Apparently, one of the King's men had made the ride from Edwinstowe around midday with the order for the poster. He wanted it finished today. I managed to convince Brother Thomas I'd seen you on my travels within the forest, and that your nose was much larger, your forehead higher, and your lips thinner. He started on a new copy of the picture while I was visiting. I took this one from the rubbish when he went out to get more mead."

Rob closed his eyes briefly, a small and single indication he'd been worried about what was on that page.

As John laughed and slapped Michael on his back for his quick thinking, I looked from one to the other, their faces planes and angles in the firelight. If Rob really was Robin Hood, then his friends were part of the legend, too.

"Miller's not your first name, is it?" I stared at the boy, noticing him properly for the first time. He was young, maybe around thirteen, with strawberry-blond hair and a healthy dose of freckles covering his cheeks.

Miller grinned, his brown eyes glowing. "That's rather a personal question given we've only just met, don't you think?"

I shrugged. "I could think of something more private to ask, if you prefer?"

Miller's cheeks turned bright red, and the others laughed. He licked his lips, trying to hide his embarrassment. "No, milady. That question will do just fine. Much is my first name."

"Your father was a miller, then?"

He nodded. "God rest his soul."

Much, the Miller's son. I turned to John. He wasn't the giant-like man of the legends, slightly shorter than Rob and skinnier, too, though I doubted he'd finished growing. "Let me guess. You're surname's Little?"

John gave a twist of his head, agreeing. "Our Robbie's been telling you all sorts of things, hasn't he?"

"I'm fairly sure I shouldn't believe anything *Robbie* has told me so far." I turned to Rob, pulling my face into a sarcastic smile.

Rob met my eyes with a slow blink, his face softening until he was almost smiling as if he knew he'd annoyed me—as if it pleased him.

Already knowing the answer, I turned to Michael. The brown robe he wore had less to do with fashion choices and more to do with career choices. I was fairly sure he was a friar. "And you're Michael Tuck? Friar Michael Tuck?"

Dad had always shared his version of the Robin Hood legend with us, right from when we were small. For Carrie, Josh and I, tales of Dad's stories of Robin Hood were our fairytales, the stories we fell asleep listening to. The true version, the one from history that my friends knew, the version from novels and movies, told of a group of men whose estates were some of the biggest and best in the forest, and who murdered and pillaged to keep it that way. Those stories weren't welcome in Dad's home. Which, of course, made me read every novel and watch every movie I could get my hands on.

The one place where Dad's stories were the same as what everyone else knew, were the people in it. That's why I'd known their names. The obvious absentee from this current group was Maid Marian. She was most definitely still absent, because, despite having a similar sounding name, I was certain I wouldn't be here long. I was not her.

I kept my eyes on Michael. In my time, Tuck was portrayed as a merciless killer, as lethal as Robin Hood himself, while Dad's stories pegged him as kind and caring.

Michael swallowed, then nodded.

Based on the stories I knew, I should be terrified of these people, but nothing about them so far made me feel that way. I was going to believe they were the people Dad had told us of, and this small group of boys was going to get me back home.

Rob cocked his head to one side. "You ask a lot of questions, Lady Maud. Now it's my turn. You were looking for me. What exactly is it you want from us?"

That was an answer I'd never be able to give. So, I said the first thing that came to my mind. "I heard the four of you were sympathetic to the plight of the poor."

The messy-haired boy, John, had just taken a drink from the wooden mug that had been sitting on the ground in front of him. The contents of his mouth sprayed across the fire as he laughed so hard I wondered if he might topple backwards. "Spoken like a true aristocrat."

I stared at him, confused.

Rob leaned forward, watching me carefully. "What John means to ask, Lady Maud, is what exactly would you know of the plight of the poor?"

I straightened my back. "Plenty." But probably not enough to bluff my way through this particular conversation.

"So, you're telling me, two years away from your father, and you no longer agree with a system where the rich sit on their butts and continue to get rich, while the poor do all the work and get poorer?"

My eyebrows rose. That sounded exactly like something Dad's Robin Hood would say. This might be easier than I'd thought. "Of course I don't agree with it. Who would?"

Rob rubbed a hand against his temple. "Plenty of people. Usually those born into riches."

It was on the tip of my tongue to mention he was exactly one of those people, but then I saw his threadbare tunic and the fact he was going to sleep rough tonight, and held it in. Just because his father had once lived in a manor house, didn't mean Rob did. "I saw the way you tried to help the people in Edwinstowe today. I know you care, whether you want to admit it or not."

Rob shrugged as if it had been no big deal.

"I'd like to see how well those soldiers would do against armed fighters, rather than unarmed farmers." Miller spoke around a chunk of the bread I'd brought from the future, which he'd just shoved into his mouth. He glanced at me. "This bread is the best I've ever tasted."

Rob tossed a stick into the fire, watching as it burst into a bright orange flame. "Wouldn't we all."

There was a chorus of grunts in agreement.

"I still don't understand why the soldiers have started attacking villages again." Miller looked between Rob and John for an answer. "What does it prove?"

John rested his hands on his knees. "The Sheriff isn't trying to prove anything, Miller. He's sending a message. The same as he did almost four years ago, when he did the same to our villages."

"But...he stopped destroying villages a long time ago." Miller shook his head, as if that would stop the truth of John's words.

"Times are tough. Low crop yield means the villagers have no gold to pay taxes to the crown. Less tax coming in, means the cut the King gives the Sheriff for enforcing the law in his absence is less, which means the Sheriff needs to tighten his belt." John lifted one shoulder. "And he really doesn't want to do that.

Miller's face was blank. I felt much the same level of understanding. How as that a reason for killing the inhabitants of an entire town?

"The Sheriff is burning villages again because he can." Rob's voice was bitter.

John shook his head, a slight grin forming on his face, although by the way his hands balled into fists, he seemed anything but amused. "No, Miller. What I meant was, he's telling people to pay their taxes or suffer the consequences. Nottingham is letting everyone know he won't tolerate late payments, no matter how hard the season's been."

"Same thing." Rob glared into the darkness beyond the fire.

Here it was. The opportunity to make these boys into the legends they were supposed to become. And send myself home. "So, fight back." Legend-making aside, it did seem like the obvious answer to something that upset them all so much.

"Nice idea, Lady Maud." John gave me a grin. "And easy for you to say, since it would be us, rather than you, risking our freedom by raising a bow in the King's forest."

Somehow, I didn't think it was being dragged to the dungeons for using a bow that scared Rob. Something else possibly, but not that. He'd used his bow today against those soldiers.

I looked at the ground, speaking quietly. "Only if you get caught."

There was a beat of silence.

Then John burst out laughing, a rolling sound that came from deep in his belly. "Only if we get caught," he repeated through his laughter. "So true."

Rob cleared his throat. "That's a dangerous thing you suggest, my lady. Many would say treasonous." He twisted slightly toward me. I felt the movement rather than saw it.

My head jerked up. Stupid. Of course a comment like that would be considered treason in this time. I needed to think before I spoke, rather than simply worrying about getting home. "I...I didn't mean to..."

"Though, it would seem you're not worried about treachery given the way you used my bow earlier today." His lips twitched at the edges as he watched me. With his bright green eyes, blond hair and high cheekbones, he was what the girls at my school would have called *hot*. Not me. I never looked twice at guys. I didn't need guys, or friends for that matter. And I didn't need to be noticing those things about Rob, either.

Still, I let out my breath, glad I hadn't offended him. "Perhaps that makes us two of a kind." If he was going to tease me, then it was coming right back at him. "I was just trying to keep us safe from the most dangerous thing in this forest." That's what he'd called the deer. I shrugged. "Someone had to."

Rob lifted his eyebrows. Perhaps he'd expected me to stammer and blush. Then his lips twitched again. "I believe I had my hands full with—"

"Your hair? Lucky one of us could act, then. Otherwise, who knows what might have happened." I gave him my sweetest smile, my voice high and innocent.

John let out a burst of loud laughter. "It's like she's known you for years, Rob."

Rob licked his lips, the shadow of a grin forming. "I'm not sure everyone would agree your shot saved our lives. In fact, it could easily be argued it would have been safer had you *not* taken it."

Suddenly, my words dried up. *Safer if I hadn't taken it.* His comment hit a little too close to home. I wasn't any good at this sort of verbal sparring. Carrie was an expert, witty responses falling from her lips almost before the other person had stopped talking. I, on the other hand, could often think of a response, but then as I was reminded what a terrible person I was, the words would disintegrate. Where Carrie received raptured laughter from her school friends, the reaction I earned was usually mocking smirks closely followed by someone wondering aloud if I was about to "lose it" and hurt them all.

It seemed my reaction was no different in the twelfth century.

"You really can shoot a bow, Lady Maud?" Miller's voice was incredulous.

I shook my head, pushing off the memories. "I...no..." Today's shot was something I had no intention of replicating.

"She can." Rob answered for me, smiling in my direction. A proper smile that softened his features and stole my breath.

"But..." Miller looked around the circle, a crease forming between his eyes. He shook his head. "But. She's a girl!"

"Yes." Rob ran his fingers slowly down his jawline, glancing my way. "She does seem to be." His eyes were on me, and he was trying to keep his face straight. But as he began speaking, he broke into a huge smile. "And she's a far better shot than you."

Quiet laughter erupted around the fire and Miller's mouth opened and closed like a fish out of water.

As they laughed, Rob leaned over and spoke quietly in my ear. "In fact, she's one of the best archers I've ever seen." He fixed me with his intense stare, making me shift uncomfortably. As much as I wanted to out-stare him, I found the dirt beneath my shoes suddenly much more appealing.

Six

THE conversation moved away from me, which was exactly the way I liked it, and on to more benign topics: Miller tripping over his own feet as he tried to catch a fish earlier today and falling headfirst into the river, John stressing about the need to barter for more arrowheads the next time they were in town, and a retelling of how Tuck's quick thinking had stopped Rob's face being plastered on the wanted poster. There was no opportunity to steer it back to how they might become heroes.

Rob was mostly quiet, laughing from time to time. I could feel him watching me though, a presence so strong it was like a physical touch. I turned to meet his eyes once, but he looked away. After that, I kept my own eyes on the fire.

Until he nudged my arm. "I believe we have a conversation to finish."

I stared blankly at him, certain I should know what he meant, but my brain failed to click into place. It had been a long day.

"A lover's quarrel, I think Tuck called it," John called from across the fire, laughter in his voice.

My face reddened. "We're not lovers——"

Rob took my arm, pulling me gently to my feet, and throwing a pointed glare at John as he spoke. "He knows."

I shook my head at Rob. I wasn't up for this right now. "I'm too tired for another argument."

Rob grinned. "Why? Scared you might lose? Again?"

A surge of frustration rose in me. "I didn't lose the first time. Or the second." I huffed out a breath.

He raised his eyebrows. "Follow me."

I glanced at the boys sitting around the fire, each of them watching the exchange with un-abashed interest. "I don't think I should..." The grin on every face said exactly what they thought the two of us would be doing if I followed Rob, and they didn't expect us to talk.

"Relax." Rob ducked to catch my eye, his glance reassuring me that talking was all he intended to do. "We'll be at the edge of the clearing where the trees don't have ears." He turned to glare pointedly at his friends, who dropped their gazes and took great interest in their fingernails.

Time alone with him might give me another chance to talk him into becoming Robin Hood. Tired or not, it wasn't something I could pass up.

Following the sweep of Rob's arm, I found a place just outside the clearing and sank down, a huge tree behind my back. We were close enough to see the light of the fire through the bushes and hear the murmur of voices. The full moon dappled the ground, casting strange shadows through the trees.

Rob sat beside me, a shaft of light falling across his lips. "Any time you're ready."

I frowned. "For what?"

"To explain yourself. Missing lord's daughters don't usually spend their nights sleeping rough in the forest."

True. And not a question I could answer on the fly. I needed time to come up with a story he might believe. "Sure. Once you've told me why you lied about who you were."

He met my eyes, not even the hint of a smile on his face. His jaw worked, but finally he spoke. "You, Lady Maud, are part of a very small and select group. Most of the world thinks I'm dead.

And that's the way I'd like to keep it, thank you very much. I'm sure you know my story."

"The story of how you supposedly died?" I shook my head. If only.

His voice hardened. "Do you think I'm stupid, my lady?" He tilted his head to the side. Anger never seemed far from his grasp.

"I...no." The rapid change in subject and aggressive note in his voice had me confused. "Do you always answer a question with a question?"

"No. Do you?" As he realized what he'd said, his shoulders dropped and his face softened. "One more question. And if you answer it, perhaps I'll answer yours."

I nodded. I could work with that.

"Are you Lady Maud Fitzwalter?"

I drew a deep breath. To make him Robin Hood, I needed him to trust me. Surely he'd trust a known noble over someone who couldn't tell him where she came from, had no family or friends, and nowhere to live. But it was a risky game. 'Tell me why you think that." My voice was soft, perhaps a little pleading. I needed to know what I was dealing with before I jumped in boots and all. "Please."

Rob retied his hair, then picked up a stick and began to skin the bark from it with his fingernails. We were sitting too close. I could feel the heat radiating from his body and should have shuffled away. I didn't.

He shrugged. "You look like her. Except maybe your hair. Same brown color that goes red in the light, but I seem to recall it used to be curly."

I ran my fingers self-consciously through my long and very tangled hair. I'd always wished for curls but never had them. "Even if I do look a little like her, why wouldn't you assume she's tucked up safe and warm in her bed right now?"

As a hedgehog snuffled in the undergrowth nearby, he gave the ghost of a smile. "Let's be clear. You look *exactly* like her. There wouldn't be a person who passed you by who would not recognize you as her." His eyes narrowed. "If you're not her, how is it no one has ever confused the two of you before now?"

If I was going to do this, I might as well start now. "They have, believe me."

His brow furrowed and his eyes reflected his confusion as he searched my face. After what felt like forever, he sighed. "I know she's not safe in her bed because she, the other Lady Maud...you...disappeared in Sherwood Forest two years ago. Your...her father spent a large fortune and a lot of time searching for her, but no one has seen her since that day, nor has her body ever been found. Her parents, believing her dead and lost in grief, went to visit family in France, and have never returned."

I wasn't sure what to say. For all the hours Dad and I had once spent in Nana's little study learning about the Lord Fitzwalter, somehow, we'd never come across this information about his daughter. "She died? Out here in the forest? How?"

Rob tilted his head to the side, his smile becoming more obvious. "Well, until today, I assumed like everyone else, she'd drowned in the river and her body had washed out to sea. But now..." He raised an eyebrow. "Now, perhaps, I'm going to hear what really happened?"

That piece of hair had come loose from its leather tie again and framed one half of his face. The untidiness suited him.

I swallowed. He wasn't going to get what he wanted from me. I couldn't give him any insight into Maud Fitzwalter's death. "I don't know."

Rob's nostril's flared and he jumped to his feet. Like a curtain falling over him, his anger returned. "I should have known. People like you, you're all the same."

I couldn't let him walk away. He was my ticket out of this place and if I didn't act now, I didn't know when I might get another chance. I grabbed his wrist and pulled, hoping he'd sit down. "Hear me out," I said quietly, my brain working double-time to come up with something that would sound feasible.

His stare, violent and fierce, rolled over me. I drew my hand away.

"Please." My heart was racing so fast, he could probably hear it. I just hoped he didn't hear the tremor in my voice.

Slowly, as if he didn't want to, he lowered himself back down beside me.

I took a deep breath and hoped I sounded convincing. "I don't remember what happened. If I'm honest, I don't remember anything of my old life. Not even my name, though other people seem happy to remind me of it." I threw him a wry smile while wracking my brains for the name of a town we'd driven through on the way to the forest this morning. "I woke up in this little shack in Ollerton, an old lady with long grey hair leaning over me. She told me her son had found me in the forest. He thought I was dead, but when he discovered I wasn't, he brought me to her. I remember being weak, hardly able to move. She nursed me back to health." I glanced at Rob, pleased with my on-the-spot story.

His lips were pressed together. "Your father sent hundreds of people to search the forest for you. How was it they didn't find you?"

I chewed on my bottom lip, hoping to look like I was lost in thought to buy some time. *Think, think, think.* "Ah...well...I wasn't really awake when that was happening, but the woman told me I kept screaming in my sleep, begging not to go back there." I shrugged. "She hid me."

Almost imperceptibly, Rob's face softened. The hard lines at the corners of his mouth disappeared, as did the tightness around his jaw. "You didn't want to go back to your family?"

As much as I preferred Rob when he wasn't looking at me through an angry lens, I had to risk it returning. *That* was a subject I wasn't touching. "I don't want to talk about it."

Rob sat up straight, blinking. "Oh, of course. Sorry."

"Soldiers killed her a few weeks ago." I looked at the ground, hoping he'd think it was sorrow rather than guilt that had me refusing to meet his eyes.

Rob nodded, understanding slowly creeping over his face. "That's why you were looking for someone to fight back against them."

I let out a very slow, deep breath. Somehow, I'd managed to fit my lies together like puzzle pieces. "Yes."

"Who told you my name? You asked for me in Edwinstowe. Most people think I'm dead."

So. Many. Questions.

"I don't know." I shook my head, my eyes on the ground.

There was silence for the longest time, just the sounds of the forest at night around us; snuffling animals, crunching leaves, buzzing bugs.

"How exactly do you propose we fight back?" He said it quietly, as if he was almost too afraid to ask.

My head shot up. "Are you serious?" He was interested. I wanted to do a happy dance. It was a step forward, a step closer to home.

He grinned. "Extremely."

I was about to ask him to become a thief, though I didn't intend to pitch it that way. I had to tread carefully. "What do the villages need the most?"

He frowned. "Food. Clothing. Gold."

I nodded, leaning my head against the rough bark of the tree at my back. *Please let this work.* "And who has plenty of all those things?"

His eyebrows were still squished together. "Nobility, the Sheriff, the King."

"If we could get the gold from the rich and give it to the poor, that would solve some problems, right?"

"Yes, but how would you do it?" He tapped his knuckles together, thinking. At least he was considering it.

"Stop their carriages as they come through the forest. Pretend you have more people in the trees who'll shoot if they don't hand over their gold." Wasn't that how Robin Hood did things?

"You've thought a lot about this." His face was unreadable.

I hoped mine was the same. "It means a lot to me." Like being able to see my little brother again.

He nodded slowly. "It might just work. Tuck could hide in the trees with his bow in case something goes wrong. The rest of us could stop the carriage on the trail."

This was more like it. I smiled enthusiastically. "And you shouldn't kill anyone." I didn't want to risk him becoming the lethal killer from the legends in my time. To be the Robin Hood of Dad's stories, he had to be a fast talker. A charmer, not a thug.

"Why not?" That frown returned to his face.

"Because then you'll be wanted for murder, rather than just theft."

"You have a strange sense of morals, my lady. A conviction for either will end with the same punishment."

"Yes, but at least if I'm hanged for theft, I won't have an innocent death on my conscience." I lifted my eyebrows. "Some would say it's you with the strange sense of morals."

He sighed loudly. "If we're not killing, how exactly do we get the gold?"

I shrugged. "Ask for it?" At least that's what Dad's version of Robin Hood had done.

Rob snorted. "You're joking, right?"

I shook my head, sharing his skepticism and trying to hide it.

He untied the piece of leather fastening his hair and ran a hand through it. Rob might be scoffing, but he hadn't walked away yet. "Would you care to explain how asking for a rich man's gold works, because I've never found it profitable in the past."

I tried not to smile. It did sound impossible, but that's what Dad had told me. "I don't know. Maybe a threat will work? Something like, *give me your gold or I'll shoot.* Or maybe it's the women who hold the purse strings? You could try smiling at them. Say something nice. Compliment their clothing, their hair." I tilted my head back and looked down my nose, the bark digging into my scalp. "It might be a foreign concept to you, but perhaps you could give it a try?"

Rob watched me for a long moment, then he got to his feet and held out a hand to help me up. "Compliment them, you say? Why ever would you think that would work?" His face was serious for a long moment before shattering into a grin that stole my breath.

Seven

I FOLLOWED Rob and the others down the trail the next day, wondering how long until we would stop. We'd started out early this morning and the sun was now high in the sky. Other than me, no one showed any signs of needing to rest. After the hours of walking I'd done yesterday, I was more than ready for a break.

The boys asked me to travel to Nottingham with them as Rob and I returned to the fire last night. The Sheriff of Nottingham was holding a tournament in a few weeks, and the prizes—gold and gems—he offered were too good to pass up, especially because, according to Miller, Rob was the best archer in the forest. I did wonder if Rob had another reason for wanting to attend. He'd been silent and somber for the duration of that conversation, only snapping out of it when he met my eyes and agreed I should travel with them.

Though the idea of going to the tournament appealed—if only to see one in real life before I returned to my own time—it was the idea of traveling through the forest with the boys that had me excited. Day after day walking the forest trails toward Nottingham would be the perfect time to make Rob into his legend. Especially with many rich nobles also heading to the tournament. Rich nobles we could rob.

But expectation and reality were parted by a wide gulf. Walking the trails sounded good, but not after a night of little sleep on the uncomfortable ground. No matter how many times I'd shifted a stone out from under me last night, it seemed another rose to take its place.

When I finally got comfortable, I dreamed of Josh, knowing he already missed me. Sometimes, when he had a bad dream, he would creep into my room and climb in bed with me. All last night, I'd wished his warm little body was lying beside me. Even now, I wished he was near enough that I could describe the way the whole forest sparkled in varying shades of emerald green. He'd have gotten a kick out of it.

Up ahead, Rob and Tuck's pace suddenly increased, Rob gesturing at something in front of him. Miller dropped back beside me, nervous energy dancing off his skin.

"What's going on?" My heart thudded, images of caped soldiers flooding my mind.

He pulled his shoulders back and raised himself to his full height, which brought him up to my nose. There was an echo of Rob in his posture. "Seems you made quite the confession on our Rob. He's taking the advice you gave him." Miller's eyes were glowing as he urged me to walk faster with a flick of his hand.

"Confession?" I frowned. *What the…?* "Oh! You mean impression?"

Miller nodded, indicating with his head that I should walk faster.

Rather than moving faster, I stilled. "About what exactly?"

"About fighting back."

"What?" A mixture of dread and excitement ran through me. This was exactly what I wanted. Yet it wasn't. We had no plan. Rob couldn't just fly by the seat of his pants. Things could go wrong. People could get hurt.

Miller reached out and placed a hand on my shoulder, his face growing serious and a frown forming between his eyes. Physically, he looked nothing like Rob. But once again, he held himself in a way that made him a mini replica of his friend. "He thinks your idea has merry."

I stared at him, unsure what the hell that meant, but almost wanting to smile. It was clear he was trying to imitate Rob. And it was sweet, even if the current subject matter was a little concerning.

Miller shook his head as if to clear it. "I mean merit. I think the word he used was merit."

"You're stopping a carriage?"

Miller nodded.

They couldn't do this. I couldn't let them. If they died through lack of planning, if Rob died, I'd be stuck here. And I wasn't having that. I pushed past Miller, running to catch Rob. Taking hold of his arm, I forced him to stop. "What's going on?"

Rob shrugged, his shoulders tense. "John saw a carriage on the main trail. This trail," he indicated to the path in front of us, "is quicker but not wide enough for a carriage. If we hurry, we can beat it to Lucas Flat."

"And then?" I already knew what he was going to say, and I didn't like it.

His eyebrows rose. "We ask them for their gold. Like you suggested."

"You can't! What if there are soldiers around? Have you even checked? What if the soldier from yesterday sees you?" I'd lowered my voice, but it still came out in a rush in my attempt to make him see sense.

Rob pulled his arm gently from my grasp. The corners of his lips were tight. "I think you already know the answer to that, Lady Maud."

I did. And it was exactly what worried me. It wasn't worth the risk. There were other ways, safer ways of achieving the same thing. Just not today. Not without planning.

"Anyway," Rob folded his arms. "Weren't you the one suggesting we do this? Or was that just campfire talk? The sort of thing you say, but never do?"

"If you can find a way to help the poor, you should. But...it's dangerous to do this on a whim! The soldier..." It didn't take much effort to imagine him dragging Rob off to be hanged.

He let out a deep breath, some of the tension in his posture leaving with it and started along the thin trail. "We'll be all right. That soldier won't be here today. I promise. And once we're done, we'll be able to help the people from one of the villages the soldiers razed. Besides, if that soldier ever finds me again, I'm as good as dead. Might as well do something useful before that happens."

I followed behind him, all sorts of reasons this was a bad idea on the tip of my tongue, but none making it out my mouth. I had the feeling Rob wouldn't listen anyway. His mind was already set.

When the wider trail came into view, Miller ran up and stopped beside me. "Now, Rob says you're a fine shot with the bow?" He said the words as if he still didn't believe them, but he didn't give me time to answer. "If this doesn't go well..." He dropped his bow and quiver on the ground at my feet. "You know what to do." Then he turned and skirted the edge of the wider trail toward the place John was hiding, behind a huge tree.

Rob raised his eyebrows, a small grin on his lips, then followed Miller without another word.

"Wait!" I didn't even know how they were going to do this. How would I know if it went wrong? But they were already gone, all of them hidden somewhere along the trail among the bushes.

The forest was peaceful today. The sun shone through the leaves, dappling the forest floor with light. Birds sang and insects hummed. It was a far friendlier place than it had felt covered in fog yesterday.

I concealed myself behind a huge leafy tree just as a horse-drawn carriage bumped loudly over the rough ground toward me. Miller's bow lay untouched at my feet. Nerves jumped in the pit of my stomach, but I refused to give my imagination time to consider everything that might go wrong.

As the carriage drew closer, Rob, John and Miller stepped into the middle of the trail. All of them had pulled the large hoods of their cloaks over their heads, and with the shadows cast by the trees, it was almost impossible to see their faces.

Rob held his hand up, telling the coachman to stop.

The coachman flicked his wrist. "Get out of the way! I'll not stop for you, or anyone."

The carriage was large and heavy-looking with a curved roof that might have been leather, and walls that were thick, roughly stained wood. The only ornament that adorned the outside was a large black *G* painted on the door.

"We don't want to hurt you, but you must stop." The hum of Rob and Miller drawing their swords cut through the air. John, who didn't seem to carry a sword, thumped his wooden staff upon the ground.

The coachman pulled reluctantly on the horse's reins. As they slowed to a stop, he stood and drew his own sword. "My lord and his soldiers will be along shortly. You would do well not to anger him by upsetting his lady in the carriage."

I took another look at the bow at my feet, and my imagination wriggled out of the tight grip I'd held on it. I could see clearly how this would go. Rob was good with a sword so the coachman wouldn't be a problem, if it came to that. But for all of us to walk away from this, it would depend on who and how many were inside that carriage, how good Miller was with a sword, what John could do with that staff. And whether the coachman's lord came past while the carriage was stopped.

Too many variables. I should have tried harder to stop them.

Rob moved to the side of the carriage. He paused, staring at the door, and for a moment it seemed he might change his mind and walk away. Just as he made his decision, raising his arm to knock, the door swung open and a woman poked her head out.

I glanced at the bow. I should at least try to be ready in case they needed me.

Apart from yesterday, it had been a long time since I'd touched one of these. The only reason I'd been able to do it yesterday, was because I'd been certain we'd die if I didn't. If I closed my eyes, I could still see the arrow protruding from the body of the deer. And from years of experience, I knew I didn't have to close my eyes to see another arrow protruding from a different body. I doubted I'd be able to pick up that bow lying at my feet today.

The woman and Rob spoke too quietly for me to hear, then she handed him something. He inclined his head in thanks. The woman's melodic giggle forced me to remove my eyes from Rob, and properly notice her for the first time.

A surge of adrenalin rushed through me and I jumped to my feet. She wasn't the old woman I'd expected; she was a teenager. Tabitha, the girl from the Major Oak, to be exact. She was dressed differently from yesterday. Her black hair was pulled tightly back into a high bun, and she wore a beautiful yellow dress with billowing sleeves that accentuated her tiny waist and blue eyes. Her cheeks were flushed slightly pink, and she kept glancing between Rob and her feet.

I took a step closer, my shoulders relaxing for the first time in more than twenty-four hours. *She was here right as Rob was becoming Robin Hood.* She'd be able to watch, then send me home. And her being here meant I didn't need to go to the tournament. I'd done enough to go home already. Tears pricked at my eyes and a surge of relief like I'd never felt before made my shoulders sag.

The girl shuffled back into the carriage and Rob slammed the door shut with such force the sound echoed around the forest. As John slapped one of the horses on her rump, I pushed through the branches of the tree hiding me. She couldn't leave. Not without me. "No!" I tripped on a root, landing on my knees before scrambling back to my feet. That carriage had to stay. The girl was going to get me back home.

By the time I reached the wide and muddy trail, the carriage had passed me by. I ran after it, already knowing I couldn't catch it. And even if I did, what was I going to do? Climb on and force my way inside?

Rob caught up to me, catching my arm and stopping me in my tracks. "Lady Maud."

I wrenched myself from his grip, wanting to scream that my name was Maryanne, not Maud. I was out of breath from running, and the tears of relief that had pricked my eyes moments ago had turned to self-pity. She had been close enough to talk to. Now she was gone.

"What are you doing?" The sympathy in Rob's voice was almost enough to make those tears spill.

I turned away. What was it about him that produced these over-the-top reactions? Or perhaps a better question, why was he so concerned? I swallowed. I wasn't going to let myself cry just because someone looked at me as if he cared I was upset, even if it was the first time anyone had looked at me that way in two years. "Leave me alone." Putting my hands in my hair, I watched the carriage rumble away. I had to go after her.

Footsteps pounded up behind us. "What's going on?" John puffed.

From the edge of my vision, I saw Rob raise his shoulders.

My eyes flew from one face to the next as Miller and Tuck joined us. "I know that girl. I have to go after her. Do you know where she was going?"

The boys' mouths dropped open, though no one made a sound. I turned to Rob. He'd spoken to her, perhaps she'd told him something.

Rob's voice was careful, like he thought I might explode at any moment. "She said she was heading to Edwinstowe."

I frowned. That didn't make sense. Why would she go there? That town was devastated. And totally unsafe. "Did you tell her not to? Did you tell her what happened there yesterday? Did you tell her those soldiers might come back and kill her?"

Rob glanced quickly at John, then back to me. He clasped his hands in front of him and spoke slowly. "I wouldn't think she has a whole lot to worry about in regard to the soldiers, my lady. You remember who she is, right?"

I frowned. "Wait. You know her?" Did that mean she traveled back to this time often?

I waited for someone to explain, but there was more silence. John wouldn't meet my eyes and kept running a hand through his hair. Looking at Miller, I shook my head, hoping he'd take pity on me and tell me whatever no one else wanted to say.

Miller clasped his hands, the exact mini replica of Rob. "Her cousin is the common of the soldiers."

I stared blankly at him, trying to decipher his words.

Tuck cleared his throat. "Commander."

Miller gave me an apologetic grin. "Everyone knows Eliza Thatcher. Even you, Lady Maud, though you never used to like her much. Her lord is the one in charge."

"Her name's Tabitha," I blurted, too distressed to make sense of anything else Miller said.

A small sound came from the back of Rob's throat, and he gave me a sad smile.

"What?" I snapped. Why didn't he just tell me whatever he wanted to say?

Rob licked his lips and stepped closer. "*That* was Eliza. Tabitha was her sister. And she died four years ago. Perhaps something else you've forgotten?"

I searched his face, trying to decide if this was a lie. And if it was, what reason he had to say it.

As if he could read my mind, he said, "It's true. Ask anyone."

I looked to John. His voice was gentle. "There was a fire. Tabitha didn't survive."

If this was true, it must have been Eliza I'd met at the Major Oak. She'd given me a different name. Seemed to be the thing to do around these parts.

I drew in a few deep breaths, trying to concentrate. They weren't surprised I knew her. Which meant Maud Fitzwalter had known Eliza Thatcher. I wasn't sure what to do with that information. It didn't help me at all, as far as I could see.

"Probably worked out best for Eliza since her uncle took her in and treated her like his daughter." Miller was the only one who wasn't looking at me as if I might combust. "You know she's Rob's——"

"Miller!"

One word from Tuck was enough to shut Miller down. He sank into himself, taking a step back. He didn't look a bit like Rob now.

"Rob's...what?" His girlfriend? His childhood friend? Whatever she'd been to him, she must think him dead. And Rob obviously didn't want to change that.

Rob looked at the ground. When he spoke, the soothing tone was gone, replaced by something lighter. "I think what Miller means is that Lady Eliza is a beautiful woman." He looked at me with eyes dancing. "And I have a soft spot for beautiful women."

I shook my head, forcing myself to ignore both his words and his wicked grin. While we stood here talking, Eliza Thatcher was rolling farther and farther away. The carriage had already turned a bend in the trail, and I could no longer see it. An invisible clock was now ticking inside my head. She might have told Rob she was going to Edwinstowe, but that made no sense. There was nothing there for her. The Big Tree was close to the village. And since I'd done what I needed to get home, it made more sense she'd actually be going there. To accompany me home.

"I have to go to the Big Tree. I think that's where she's really going." I looked at John. He'd give me answers. "If I keep to this trail, will it take me there?" I was a modern woman. I could find my way through the forest and back to that village.

The boys stared at me with open mouths again, then they spoke together, three different questions on their lips.

"Why would you want to do that?"

"Isn't she the last person you'd want to see?"

"You know what she's likely doing, don't you?"

I answered the easiest one. "Why? Because I think she can help me get home." Back to Josh. To my family. To a life away from constant danger.

Rob nodded. "Most likely. But are you sure you want *her* to take you? Nothing's changed. We're still going to Nottingham. You're still welcome to travel with us." His last words were soft. Not pleading exactly, but something else.

We were talking about different things, different homes, but it didn't matter. I shook my head. He'd just become Robin Hood, which hopefully meant I was going home. *Home.* Sure, getting him to rob that carriage and making him the legend had been easier to achieve than I'd expected, but that didn't mean anything, right? Easy or difficult, I'd done what Dad asked. I could leave this place. "You can't. It has to be her."

"No good has ever come to anyone who sought out the help of a witch." John ran a hand through his already messy hair.

"She's a witch?" Seemed plausible. Magic had brought me here. I guessed someone had to own that magic.

He nodded.

Just a few days ago, I'd have laughed at the idea. But given she'd thrown me back in time, it made sense. In fact, now I thought about it, it seemed like a necessity. "I'll be careful."

Rob ran his fingers slowly down his jaw, speaking almost to himself. "We have to go to Clipstone, and we'll spend tonight at Frog Rock." He tapped his fingers on his chin, then looked at me. "All right," he said, nodding.

As the ticking of the imaginary clock tapered off, I relaxed enough to smile. "You'll show me back to the Big Tree? But what about the tournament in Nottingham?" The Big Tree and Nottingham were in two opposite directions.

"We have plenty of time to get down south to the tournament. Certainly, enough to first accompany you." He nodded. "It's too far to go today, plus we have to check on John's sister first. But we'll stay nearby and leave in the morning. If we walk fast enough tomorrow, you'll be back at the Big Tree just after first light the following day."

"Wait. No." I shook my head. "I have to leave today. Tomorrow will be too late. Eliza will be gone by then."

"Not a chance," Rob said.

John's lips turned down. "There's not enough light left for Eliza to make Edwinstowe today."

I looked up at the sky, trying to find the sun, but the forest was too thick to see anything except the occasional glimpse of blue. I couldn't wait two more nights. I might miss her completely. I'd go alone. "If I follow this trail, will it take me back to the Big Tree?"

Miller nodded enthusiastically. "Just remember to turn right at White Hollow."

I felt my shoulders relax and inclined my head toward him. "Thank you, Miller." I looked at the other two. "And thank you both for taking me in, but I really need to find Eliza Thatcher. I wish you all luck in...your future endeavors." Without expecting or waiting for an answer, I started down the rutted trail.

I'd only taken a few steps before Rob caught up with me. He walked silently at my side for a long while, presumably to put some distance between us and the others, before speaking. "Do you really think this is wise, my lady? After what happened yesterday?"

Possibly not. Though I didn't expect him to understand. "If I hear soldiers coming, I'll hide at the side of the trail until they've passed. I'm sure they'll make plenty of noise."

Rob gave a slow nod. His voice was dry. "Of course you will. And I'm sure you'll keep yourself totally safe."

I turned to him, annoyed by his tone. "If you're going to preach some rubbish about how a *lady* shouldn't travel on her own, save it. I'm more than capable of looking after myself, thank you very much."

He put his hands in the air as if he was surrendering. "I would never suggest you weren't. You're most certainly capable of keeping a soldier at bay with a bow." He glanced at me sideways. "Or a deer."

A flush of color rose up my cheeks. I hated that I'd killed that deer. And I hated even more that I hadn't identified my target. "I thought we weren't to talk about that." He'd been the one to tell me not to, and I was more than happy not to mention it. Ever.

"We're not." His eyes danced as they crossed my face. The lightheartedness suited him so much better than the anger he often wore.

"Says the person who keeps bringing it up." I folded my arms over my chest. "Either it's dangerous to talk about, or it isn't."

He grinned, a lock of blond hair falling across one eye. "Yes. Well, the thing is..." He ran a hand through his hair, the sleeve of his shirt falling back and revealing a muscled forearm. "It *is* extremely dangerous. But your face changes color whenever I mention it, sort of like the first rays of sun hitting the morning sky. Then for a moment you go silent, like you're lost for words and, well, that doesn't seem to happen often." The intensity of his eyes made me want to look at the ground, but I was suddenly unable to move. He shrugged. "There's nothing more beautiful than the rising sun."

I blinked, finally dragging my eyes away. Had he just called me beautiful? He couldn't have. I wasn't. Eliza Thatcher's face flashed in front of my eyes: her stunning yellow dress, her smile, the way he'd said *she* was beautiful. I ran a hand through my knotty hair—how I wished I had a brush. Compared to Eliza in her beautiful cloth-ing, I wasn't worth looking at.

Rob licked his lips, drawing my eye to their fullness. *Stop.* He's just a guy. A hot guy who looked like Adonis when he held a bow, but a guy nonetheless. Plus, his love story was already writ-ten. If I was going home—and I was—I could have no part in it, no matter if I liked the way it felt when his eyes wandered over me. I looked at my feet, refusing to let myself be drawn in by his smile.

Rob gave a quiet laugh. "All I was going to say was it's going to be dark soon and it's a very long walk with two nights on your own." He lifted an eyebrow. "Possibly more, based on the speed you walk. Come with us, share our fire and food tonight. Before we make camp, we'll go to Clipstone, and tomorrow we'll start back toward Edwinstowe. By the next day, we'll be there." He turned his hands palm up. "If Lady Eliza isn't in Edwinstowe when we get there, then we'll take you to find her in Nottingham."

A warm fire, food and company did sound bet-ter than two nights' alone in the cold and dark forest. But I had to get to her. "I..."

"Good. It's settled." He took my arm and turned me back to where John, Miller and Tuck waited in the middle of the rutted trail.

Nothing was decided yet. "I never said——" I pulled at his grip.

"Yes. But you were going to." He grinned. For a moment, his fingers remained on my arm even as I tried to loosen them. Then, still grinning he let go, and I wished I hadn't been quite so quick to pull my arm from his grasp.

Eight

CLIPSTONE wasn't so different from Edwinstowe. A few homes, a church, some fields, a couple of chickens pecking on the ground. And ten freshly dug graves at the edge of the forest.

"Did you know any of them?" I nodded toward the mounds of dirt.

Rob folded his arms across his chest and nodded. I couldn't see his face. He'd insisted we all pull the hoods of our cloaks up, and though I couldn't shake the feeling he was watching me, each time I looked at him, his head was angled toward the village, eyes invisible. "That one there." He pointed to the farthest mound, one that was half the size of the rest. "That's John's four-year-old nephew, James. And the one beside that is John's brother-in-law, Lester."

"I'm sorry," I said.

Rob's shoulder's stiffened. "Why? Was it your fault?" His voice was suddenly hard with the anger that never seemed far away.

I shook my head. "I...of course not. I just meant I was sorry for your loss." Perhaps that wasn't the sort of thing people said to each other in the twelfth century.

"Not my loss. John's."

I sighed. "Fine. Then I'm sorry for *his* loss." If we were going to get petty about it.

John was down in the village, his hood up and talking to a woman. I wasn't sure why we were wearing our hoods, exactly. To stay hidden, Rob had said. But the woman with John had called him by his name, I was sure of it. She kept touching his shoulder, searching for his face beneath his hood. "Is that his sister?"

Rob nodded. "Josephine." His voice softened a little.

"The soldiers did this, too?" The field in front of us was crushed and there were five smoking piles of rubble where I assumed homes had once stood. Plus, there were those fresh graves.

Rob shrugged. "Who else?" He pointed to the fields. "Once they'd finished killing, they rode their horses through the fields."

"So, they have no crops? How will they survive?" How could the soldiers do something so cruel, knowing they might sentence these people to a slow death?

Rob indicated with his head toward John, who pressed something into his sister's hand. She pulled away and looked inside the little pouch he'd given her. Her next words were too quiet to hear but were quickly followed by a much louder, "What? No!"

"The gold you took from Eliza?" I glanced at Rob.

He shrugged one shoulder. "Some of it."

Miller, who'd been standing quietly on the other side of Rob, replicating his pose, leaned forward. "That's why he wants us to be unanimous, milady. So no one knows we took the gold and gave it to people who need it."

"I believe the word I used was anonymous," said Rob quietly, his hooded head swiveling toward Miller.

"Right. Anonymous, milady."

"So, she *did* just hand over her gold?" The shock of seeing Eliza had made me forget to ask if he'd been successful.

"After I paid her a compliment and appealed to her better nature." Rob lifted his chin. "I imagine the presence of John and Miller's weapons likely helped a little."

"Looked to me like you quite enjoyed taking money from that woman."

"I'm not fussy, Lady Maud. I'd have taken it from a man just the same." Now we were no longer talking about the soldiers, lightness had crept into Rob's voice. I imagined if I could see his face beneath his hood, he'd be smiling.

I sighed. "Did you only take her gold because her cousin is the commander of the soldiers?" Not that it mattered. I was just curious of his motives.

"No. I took it from her because she was the first person to drive past in a fancy carriage. Her being the cousin of the commander was an added bonus."

John gave his sister a hug and started toward us. Josephine squealed and people ran from their homes to her. I couldn't hear her words and I didn't need to. The newcomers jumped up and down, then looked our way and waved.

Josephine held the little pouch out in our direction. Her voice was loud and echoed across the rutted field. "Thank you, Robin of Woodhurst. The village of Clipstone is in your debt."

Rob dropped down into a low flourishing bow. "Anything for you, lovely lady."

"So much for keeping ourselves unanimous," I mumbled to Rob, trying not to smile. Even with his hood up, he'd been recognized.

Miller turned to face me, hands on his hips like a schoolteacher. "The word's anonymous, milady."

Frog Rock turned out to be, not a rock where frogs lay resting in the sun as I'd imagined, but instead a rock, which if you stood in exactly the right place and squinted, almost looked like a frog. It was a pretty area, filled with the setting sun and bright green wild grass that grew right down to a wide river. We'd walked for most of the day to get here and Rob assured me we were far from the main trail. In my mind that meant far from the danger of the soldiers.

The boys were still on a high from the success of today's robbery and, I guessed, from seeing the joy of the villagers as they realized they'd be able to feed their families tonight. None of them sat still for long, jumping up and tackling each other when they least expected it, all four then dissolving into peals of loud laughter. Even John, who was trying to cook dinner, kept jumping up and joining in. I understood. It *was* exciting knowing we'd helped so many people today. I was surprised by how good it made me feel. I'd come here with my sights on the one thing that would get me home. I hadn't expected to enjoy anything about my time here.

But as I sat amongst the sweet-smelling grass, I knew this wasn't my success to celebrate. I hadn't played any part in obtaining the gold. Besides, after two days in the company of these boys, I was itching for some alone time.

I never had to worry about getting alone time at home. Josh was the only one I could count on for a conversation. And Mom occasionally. Just sometimes—a lot of times—she was so busy with Josh that everything else came second. Not long after the accident, I'd been so excited to receive my first ever A on an English assignment, that I'd run home to tell them about it. Mom might have said, "That's nice, dear," as she cooked dinner. Dad didn't bother to look up from his newspaper. After that, I'd stopped trying to communicate at home, the same way I had at school. I'd eat in my room with the door shut, listening to music on my headphones. I'd told myself I was fine, that I enjoyed being alone.

I hadn't realized what a lie it was until I met these boys. They were more like a family to each other than my blood relations were to me.

The running water of the river called to me. I was sweaty and covered in dust, and though I would have preferred a warm bath, a cool dip in the river would do just the same.

As John and Rob wrestled each other on the ground and Tuck and Miller cheered them on, I took my bag and picked my way along the rocky riverbank, searching for a place I could wash alone.

I didn't have to go far to find a bend in the river, and just beyond, a deep place for swimming surrounded by large, flat rocks.

Kicking off my shoes, I considered diving in fully clothed. I really didn't want to be discovered swimming in my underwear. But as another peal of laughter reached me, I shrugged off the worry and my tunic. The boys were too busy to come looking for me. Throwing my tunic into the shallow water, I gave it a quick rinse and rub over with the soap from my bag. The rocks on the edge of the river were warm after a day basking in the mid-summer sunlight, and I threw my tunic on one to dry. Then I washed my undershirt and pants and placed them beside it. I'd wear my cloak until they were dry enough to put on again. Housework done, I dived into the water wearing just my underwear.

The river was deep and slow moving, and a little cooler than I would have liked, but it was bliss. I rubbed the soap over my body and washed my hair, then threw the soap up onto the riverbank. I relaxed on my back thinking about the success of the carriage robbery.

In a little more than twenty-four hours, I'd be back home. I'd done what Dad wanted and it'd only taken a couple of days. There'd barely been time for Josh to miss me. Even so, I knew he would have. Three nights without his favorite story would have him quietly crying alone in his bed. I missed him just as much.

"Maud!"

Rob's panicked voice invaded my thoughts and sent a shot of adrenaline through my body. *Soldiers!* I splashed toward the riverbank.

"Maud!" Rob yelled again, closer this time, but I was too focused on reaching the edge to answer, too busy imagining those soldiers hurtling toward us on their horses, swords slashing the way they had in Edwinstowe.

He reached my swimming spot at the same time I was scrambling barefoot over the rocks in knee-deep water. Our eyes met and we both spoke.

"There you are. Thank goodness!" He dragged his hands down his face, his gaze pained, then stopped mid-step, his eyes going round when he realized I was in my underwear.

I didn't care, tiptoeing as fast as I could toward him, the stones painful on my feet. "Soldiers? How close?"

Blinking, he turned away, mumbling, "Sorry, my lady."

I continued my slow progress to the bank, speaking to his back. "How far are they?"

"Who?" Then he yelled into the forest, "Got her."

"The soldiers."

He glanced over his shoulder, caught my eye, then turned around again. "What soldiers?"

I stopped. "Rob, why exactly were you screaming my name?" *Her name.*

"Because none of us knew where you were " He turned to me, his eyes only on my eyes. "It's dangerous out here. If that soldier from the other day found you..." His voice trailed off. I didn't need him to explain further. "But there are plenty worse than him out here."

"So, I'm not in danger right now?"

He shook his head. "No. I just thought..."

I splashed backward, sinking into the water until it covered my shoulders. "Turn around."

Perhaps sensing my relief, a slow grin spread across his face. "Why?"

"You know why." Now I wasn't frightened, a blush crept up mine.

He shook his head, his lips turning down. Something shone in his eyes. "I'm afraid I don't."

I glared. Weren't medieval men supposed to be uncomfortable seeing so much of a woman's skin? "I'm bathing."

"And?" His success had him in a good mood. A mood I would have liked to see more of. Just not when I was in my underwear.

"I'm almost naked." It struck me that I wasn't wearing anything different than if I was in my bikini at the beach back home. But something about this boy with the intense green eyes seeing my lacy black bra and underwear made me uncomfortable. I curled my knees up to my chin and pushed out a little deeper.

His eyebrows rose and he sauntered toward the water, the pained gaze gone. "Really? I hadn't noticed." He bent and picked up the bar of soap I'd thrown onto the bank and twisted his head in question.

"It's soap. You use it for washing. Your clothes, your hair, your body, though I guess you wouldn't know about that." I didn't mean it, was simply trying to get a reaction from him to hide the color in my cheeks.

With deliberate movements, he unbuckled his sword belt and lay the weapon carefully on the stony ground. Then he whipped his tunic and undershirt over his head. He grinned at me, and I wished—really wished—I could have torn my eyes away. Standing less than three meters away was a guy who was totally ripped. And totally comfortable with his body. It probably had something to do with him having muscles on top of muscles—far more toned than the guys from my time.

He dropped his tunic and undershirt into the shallow water and picked up the soap, sniffing it. "Care to explain how I do this?"

I crept farther back into the water. "Just rub the soap onto your clothes, then rinse it out in the water."

He looked between the three items. "Want to come over here and give me a lesson?"

"In your dreams." I wasn't getting out of the water until he was gone.

He bit back his smile, crouching then dunking his tunic in the water. "Quite possibly."

I pushed myself under and swam out deep to hide my cheeks. After the show he'd just put on, he'd quite possibly be in my dreams, too.

When I resurfaced, he was soaping up his tunic. He cleaned it off and threw it onto the rock next to mine and did the same with his undershirt. Then he began to unlace his fly.

I gasped. "What are you doing?"

"Washing. That was what you wanted, wasn't it?" His voice was innocent as he continued to slowly undress while watching me.

I turned away, treading water and desperately not watching—I wasn't sure people wore underwear in the Middle Ages and I didn't want to find out. He gave a soft chuckle that traveled up my spine and splashed as he dived into the water.

"You can turn around now." He was closer than I expected. Touching distance close.

Slowly, I turned to face him, careful not to look down. "Who taught you how to swim?" From what I'd learned from my research with Dad, there were bigger things to worry about in these people's lives than learning how to swim. Most couldn't.

His arms made wide, lazy circles near the top of the water. "My mother. Her sister drowned when she was ten, and Mother stood on the riverbank only able to watch as she died because she didn't know how to swim. After that, she taught herself. And when I was old enough, she taught me." He sniffed his hand. "That's the best soap I've ever used. Even smells good."

"You expect me to believe you've actually used soap before?" I grinned. This Rob, I enjoyed. The angry version, not so much.

He didn't take the bait. "It's hard to get. And never as good as yours."

I shrugged. "Maybe it'll get easier to get now." Now they knew how to rob carriages, they could keep doing it after I was gone. Then they could afford to buy better soap.

"I doubt it," he said quietly. Then, "You're cold."

I was trying to keep my teeth from chattering. Had he not come racing down to the riverbank, I'd have been out of the water by now. But since he was here and I was almost naked—and, I was fairly sure, he was completely naked—I didn't quite know how to broach getting out of the water. But I was damn sure I wasn't climbing out while he sat back and watched. "I'm fine."

"Liar." He grinned, and dived below the surface, swimming toward the bank.

I turned away and a minute later, he called, "Your turn."

When I looked back, he was wearing pants again, to my relief. "I'll get out once you're gone."

He shook his head. "Too dangerous out here for you to be alone without any weapons." He sauntered over to the rock where our clothes were drying, picked up my tunic and pants and brought them to the edge of the river, then turned his back. "I won't look. Promise."

"No! I'm not getting out until you leave."

He glanced over his shoulder, quirking an eyebrow. "Then it's going to be one very cold night for you, my lady." He turned away. And waited.

I stared at his muscular back, considering my next move. I couldn't stay in the water much longer. And he wasn't going anywhere. The only option was to get out and hope he was as honorable as his legend suggested. Besides, he'd already seen me in my underwear, and had only looked into my eyes rather than ogling my body like the boys at home would have done.

I splashed out of the water and picked up my tunic, using my cloak to dry my body as quickly as I could. All the time, my eyes were on Rob in case he should turn around. He didn't. I was fairly sure the back of his neck had turned a mottled red color, so perhaps neither of us were overly comfortable with this arrangement, no matter how cocky one of us seemed.

"How did you think the robbery went?" he asked, without turning around.

I pulled the damp tunic down over my head, the woolen fabric itchy even through the undershirt. "All right, I guess."

"All right? You're a hard one to please, Lady Maud Fitzwalter. We got her gold. What more could you want?"

"A little more planning would've been good."

I could almost hear the frown in his voice. "Planning. Why?"

"Did you know whose carriage it was before stopping it?" I pulled the pants up then sat down on the stony ground pulling a sock onto my foot and slipping Dad's dagger into it.

"No. But—"

"So, you didn't know you were going to steal from the commander of the King's soldiers? And that he and his men might have been along at any minute?"

"No. But—"

"And you had no idea who or how many were inside that carriage or if they were armed?"

"Well, not exactly. But—"

I pulled on my shoes. "And if more soldiers had turned up, how did you plan on getting out of there with your lives? I'm dressed, by the way. You can turn around now."

He turned to face me, watching silently like he was waiting for me to say something. When I didn't, he said, "Oh? You're going to let me speak now?"

"Do you have something important to say?" I asked innocently. I hadn't meant to talk over him.

He could have died today. I wanted him to understand that.

He walked slowly over to where I sat in the long shadows at the edge of the river, sitting down and picking up a stone. "I knew exactly whose carriage it was the moment I saw it. I knew there was a chance Eliza Thatcher's lord might be inside. But I also know how much that man likes to ride, so I took the risk that I wouldn't find him on the other side of that door. As for something going wrong, you were supposed to be ready with Miller's bow. Tuck was on the other side of the trail. You're both excellent shots, you should each have been able to take care of a few soldiers, had any turned up. Except—" He looked me over, his lips pursed. "Except one of you left the bow exactly where Miller dropped it on the ground. Care to explain why?"

I shook my head, a ball of dread spreading inside my chest. "I can't. You wouldn't understand."

Rob's lips remained pursed as he ran his finger and thumb along his jawline, considering. "And if something had gone wrong? If more soldiers had turned up and attacked us? What would you have done then?"

I slammed my eyes closed imagining the sort of shot I might have had to make. I could have aimed for a soldier but hit one of the boys instead. "I hope...I hope I would have been able to do something to help you, had that happened. But the truth is..." I took a deep breath. This was way more honesty than I ever gave. "I don't know if I could have. Chances are I might just as easily have curled into a ball on the side of the trail and waited for a soldier to impale me." I opened my eyes slowly, not daring to look at Rob, focusing instead on the willow across the river, its leaves dangling in the water.

The silence drew out between us, and I waited for questions. Or condemnation. What he said surprised me. "How would you have done it better?"

I turned to him and his lips tightened into a small smile. "I don't know what you mean."

"The robbery. You didn't like the way we did it. What would you have done better?"

"It wasn't that I didn't like it. I think you did a fine job."

"But...?"

I was going home tomorrow, and now I had the opportunity to tell Robin Hood how to be better. I liked this boy. I was beginning to understand why the world would love him so much if they ever heard about this version of the legend. I wanted him to be everything dad had suggested he might be. I shrugged. "Maybe you could be more...charming."

His eyebrows shot up. "Charming?"

"Yes. I know it doesn't come naturally, but maybe you could try. See what happens."

He shot me a half-smile. "And what, exactly, do you envisage my charm will achieve that we didn't get today?"

I shrugged. "Wealth. Power. Prestige."

"Well..." His smile turned to a grimace. "I'm not sure—"

"Relax, Rob. I'm kidding."

"Oh."

"Not about the charm, though. Next time you ask for gold from a woman, look into her eyes, tell her she's beautiful, kiss her hand if you need to. Pretend if you must, but make it seem sincere and I guarantee you'll come out with more gold than you did today."

Rob looked skeptical.

"Worried it's beyond you? Because I'm pretty sure Miller would give it a go if I suggested it to him."

He pressed a hand to his bare chest, his tunic still drying on the rock. "You wound me, Lady Maud. I possess more charm than the average man and I'm more than capable of using it to gain wealth and prestige."

I grinned. "Can't wait to see it." As I spoke, a pang of regret ran through me. I'd never get to see Robin Hood use his charm on the people of this forest because I wouldn't be here. I'd never see the end of what I'd helped start.

"Very well." He twisted to face me, his eyes still dancing. He took my hand gently in his and cleared his throat. "You look cold, my lady. Want to use me as a blanket?"

A laugh burst from me. "Um. No. And if that's your best effort, I'm guessing there won't be any wealth or prestige in your future." I pulled my hand back and got to my feet. It was getting late. And with my tunic and pants still damp, a little cold, too. I could do with warming up beside the fire.

Rob reached out and grabbed my hand, pulling me back down beside him. His hand engulfed mine, warm and solid, and with him shirtless beside me, I couldn't catch my breath. "I'm not sure charm is in my nature, my lady. But honesty is, and perhaps I can learn to package that up with charm." Those intense eyes stared at me, gluing me to the spot and setting my heart on an uneven rhythm. On second thought, he would probably get by simply by staring into the eyes of any woman he intended to rob.

"You're different from everyone else, Lady Maud. I've met plenty of young nobles, and most of them are more concerned with the latest fashion or hooking a rich husband than about the plight of the people around them. Most wouldn't care that there are people starving out here. But you do. And on top of that, you wear a tunic and pants better than anyone I've ever seen."

I shifted uncomfortably, my head at war with, well, my body. His hand on mine sent tingles up my arm and I didn't want to move. But, I'd known him for two days. It was far too early for declarations like this. Yet, my heart continued to hammer out its own beat and I couldn't drag my eyes from his face. "That's because my tunic and pants are clean," I quipped.

Rob's lips twitched. "Ah, well, forget I said it then, because if that's what makes them look so good, then I'm surely going to be the best-looking tunic-wearer around here now."

"Modest, too." I tried not to smile.

"Honest, I think you'll find." His breath tickled my face.

For the briefest moment, I wondered what those lips would feel like on mine.

"You're nothing like I expected." His eyes were on my lips, voice rough.

"Expectations are the root of all disappointment." I needed to move away, to find a place where the air was a little easier to breathe, but next to him, I was trapped.

"I can't imagine you being a disappointment to anyone, Lady Maud."

And just like that, whatever spell he had over me broke. I was not and would never be, Lady Maud Fitzwalter. I was Maryanne Warren, and I was a rather large step down from the English noblewoman he thought me to be. The lie knotted my stomach. Not that it should. I was leaving soon.

I pulled my hand from his grasp and jumped to my feet.

He blinked, like perhaps he was coming back from somewhere very far away. For a moment he looked stunned, then he stared up at me with a cocky grin on his face. "Do you feel more like handing over your gold to me now?"

That was what this had been about? I pressed my hands to my cheeks, hoping to cover my embarrassment. Hoping to hide the fact that those pretty words had glued me to the spot, so eager to hear someone tell me how wonderful I was, that I hadn't seen it for the lie it was. "I think you'll have to work a lot harder on your charm if you expect women not to see your words as desperate."

His grin widened as if he was pleased by my reaction. "Desperate. Not quite what I was going for. But better than pathetic. I can work with that." He got to his feet and threw his tunic on, then flourished his hand in the direction of our camp for the night. "After you, my lady."

NINE

I FOLLOWED right behind Rob on the muddy trail a day later. I'd risen early and convinced everyone we needed to leave as soon as possible. I was desperate to get to the Big Tree; hopeful I'd done enough to return to my family.

The others walked a little behind, laughing and joking, but Rob and I had little to say, so we walked in silence, listening to the birds in the trees and the others talking behind us.

Rob finally twisted around to glance at me over his shoulder. "You sure you want to go to the Big Tree? Not Edwinstowe?"

I nodded. I was certain the tree was where I'd find Eliza, no matter what she'd said to Rob. "You don't need to come. Just point me in the right direction."

"And what happens when you find her? You'll go home with her? If she'll take you?"

I nodded. "I miss my family." He was talking about Maud's home. I wasn't.

"If you're certain." He turned and pointed. "Big Tree's up that trail to the left. I'm going to wait here for a few minutes. Until you're safe."

I nodded again as Rob walked away to stand on the far side of the trail. My chest ached as I watched his back. He was the first friend I'd had in two years, and I would miss him. "Thank you," I called. "For…everything." I couldn't even begin to list the things I was in his debt for after these few short days. Nor could I bring myself to put into words how much his friendship had meant.

He nodded without turning, instead focusing on the others as they made their way up the trail toward us. It was a strange feeling, standing and watching them all. I wanted to go home more than anything, but the desire to stay here, to stay with Rob, was almost as strong. Stupid, since I barely knew him.

Shaking it off, I gave the boys a final wave and started up the narrow trail that would take me to the Big Tree. I pulled my hood over my head, drawing my cloak tight around my shoulders. The wind had risen as we walked and the trees shrieked and moaned, whipping tufts of hair across my face.

Walking the trail to the Big Tree reminded me of the soldier who'd found us here. I bent and pulled the little dagger Dad had given me from my sock, just in case. Not that I had any idea if I could use it, but it made me feel better to hold something solid for protection.

The area around the Big Tree was as beautiful as it had been when I arrived, surrounded in bracken, brambles, oaks and birches, all of them dwarfed by that tree. Even the wind seemed to respect this place, its shrieking howls lessening the closer I got. Perhaps that was my imagination, or maybe it was the magic of the tree.

I'm coming, Josh.

I walked slowly around the Big Tree, trailing my fingers over the rough bark of the trunk. Eliza wasn't here, not that I could see, anyway. I bit down on the disappointment that rose inside me. I'd wanted her to be here already, but she would come. I just had to knock, the same way Dad had. It had taken him a few tries. I would do the same. I stopped where I'd woken up, took a deep breath. And knocked.

Nothing.

I tried again, knocking hard and ignoring the pain that shot through my fingers, grazed by the bark. Then softly. Then moving to the left, in case that helped. To the right.

Nothing.

Nothing. Nothing.

I tried fast and slow knocks, high on the trunk and low to the ground.

Nothing. Nothing. Bloody goddamned nothing!

This couldn't be. I'd done what I was supposed to. I'd done what Dad had asked. Rob had stolen from a carriage and given the gold away. He was Robin Hood. I'd done it. I could go home now. I could. He'd promised.

"Eliza!" I yelled her name, screaming at the wide trunk of the tree. "Tabitha! Whatever you call yourself. Come out. I've kept my end of the bargain. I've done what I was asked. Take me home!"

Nothing.

"TAKE. ME. HOME!" I slapped my hand against the tree, my throat burning from screaming.

My anger created a roaring in my ears that blocked out everything around me. The chirping of the birds and insects were gone. The wind on my face, gone. Yet I was still here. Still in this godforsaken dangerous place. Still far from my family.

"Help me. Eliza, send me home!"

Someone help me.

Someone send me home.

Someone.

TEN

SUDDENLY, there were arms around me. Arms pulling me toward a muscled chest, arms holding me still. "Maud. It's me. It's Rob. You need to stop. Whatever is happening here, you need to stop it." His voice was soft, a command and a request all at once.

Still I fought. Even as I knew I shouldn't. "No. Let go of me! I have to find Eliza." I balled my hand into a fist and beat his chest.

"She's not here. She's not here." His voice, his presence, bored deep down to a place inside me no one had found in a very long time. Soothing, soft. Over and over he spoke, until I finally heard him. Until I stilled.

"But..." I looked at the massive tree. "But she has to be. She has to take me home." There were tears on my cheeks, tears I couldn't remember crying.

"We'll find her, Maud. We'll find her." His arms remained strong, warm, keeping me in place. Keeping me safe. Slowly, he guided me to a nearby stream, pulling me down to sit on a rock beside the trickling water.

With gentle hands, he unfurled the fist I'd curled around the dagger. The blade of the little weapon was bent and battered, and as I looked at it, I vaguely recalled slamming it into the trunk of the tree again and again. He dunked a piece of cloth into the stream, took my right hand and cleaned away the blood from my grazed knuckles, all the while his eyes stayed on his work, a muscle in his jaw moving.

I watched him quietly, embarrassed he'd seen me lose my shit, and wondering what he must be thinking. Until he finished and finally looked at me. Then I knew.

His normally gentle eyes were filled with an icy rage, and his jaw was taut with it. But he blinked and it was gone, replaced by a compassion that made my heart crack. He pulled his knees up to his chest, his arm grazing mine. "What did she do to you, Maud? What did Eliza do?"

I shook my head, desperately trying to keep my tears inside. "Nothing." I sighed. "She did nothing. Except tell me she would take me home." I held up my raw hands. "If you want to blame anyone for this, blame my father." I shrugged. "Or blame me. I should have known better than to believe him. I should have known not to get my hopes up. I should have been able to keep a better lid on my emotions." I let out an unhappy laugh. "It's usually my best party trick." I ran my hands down my face. I couldn't remember the last time I'd let myself get as upset as this. "I'm sorry."

Rob's body still hummed with anger, but the ice had disappeared from his eyes. We sat in silence for a long time as my tears dried and my breath evened. He nudged my arm. "Come on, those tears weren't really about that. You're just upset that you got your tunic all dirty."

From down somewhere deep, the tiniest laugh rose inside me, his comment so totally unexpected. The right sleeve of my tunic *was* covered in my blood. The almost-laugh felt good, normal, holding at bay the desperation that had been creeping over me. I didn't want to go there, couldn't give into that hopelessness. So, even though it was the last thing I wanted to do, I forced some light into my voice. "You're good at washing now. How about you clean it up for me?"

He held out his hand. "I'd love to. You'll have to take it off, though. And how about I look after that cloak for safe-keeping while I'm at it?"

Now I really did smile, which, I knew, was the point of his teasing. "I already told you, that'll only happen in your dreams."

He shrugged, a smile tugging at the edge of his lips. "Ah, well. It was worth a try." He got to his feet. "Tuck has some salve that will make your hands feel better. Wait here, I'll get it from him."

I watched Rob jog down the trail, back to the place I'd left him earlier where the others were waiting. As he disappeared around the bend, my eyes landed on his bow resting against the tree.

I'd held a bow more these last few days than I had in the previous two years. I'd never thought I would touch one again. Even as I told myself it was a bad idea, I was drawn to it, the desire to touch it stronger than my wish not to.

A quiver full of arrows lay on the ground, beside the bow. Crouching, I took one in my hand, marveling at the wooden shaft and the crudely formed arrowhead.

When combined with a bow, this was a deadly weapon. In my time, they were deadly too, but we used them for sport. Here, this weapon could be the difference between life and death—it could provide food or kill an enemy—and it wasn't even half as fancy as the ones I'd used.

"You know, they work better when you put them into the bow to shoot them." Rob was suddenly behind my left shoulder. His voice was low, pitched just for me, and the warmth of his breath on my neck sent a shiver down my back.

Startled, I dropped the arrow on the ground. I rushed to pick it up, thrusting it out toward him. "Sorry. I was just...looking. I shouldn't have touched it." I felt like I'd been caught red-handed stealing from the cookie jar. And now I was red-cheeked, too.

He didn't take the arrow from me, and my battered hand wavered in the air. Over his shoulder, Miller, Tuck and John wandered up the trail, talking quietly to each other and ignoring us.

Rob's mood was still as light as it had been moments ago. "And here was I thinking you were going to use your bare hands to shove that arrow into my head for making you stay behind."

My grip on the arrow loosened and it dropped softly onto the leaf-strewn ground. Rob was still speaking, an almost-grin on his face. His lips moved, but I couldn't hear his voice. Could hear nothing but six words repeating over and over.

Shove that arrow into my head. I blinked, the vision of another day assaulting my senses.

No.

I would not think about it.

I sat down and pulled my knees up to my chest, pressing my hands so tightly into my eye sockets that I saw psychedelic colors. Then I forced myself to breathe slowly, to relax. To forget.

I was being stupid. Somewhere in the depths of my mind, I knew it. Rob's words meant nothing. He hadn't accused me of anything. He didn't blame me.

Still, those six words brought everything rushing back, and now I had to push it all into the little box inside my mind without looking too closely at the contents as I packed. I was not going to relive it. I never wanted to relive it.

Instead I let a happier memory take over; a day I'd come back from the beach wet and covered with sand from the castles I'd been making with Carrie, searching for Dad. He'd loved me back then, had loved to spend time with me. That day, he hadn't come with us. He'd stayed down in the little study at Nana's house, searching through one of her many boxes crammed full of memories. I'd raced down to see if he'd found anything new, anything exciting about Lord Fitzwalter. He hadn't. What he'd found instead was a coin. Small and copper, it had a hole in the middle and a triangle stamped into one side. I knew it was old without him saying so. It wasn't even a perfect circle like our modern coins.

That coin was now wrapped around my wrist on a piece of leather.

Dad hadn't let me touch it that day, but somehow just looking at it had felt like home. Like it was part of me.

If only I'd known why.

The memory shifted, and I saw another family day at the beach, years later. The five of us had lined up in front of the dunes for a family photo. As the moment was about to be captured, a gust of wind had scooped my hat from my head and sent it flying down the beach, and I'd chased after it. The resulting photo was of Mom, Dad, Carrie and even Josh, laughing, while I, off camera, chased that hat. Dad had loved that photo so much, it sat in a silver frame on his desk. A family photo. Without me.

"Lady Maud!"

I pulled my head from my hands, blinking at Rob's concerned face. At some point, he'd crouched beside me. His hand rested gently on my shoulder.

He closed his eyes and blew a deep breath out his nose. "Are you alright?"

I nodded.

"You just, sort of, blanked out. You sure?"

I nodded again, dazed at being pulled from such vivid memories so suddenly.

Rob drew his hand away and sat next to me, his arms sitting lightly on his knees. "You know, I'm not sure what to think."

"About what?" My voice wobbled, the fear and guilt I'd felt when I touched his arrow still lingered in my body.

His eyes roamed across my face. "You."

I swallowed and forced myself to focus.

"You look like her. But you don't act like her." He let his gaze drift to the high branches of the Big Tree. "And the bow, I know you can use it, but I can also see how much using it bothers you. Yet you won't talk about it."

Silence drew out between us. There was nothing I could say.

"Did you kill someone? Is that why you're scared of it?" Rob's voice was gentle and far from accusatory, but still the question startled me. He glanced quickly my way, before watching a bird dart from tree to tree above us. "I mean, other than the deer."

I had a standard answer and tone whenever anyone asked me about this—*I don't want to talk about it.* Usually when people asked, they would stare solemnly at me, hoping to be the one to finally hear it from my lips so they could be the first to post it on social media. But seeing him sitting quietly, relaxed and not seeming to care whether I answered or not, made other words spring from my mouth.

"He didn't die."

Eleven

ROB'S face showed no emotion. "Did you want him to die?"

"No! God, no." I ran my hands down my face. "I didn't want any of it to happen." There was no way I could explain it, and I found myself wishing I'd used my normal response.

"Do you want to tell me?" His voice was soft, like the wind in the trees. It didn't feel like he was pushing. It felt like…like he wanted to help.

I shook my head. "The last time I shot a bow, there was a terrible accident. I'm sorry, but I don't want to talk about it." I'd never talked about this. I couldn't do it now. All I could do was change the subject. "Tuck said you hadn't killed anything before the other day."

Rob took a breath, looking like he wanted to continue questioning me. Then he blinked. "No. Tuck said we'd never been caught. There's a difference." No wonder he hadn't been as upset as me at Edwinstowe.

"We'd all be dead fifty times over living in this forest if we couldn't use a weapon." He glanced over his shoulder as Miller and Tuck drew their swords and started practicing with them. To make his point, Rob met my eyes. "I'll never forget the first person that died because of me."

"You remember him?"

Rob tilted his head slightly to one side, his gaze running across my face. "His name was Edward. We grew up in the same village."

My eyebrows shot up. I hadn't expected him to tell me about it. I did everything possible to avoid talking about my own situation. I could never trust anyone as quickly as he'd chosen to trust me with his story. Then again, I'd given up on friendships lately, too. "There was an accident?"

He dropped his eyes to the ground. "No."

For a moment, I'd forgotten he was from a different time, with a different life. In those few seconds, I'd thought perhaps we were alike, that something equally horrific had happened to us both. But accidents like mine didn't happen in the twelfth century.

He gave me a humorless smile. "Worried for your safety now, Lady Maud?"

"Should I be?" I wasn't. At least, I wasn't any more worried than I had been since the moment I arrived in this time. I trusted Rob. I was, however, curious.

"Not unless my stepfather is around and wants to teach me a lesson." His voice was bitter, and his eyes shone with anger.

I frowned, unsure what he could mean, or how to ask him to clarify.

Rob gazed into the distance. His hair fell across his cheek hiding most of his face, but not the pain in his eyes. I wanted to reach out and touch him, to let him know he wasn't alone, but I wasn't used to this friendship thing that seemed to be happening between us. It had been two years since I'd wanted friends, and never a guy. I wasn't sure how I was supposed to act. So, I kept my hands to myself and waited for him to speak.

"When I was eleven, my stepfather decided to prove I was lazy and not as good with a sword as I thought I was." He put on a deep nasally voice as he said the last words, imitating his stepfather, I imagined.

"You thought you were better than you really were, and you bragged about it?" Perhaps his story *was* like mine.

Rob shook his head. "No. I was fairly good." He flashed me a grin before turning serious again. "With a wooden sword, that is. Maybe I might have bragged a little." He shrugged. "But I wasn't lazy. I loved my sword and practiced every spare moment I had.

"He brought a boy who was taller and older than me to training, handed us both a real sword, then looked me in the eye and said, 'Fight. And don't stop until I tell you to stop.'"

He licked his lips. When he spoke again, his tone had changed. The soft-spoken Rob with the caring eyes was gone, and it was with a hard, angry, violent voice that he continued.

"So, we did. People came out from their homes and stood around us, cheering each time our blades clashed. Edward was strong and fast, and much better than me. Mostly I just blocked his blows, waiting for Father to call him off. I knew he'd yell at me for not trying, but Edward was too good, blocking was all I could do."

He turned to me. "Edward came at me with blows so hard they jarred right up to my shoulder and almost knocked my sword from my hand. I thought I was going to die. Eventually his sword hit me here." He ran a finger across his upper arm, halfway between his shoulder and elbow, before rolling up his sleeve to show me the scar.

It was white and old, puckered around the place the blade had sliced into his skin and a little longer than my hand. I ran my fingers along the length of it. He closed his eyes, inhaling deeply, and gently grasped my fingers with his. His hand was warm and his grip didn't hurt my battered hand, but it did set my heart pounding. I was suddenly embarrassed I'd touched him, couldn't meet his eyes. Instead, I kept my gaze fixed on the scar.

"Looks like it was deep." My voice had stopped working and the words came out as a whisper. "How did you not die?"

He shrugged. "Had a good nurse, I guess." The pressure on my fingers increased until I gave in and looked at him. His face was close enough I could feel the touch of his breath on my cheek. "Your eyes are the most beautiful color. Like an oak nut at the end of summer. Yet, you never want to meet my eyes. Why not?"

I blinked. A long, slow blink that was more akin to closing my eyes and not opening them again. He was right—I couldn't meet his eyes, not just now, but almost always. There were so many reasons, like the way my heart was currently hammering in my chest, or the fact he was, or was soon to be, Robin Hood. How I was lying to him about who I was. And how he'd almost tricked me into believing his words the other night.

He squeezed my fingers and I reluctantly opened my eyes. He was still watching me, waiting for an answer. "Why not?" he whispered.

"You make me nervous." It wasn't a lie. Nor the whole truth.

He leaned forward. "You have no cause to be nervous." His breath touched my ear and a shiver went down my spine. If I turned my head, our lips would touch. I didn't move, barely breathed as I held myself still. This was no different to the other night. He was playing with me again and I wasn't going to fall for it.

As if he'd read my thoughts, he dropped my hand and leaned back, putting some distance between us.

I wasn't sure if I was relieved or disappointed.

"I don't show just anyone that scar, you know." His tone was light. I knew if I were to look at him, he'd be trying to hide his smile.

I couldn't answer, didn't trust my voice.

"Only you." He let out a quiet chuckle. "And maybe if Eliza Thatcher asked, I'd show her."

A jolt of lightning went through me as I recalled the way he'd smiled as he spoke with her. "Perhaps you can show it to her later today, if I find her." My voice was crisp. I hated how easily he could draw me in.

He gave another chuckle, his smile saying my reaction pleased him.

Flustered, I sat up straight, angling my body away from him. "You were telling me about Edward?"

He hooked his arms around his tucked-up knees. "That's right. Where was I...ah. the scar."

The heat of his gaze transferred, igniting my cheeks, but I fixed my eyes on the low branch of a nearby oak. What had I been thinking to have touched him? Something about him had me acting as if I were someone else completely. I needed to rein it in, regain control and stop fawning over the color of his eyes or the muscles in his arms. There was no point crushing on him. I already knew his love story. After I went home, he'd fall for his Marian and I'd just be the girl who'd talked him into halting that first carriage in the forest. If he even thought of me at all.

Rob started into his story again. "It didn't hurt straight away, when he hit me. What hurt was the village kids cheering for him. He was a bully. He'd hurt every one of them in different ways more than once, yet they were happy he was beating me." He glanced at me again, I saw it from the corner of my eye. A quick gesture, to check I was still listening.

"Now, I know they feared upsetting my stepfather, but back then I had no idea. It made me mad." He shook his head. "I couldn't lift the sword with my right hand, the wound hurt too much. But it didn't matter, I'd practiced with my left. While Edward was saluting the crowd, I swung at him. He didn't have time to block, and I managed a glancing blow that did little more than graze his side. He came at me again, but this time I dodged then attacked. If Father wanted to see me fight, then I was going to show him exactly what I could do." He gritted his teeth together and spoke through them. "When I hit Edward the second time, the crowd cheered. For me. I still remember how it felt to push my sword into the soft flesh of his thigh." He looked at the ground, some of the tension left his shoulders, and his voice became soft. "I didn't hate doing it, even though I should have." He ran a hand over his eyes.

"I looked to Father, but he wasn't ready for me to stop. So, I hit Edward again. And again. And again. I don't really remember much of it. Just coming back to myself at the end to see Edward, bleeding and bloody on the ground. Not moving. Not breathing. That's when the guilt hit, the realization I'd just killed someone in a crazed fit, trying to get respect from the surrounding crowd and a man who hated me. I turned to Father, I think I was crying, wanting him to make me feel better. He looked at me and said, 'Well fought,' and walked away."

"He hadn't told you to stop?"

Rob shook his head. His voice was derisive. "If I'd been a stronger person, I would have stopped though, wouldn't I? I wouldn't have been so intent on winning that man's respect or making the crowd cheer for me. If I was a better person—"

"You would have died. If your stepfather didn't call off the fight when Edward sliced into your arm, he probably wasn't ever going to stop it "

"Do you know what makes it worse?" he asked quietly.

I shook my head.

"That man wasn't just my stepfather." Rob swallowed hard, as if the words were stuck in his throat. "He was my uncle, too."

I forced my eyebrows not to shoot up at the revelation of his somewhat twisted family tree. "Your mother married your father's brother after your father died?"

He nodded. "She thought she was protecting me and keeping our land and titles in the family."

Somewhere behind us, Miller and Tuck's swords clashed again and again, but they seemed so distant from my conversation with Rob. "What about your real father?" The man my father owed such a debt he'd risked his daughter's life.

Rob shook his head. "Didn't know him. Died seven months before I was born." He gave a humorless laugh. "Ambushed in the forest by my stepfather."

I drew in a breath. That was the fight my own father had run from. The fight that had caused me to end up here.

Dad had come back in time to help make Robert Fitzwalter the rebel he would become early in the thirteenth century. And while he'd completed that task, he'd preferred the company of Robert's friend, Avery Woodhurst.

Dad never told us why he and Avery were in the forest the night Avery was killed, only saying that if he'd stayed, he too would have been killed, whether that night, or another. He'd also never mentioned that the man who'd led the ambush that day was Avery Woodhurst's brother. Not that the details mattered, I supposed. They didn't change the fact that Dad had run like a coward. Or that Avery Woodhurst had bled out alone on the forest floor. They only served to make me hate the man who had done all this, Rob's uncle. "And your mother still...?" I couldn't bring myself to ask what I wanted to know without sounding like I was judging her.

"Married him? Yes. She never found out who killed my father, never got to see the other side of her new husband before she died. But I did. I was still just a kid when I realized he'd killed my father for his land, without knowing my mother was pregnant and my father had an heir."

"You?" I asked quietly.

He nodded.

"Explains why he was so cruel to you. With Edward."

Rob smiled tightly. "He was cruel to me always."

"Do you miss her? Your mother?"

He shrugged. "She's been dead a long time. But, yes. I miss her." He pulled a chain from inside his tunic and held it up. The thin silver band had been designed to look like it was knotted in the front. "This was her wedding ring to my real father. I wear it every day to remember them. As if I'm ever likely to forget." He dropped the chain back inside his tunic and shook off his memories. "Your turn."

I blinked. "My turn for what?"

"I thought maybe you understood how it felt to be so sick with guilt you can barely get out of bed in the morning." He waved his hand at the tree behind us and at my damaged hands. "I thought all this might be because no one had ever asked you to talk about it." He licked his lips. "Perhaps I was wrong?"

"You're not wrong. I just..." I'd never talked about what happened to me. Except to the police. And a psychiatrist while she tried to work out if I'd done it on purpose. But I'd never talked about it willingly. Hadn't thought I ever would. "My little brother was hurt in the accident. I haven't picked up a bow since." I stared past him, trying to keep the wobble from my voice that happened whenever I thought of that day. "I can't talk about it. I'm sorry."

"Ah, well. I guess it doesn't matter." The warmth in his voice dried up. I'd offended him by not sharing, and just like that, the anger and distance that had been there when we met, returned. He stood and marched over to where Tuck and Miller were still fighting their duel.

Even if I'd wanted to tell him, and I wasn't entirely sure I didn't, I'd missed my chance.

And now I was sitting beneath the Big Tree feeling sorry for myself. That may have been how I did things in my own time, but it hadn't done me any favors then, and wouldn't in the twelfth century, either.

If I wanted to go home, I had to get off my butt and do a better job of completing Dad's task.

Clearly, I needed to do more to make Rob into Robin Hood. How much more, and exactly what, I wasn't sure. But I was going to find out.

I stood and wandered over to where Miller and Tuck were still fighting their battle. Their faces were serious, foreheads dripping with sweat. John watched with folded arms. I stopped beside him while Rob stood a little distance away, adjusting his sword belt.

"Training?" I asked.

John nodded, his eyes never leaving the battle.

Despite the size difference between Tuck and Miller, it did seem like an even match. "Miller's doing well."

Miller blocked a shot from Tuck then shuffled backwards.

John twisted his head. "Aye. He's not bad. Tuck's going easy on him."

"I didn't think Tuck would know how to use a sword." Being a friar and all.

"He doesn't like to, if he can help it. But he's almost as good with a sword as Rob. They had the same teacher."

"Rob's stepfather?"

Tuck's movements were quick and sure as he forced Miller another step backwards.

"Stepfather, uncle, father's brother—whatever you want to call him." John's focus shifted from the fight to Rob, whose lips were pressed tightly together. "You and Rob been arguing?"

"No." I focused on the sword fight. Rob was annoyed with me because I wouldn't tell him why I couldn't pick up a bow. I could feel him wanting to trust me but needing something from me before he could. I'd failed to give it to him again, but it was hardly an argument.

"Huh. Here I was thinking Rob might have found another focus for all that anger." He glanced at me, eyebrows raised as if I should understand what he meant. "I guess not."

"I hope you'll still allow me to travel to the tournament in Nottingham with you." I had to stay with them if I was going to complete the task Dad had set and go home.

"Of course." John nodded.

Hopefully I hadn't upset Rob enough for him to withdraw that offer. Especially because I had one more favor to ask first. "But I need to talk to Eliza Thatcher before we go. Would you show me to in Edwinstowe?" I might have found my own way there yesterday, but I'd been following the sound of the soldiers.

"I don't think that's wise, milady." John looked at the ground.

They seemed scared of her. Or scared to go and find her. Didn't matter. I needed to talk to her about what else I needed to do to get home, and I needed them to wait somewhere I could find them while I did. "Or can you point me in the right direction? I'll come back to you once I'm done."

Rob looked up, Tuck and Miller fighting between us. His stare fell on me as he made his way around them to where I stood with John. "You still want to go home? Even with all those things you said earlier about your father, you still want to return to him?"

I could write an entire book about all the ways Dad had disappointed me these past two years. Like the time he'd promised to take me to the movies but when I got out of the shower and came down ready to go, he'd already left and taken Carrie instead. Or how he never came to watch my football games. Or my birthday last year, which he hadn't acknowledged with either words or a card. I deserved it, so I never let him see how much it hurt. Besides, he was my family. I had to go home to him. Hopefully Eliza would tell me exactly what else I had to do to make that happen.

"Eventually. But not today. Today, I just need to talk to Eliza Thatcher."

He watched me for a long moment before finally nodding. "Fine. We'll wait."

I arrived at Edwinstowe alone. John had walked me halfway, stopping in the middle of the trail and refusing to walk any farther. He promised not to leave that spot until I returned. I was a little disappointed Rob hadn't walked with me; I might have found the courage to tell him about my accident. But he'd remained at the Big Tree with Miller and Tuck, barely evenly speaking a goodbye as I left.

The village of Edwinstowe, what was left of it, was still, despite the wind. All but three of the huts had been destroyed from the fires the soldiers had lit, the occasional plume of smoke still rising from what were now piles of rubble.

Bodies lay on the ground, just as they had three days ago. Eliza and her coachman were wandering through the village, stopping and surveying, sometimes crouching beside a body as they passed.

My chest tightened until I could barely breathe. It was really her. She wore the same yellow gown she'd worn when the boys stopped her carriage, and her long black hair was pulled off her face and fastened at the back of her neck.

I pushed my way between two ferns and out of the forest, wishing my legs would carry me faster. Seeing her was indescribable——she was a real person and not a figment of my dreams, a person who could send me home. The hood of my cloak flew off as I ran, but it didn't matter. I'd found her and I could have hugged her.

The pounding of my feet against the ground made her look up, and she stared with her mouth open. Then she stood. "So she returns." Her voice was deep for a girl, and strangely melodic. I hadn't remembered that about her from the other day. She glanced at her coachman and circled her hand, telling him to continue with whatever he was doing. But he stared at me with wide eyes, no longer concerned with the dead child at his feet.

I put my battered hand up, gesturing for her to stop, even though she didn't appear to be going anywhere. "I need your help." I was out of breath and after my meltdown at the tree, anxious she didn't turn and leave.

Up close, I could make out three faint scar lines running across her left cheek. I didn't remember seeing those the other day. "I met you a few days ago. At the Major Oak. Remember?"

Her expression was neutral, but her eyes narrowed as she sized me up. This was not the way it was supposed to go. She was not supposed to act as if she'd never seen me before.

"You know, the Big Tree?" A frantic note crept into my voice. If she was the person who sent me here, she'd have known the tree by its modern name.

She took a step forward, suddenly interested. "What did you say?"

A wave of nausea rolled in my stomach, and my voice wavered. "The Big Tree. You talked to the man I was with." I spoke so fast my words were almost incomprehensible, the whole time wishing this girl was the one who sent me here, while already knowing she probably wasn't.

She took three more graceful steps, gliding across the uneven ground with her eyebrows raised hopefully. "Have you figured it out Lady Maud? How to travel?"

No! I wasn't Maud. I was Maryanne. How I wanted her to recognize me as me.

As she neared, she reached out as if to stroke my cheek, but her fingernails were long and filed into sharp points. I stepped back, fighting the sudden urge to run.

She bowed her head gracefully, ignoring my reaction. "Did Tabitha give you a message for me?"

My mouth dropped open and my mind filled in the few blanks I had hoped not to see. This wasn't the girl who'd sent me back in time. This was her sister. "Tabitha?" I whispered.

"You said you saw her at the tree."

"Isn't she dead?"

Eliza shrugged. "Did she seem dead when you saw her the other day?"

I let out a deep breath. I'd come to Edwinstowe in search of answers, and I had found some. Just not to the questions I'd hoped to ask. I guess it didn't matter. It seemed clear that one carriage robbery wasn't enough to make Rob a hero. I'd been hoping for verbal confirmation and perhaps a few clues on the best way forward, but the fact that Tabitha hadn't been at the tree should have been confirmation enough.

Behind Eliza, a movement from her coachman caught my eye. He was crouched on the ground beside the boy, some sort of tool in one hand and the dead boy's wrist in his other. With a quick chopping motion, he sliced through the boy's finger, held it up for inspection then placed it into a bag at his waist.

I stifled a scream, forcing my eyes back to Eliza. John had said she was a witch. Perhaps that explained her coachman's actions. I straightened my back and started to turn away. There was nothing for me here. I was going to have to figure out how to make Rob into an acceptable Robin Hood on my own.

"You were telling me about Tabitha?" Eliza called. I turned to see her eyes narrow as she looked me over from head to foot, then gave a small nod. "She sent you back through the portal."

Or maybe she could help me. I stepped toward her. "Do you know how I get back to where I came from?"

Her smile was slow and beautiful but didn't reach her eyes. "You require a key." She blinked slowly. "Do you have a key, Lady Maud?" She put her hand out in front of her, palm up, waiting for me to hand it over.

My coin. Dad had called it a tether. But it was the thing that would help get me home, so I guessed it was a key. Perhaps I had to use it somehow.

I slipped the bracelet off my wrist and held the little piece of tainted copper out toward her. "This? Do you mean this?"

As she reached for it, a gust of wind whipped around us. It pulled at my cloak and whipped my hair around my face. And it cleared my head. That coin wasn't for her. Dad had told me to keep it on me at all times. I closed my hand around it. But she was faster and had it between her fingers before I could stop her.

She held it up to the sun, turning it over and inspecting each side.

Swallowing, I tried not to let her see the panic that was blooming in my chest. "That coin is very important to me. I'd like it back, please." Tears pricked at my eyes, and my voice wobbled even as

I tried to keep it steady. I might have just handed over the most important thing I owned.

Eliza closed her fingers around it. "It's very important to me, also. And I think you'll find you don't require it any longer."

That coin was my link to Josh, to my family. She was not taking it. "Give it to me!" I launched at her, a scream in my throat. She pulled her hand back, pushing me away at the same time. I stumbled and fell. With a growl, I jumped up to attack her again, just as a soldier rode out of the forest toward us.

He wore the burgundy and gold of the other soldiers, but his cloak was more detailed around the hem, more ornate. It was drawn out behind him so it covered the rump of his white horse. He was either wealthier than the other soldiers I'd seen, or a higher rank. Or both.

The commander of the soldiers perhaps? Eliza's Lord?

The handle of his sword glinted in the sunlight. I started to run, hoping I could make the forest before he saw me, but Eliza grabbed my wrist. I pulled at her, trying to get free, but her grip was like a vise.

"Let go of me," I growled. Although my back was now to him, I was certain that soldier was already galloping down here to shove his sword between my ribs.

She gave a slow nod, somehow remaining graceful even as she gripped my arm. "Give me the message from my sister. Then I'll let you go." The trees shrieked as another gust of wind whipped through the forest, leaves and dust pummeling my face. Eliza looked over my shoulder, toward the soldier. "Once Gisborne knows you're back, he'll not give you the chance to leave again. And since he's only moments away, you might as well tell me what I need to know. So I can go get my sister." Her smile was tight.

I stepped back, shaking my head. "She didn't...I don't..." I wanted to tell her there had been no message from the girl at the tree. But something tugged at my memory. Words I didn't remember, that didn't mean anything, sentences that had been running through my head as I fell backwards through time. Like waking from a dream, the memory was dancing just out of reach.

Her beautiful, serene face twisted into something menacing and she leaned in until her breath touched my skin. "Give it to me. I can see you know something. I know there's a message."

Perhaps there was. But the words skittered away the moment I tried to recall them. "Give me my coin. Then I'll tell you."

"Eliza!" The soldier's voice was a command spoken by someone used to being obeyed.

I struggled to break free, but her grip remained tight.

"Tell me what she said." She spoke into my ear, her jaw clenched.

"Give me my coin." My heart was racing. That soldier was almost here. I could imagine him raising that exquisite sword, bringing it down on my neck. Killing for the sake of killing, that's what they did. I pulled against her hold. "Let go of me!"

"Lady Eliza. Please unhand this poor girl. She looks positively petrified. I thought the reason you begged me to accompany you here was so you could collect your...medicines." He glanced at Eliza's coachman and a shiver ran up my spine. "Not so you could scare the locals."

My legs were trembling so hard I couldn't have run even if I'd been free. Oh, God. I was going to die.

Eliza looked up at him. "My lord." There was a tone in her voice I couldn't decipher— resignation, anger, love, it could have been any of those things or something else entirely. Her face had shifted back to serene, almost regal. "That's exactly what I'm doing. Collecting ingredients." She let go of my arm and walked away, calling over her shoulder. "I think you'll find this one isn't a local."

"I see you've met my cousin." The soldier's voice held a touch of amusement as he watched Eliza's back.

I looked from Eliza, to the soldier, to her coachman, to the far-away edge of the forest and a possible escape route. I couldn't decide who was the bigger threat. The soldier hadn't drawn his sword yet, that had to be a good thing. Unless he was planning to draw out my pain. I pulled my hands inside my cloak to hide their shaking. Stupid. I was stupid for coming here. Of course there would be soldiers. Eliza's coachman had said as much yesterday.

It wasn't only my safety that worried me. Hearing the soldier's name had made the hair on my arms rise.

Even from high on the back of his horse, I could see he was tall. He sat with a straight back, his chin somehow aloft even as he looked down at me. He had high cheekbones and jet-black hair, and looked nothing like I'd ever imagined of Sir Guy of Gisborne.

Because that's surely who he was.

And if Dad's stories were right, he was Rob's enemy.

Eyeing up the edge of the forest, I started to run. Within seconds, Gisborne's horse was in front of me. He slid off in a single movement, standing before me with round eyes. "Lady Maud?"

If I hadn't been so petrified, I might have rolled my eyes. Was there anyone around here who didn't know Maud Fitzwalter?

He reached out, then thought better of it, dropping his hand back down by his side. "Is it really you?"

I suddenly wished I knew more—or anything really—about Maud Fitzwalter. It had always been her father Dad was interested in, and so it had been Robert Fitzwalter we'd researched.

I licked my lips, suddenly all too aware I had no idea how the daughter of a baron was supposed to act, especially when talking to someone whose name began with 'Sir'. But since he was off his horse and staring as if he'd seen a ghost, I guessed perhaps I had the upper hand. "Sir Guy of Gisborne. It's been a long time."

"It's really you." His voice rose in surprise, as if he couldn't believe what he was seeing. Given what Rob had told me about Maud's disappearance, it was little wonder. "Your father had hundreds of people searching for you in the days after you left, and here you are, acting like a peasant in the forest."

I raised my chin, hoping he didn't notice my shaking hands. "Here I am."

He took a step forward. "It's good to see you, my lady."

I shuffled back. He might think he knew me, but all I saw was a soldier. I'd seen nothing so far to make me believe any soldier could be trusted.

His face fell, but he recovered quickly. "Where have you been these last two years? What have you been doing? You owe me an explanation after the way you left."

Maud may owe him an explanation, but not me. "I don't believe I owe you anything." I turned away, glancing at the edge of the forest. As I considered running again, Gisborne stepped in front of me.

He pushed a smile back on his face and held out a hand. "Come on. I'll take you home."

I glanced at the sword fastened to his hip. It was too easy to imagine him using it. I shook my head. "No, thank you."

"Come on, Lady Maud. Your father has offered a reward for your safe return. We'll use the money for whatever you want. Nottingham's where you belong, not out here."

I folded my arms over my chest, disliking the way this man assumed I'd do as I was told. "There are many places I *belong*. I don't believe any of them are with you."

He held up his hands, his voice softening. "I'll do anything, my lady. I've missed you so much. More jewels, beautiful dresses, whatever will make you happy." He must have caught my astonished stare because he hurried on, his voice pleading. "If...if it's still my cousin you want gone, I'll do it this time. I'll tell her today and she'll be gone from our lives by tonight."

I shook my head. It didn't matter how he bribed me, I wasn't going with him. Dad said he was Rob's enemy, and I was surprised to realize I considered him my enemy, too. "I have to go."

He took hold of my left hand, sucking in a breath as he looked at my fingers. The confidence on his face evaporated. "You're not wearing it. Did you lose it? I...I can get you another."

I pulled my hand away and straightened my back. "I'm sorry, my lord. But I have no idea what you're talking about." I tried to step around him, but he was standing too close. He took my hand again as if to double check.

"It's okay. I can get you a new ring, a new emerald. Or a different stone, if you prefer. It can be a homecoming gift *and* an engagement gift. If you're worried because you lost it, it doesn't matter to me." His smile was hopeful, his voice close to pleading.

I yanked my hand from his grasp and stepped back. "I suggest you listen carefully, my lord, because I'll say this only once. I will not go anywhere with a man who kills innocent people. I don't care if it's your job or if you do it for fun. It's deplorable, and I'll have no part of it." I hoped he would consider that a good enough reason for Maud to walk away from him. Without giving him time to answer, I started for the forest.

Wordlessly, he drew his sword, the hum of metal on metal ringing through the air.

Run. The instruction made it to my brain but not my limbs.

Gisborne pressed the sharp tip of his sword between my shoulder blades. Then his fingers clamped around my arm.

Twelve

I WENT still. It was only about fifty steps to the edge of the forest, but it might as well have been a thousand.

"Lady Maud. We can do this the easy way, or the hard. Either way, you will be coming home with me today." Gisborne's voice was like steel.

I lifted my chin and hid my shaking hands in my cloak, refusing to let him see what that blade did to me. "Let me guess. The easy way is where I turn around, take your hand and insist we leave right now, while the hard way is where you throw me over your shoulder and drag me to Nottingham?"

Gisborne moved closer. His sword pressed through the fibers of my cloak, digging into my skin. "It would appear you're still angry with me, so let me apologize. I'm incredibly sorry for hurting you, Lady Maud. I hope to never do it again. I've missed you and I want you to come home. I want everything to be the way we've planned since we were children." He didn't sound at all sincere. It sounded more like he spoke of a business transaction. He turned me to face him, keeping a tight grip on my upper arm. Though his sword was no longer touching me, it was still dangling in front of me, like a snake waiting to strike.

"If you think I'm going to accept an apology from a man holding me down and pointing his sword at me, you're sadly mistaken." I pulled against his grasp.

"Yes. I suppose it doesn't look the best." He tilted his head to the side. "I do mean it, though. I'm sorry I hurt you, Maud." This time, he met my eyes and there was sincerity in his voice. Perhaps he really had loved Maud. I wondered what he'd done to piss her off. Perhaps it had been a fight with him that had caused her to run into the forest to her death.

"Gisborne! Let her go!" Both of us started as Rob strode out of the forest. I closed my eyes in silent thanks. Not that I needed to be rescued—I was a strong, independent twenty-first century woman. Still, it was good to see him.

With the brown hood of his cloak pulled over his head and his bow balanced lightly in his left hand, Rob was ready, itching to pull an arrow from the quiver on his back. That he could do it so quickly and with such accuracy, his target would register the pain of the arrow hitting his chest at the same moment he realized the bow was pointing at him.

As Rob marched deliberately toward us, a gust of wind whipped the hood from his head. His eyes were on me, filled with cold rage. He tilted his head in a silent question, which I was surprised to find I understood.

I nodded. I was all right.

His mouth formed a thin, tight line as he stormed toward Gisborne.

Gisborne gasped. The sword fell from his hand and onto the leaf-strewn ground. His lips worked, searching for words. "Woodhurst? But...but you're dead."

Rob raised his chin, calling across the distance between the two of them. "Clearly your information on that matter is incorrect."

For a split-second, I was as still as Gisborne. Then I dropped to my knees and scooped up Gisborne's sword. I had the hilt in my hand and was climbing to my feet before he dragged his eyes from Rob. He snarled at me, then kicked at the sword, trying to dislodge it from my grip. I saw it coming and dodged. I was so pleased with myself I didn't see his second kick.

I felt it, though, his boot colliding with my right cheek.

My jaw throbbed, and blackness and bright lights engulfed me. Blinking them away, I found myself sitting on my butt in the wet grass, Gisborne's sword clenched in one hand.

Gisborne put a hand over his mouth. "Lady Maud. I'm so sorry. I meant to kick my sword from your hand. I never..." He stepped closer. I scrambled backwards, the world spinning.

"Get away from me," I growled.

Gisborne put his hands up in front of him, still advancing and ignoring my words. "I'm sorry, Lady Maud. I didn't mean to hurt you."

I backed up farther, still on the ground. I did not want that man anywhere near me. My empty hand—the one without Gisborne's sword in it—closed around a rock hidden among the long blades of grass. "Stay where you are." My voice was hard. I would hurt him if he came any closer, and I hoped he knew it.

He shook his head, his step not faltering. "Lady Maud." Another two paces and he'd be leaning over me.

Something inside me snapped. This man had kicked me hard enough to give me a concussion. He wasn't coming any closer. I picked up the rock and threw, hoping my aim was good enough to stop him, ready to jump to my feet and run if it was.

One minute, Gisborne was standing in front of me. The next, the stone hit his temple, his knees crumpled and he fell silently to the ground, out cold.

I'd done it. I'd stopped him.

All on my own.

I allowed myself a single congratulatory moment. Then, using Gisborne's sword like a walking stick, I pulled myself to my feet and started for the forest.

"Maud!" Rob's feet slapped against the grass as he ran down the hill toward me.

Everything was spinning. I leaned on the sword and met Rob's eyes. This time there was no question in his gaze. He didn't have to ask if I was all right, he could see I wasn't. "Can you walk?"

I nodded.

Taking Gisborne's sword from me and wrapping his other arm around my waist, Rob helped me up the hill. "You're okay. You're also mighty handy with a weapon, Lady Maud. Great shot." With his eyes, he assured me everything was going to be all right. And with his arm around me, I almost believed him. But there was tension in his face, tension humming through his body, and I doubted he believed his own words.

The moment the cool darkness of the forest closed in around us, John appeared on the trail. Without a word, Rob threw him Gisborne's sword, his own bow and the quiver from his back. Then he scooped me into his arms and carried me down the trail.

A small part of my brain told myself to focus on the moment, to enjoy being held tightly against his chest. But every step made my brain rattle until I thought it might explode. All I could do was close my eyes and wish he'd put me down sometime soon.

"Not much farther, Lady Maud." His voice was soothing, like honey on a sore throat.

"Keep going." I spoke between each step, not opening my eyes. "Don't. Want. Gisborne. To. Find. Us."

He let out a quiet laugh. "No need to worry about that. On a day like today, he'll not come far into the forest. He's afraid of the ghosts." As he spoke, a gust of wind howled through the trees, sounding very much like one of those ghosts.

Finally, he placed me gently onto a carpet of thick grass, and I opened my eyes to find we were beside a trickling stream. He crouched in front of me, taking my chin between his fingers and turning my head toward a shaft of moving light falling through the windblown trees. His forehead creased with concern.

"Is it bad?" At least now that we weren't walking, my brain wasn't trying to jump out of my head.

He removed his cloak and dunked the corner into the water. "Could have been worse." Turning back to me, he crouched and gently placed the cool cloth against my chin. I waited for him to smile, maybe tease me a little because of the lump forming on the side of my face, or for getting in the way of Gisborne's foot. But he remained serious, angry even.

The effect of the cold cloth against my skin was almost immediate, drawing the pain out of my jaw. It felt so good, I sighed loudly. Then felt my cheeks redden as Rob chuckled.

"I'm sorry, Lady Maud." The laughter was gone, and he was as serious as I'd ever seen him.

I frowned. "For what?"

He nodded at my jaw.

I had no idea why he felt the need to apologize. "Why? Did you do it?"

A tiny smile flicked over his face as I used his words back at him, quickly replaced by the anger he'd worn since Edwinstowe. Since my meltdown at the Big Tree, even. He ran a hand through his hair. "I should have known. Gisborne is—"

"What were you thinking, showing Gisborne your face like that?" Tuck pushed between the trees at our backs, already yelling before he reached us. "You could have ruined everything!" He put his hands on his hips and glared down at Rob.

If I'd thought Rob had been angry before, it was nothing compared to the way he looked at Tuck at that moment. He got slowly to his feet, jaw set. "Everything is already ruined. I'm fine with it. You should be too." His voice was even, but rage bubbled beneath every word.

Something had happened to put these two on opposite sides of what seemed to be an old argument. Likely, it was to do with my confrontation with Gisborne, but why my actions would have either of them this angry was anyone's guess.

Tuck stepped toward Rob. "You're only fine because you *like* her." He spat the final words at Rob, then glanced at me.

If that was Tuck's problem, then he could get over it. Rob didn't *like* me. Not the way he was suggesting.

Tuck poked a finger into Rob's chest. "Girls like her don't stick around for outlaws. Are you going to be happy with everything that's happened when she goes back to *him*?"

Rob stilled. "Is that all you think of me, Tuck? That I'm nothing more than an outlaw?" He turned his head to the place Tuck had come from, calling loudly. "John."

John appeared within seconds, clearly close by.

"Watch over Lady Maud."

"Rob! Wait." I got to my unsteady feet, wanting to step between Rob and Tuck, but too wobbly to move fast. "He doesn't care that you're an outlaw." If he did, Tuck would have been gone the day he found the poster.

Rob turned to look at me, blowing out a deep breath, the effort of keeping his voice even slowing on his face. "He does. But that's not what this is about. Not totally." He started to walk through the gap in the trees John had used.

"What are you going do to?" Because with both of them as angry as they were, the best thing would be for them to stay far from each other.

He didn't even turn as he spoke. "Relax, my lady. I'm just going to work through my anger."

As Rob stormed away, my chest tightened. I wished he'd stayed with me.

Before I could ask John what was going on, Tuck was leaning over me, his finger pointed at my chest. "This is all your fault. In three days, you've managed to ruin everything, in so many ways." His nostrils flared. Then he turned and followed Rob through the trees.

John sat, patting the ground beside him until I gave in and dropped down beside him. "You all right, milady?"

I nodded then winced as my head throbbed. "I don't understand. What's happening?"

"Rob just saw his little brother for the second time in six years." He paused. "For Gisborne, it was the first time he's seen Rob in the same amount of time. Seeing him has made Rob a little angry, and he's taking it out on everyone." He glanced at the dampened edge of Rob's cloak I was holding to my face. "Except, perhaps, you."

My attention caught on one word. "His brother?" I frowned. "You mean Gisborne?"

John nodded, his eyes going to the place in the trees where Rob had disappeared. "The one and only."

"But..." I wasn't sure I was making sense of John's words. Perhaps the kick to my jaw had damaged my hearing. "Gisborne thought Rob was dead. If they're brothers, why weren't they happy to see each other?"

"Surely you remember what happened to Gisborne's brother, milady?"

I shook my head, then sucked in a breath as a sharp pain stabbed behind my eyes.

If only I did.

John shrugged. "He died, lost in the forest." He stared at me as if there was more to say. "That's what the public were told, anyway." I met his gaze with a blank stare, and he sighed. "Gisborne tried to kill Rob the last time they saw each other. Until today, he thought he'd succeeded." He turned suddenly to me. "Don't listen to Tuck, milady. None of this is your fault. Rob would have gotten to this point on his own at some stage."

"What point?" What exactly was I being blamed for?

John spread his arms wide. "The point where he realizes he won't ever get the thing he's been focused on for the last six years." He gave my shoulder a squeeze. "I know Rob, milady. He won't be angry for long, and he's not angry with you. He just needs to get this out of his system."

I was so confused, but John had climbed to his feet and was following Rob and Tuck. "Wait! Where are you going?"

"To help Rob work through it."

I let him leave, unsure if I could get up without falling over. My head was throbbing. As I sat in the sweet-smelling grass, John's words replayed in my head. Rob and Gisborne, brothers? They looked, and from what I could tell, acted nothing alike.

Raised, angry voices had me on my feet before I realized I'd stood. Rob and Tuck. I wobbled but remained upright, and pushed my way through the undergrowth toward the sound.

Beneath a large tree where nothing grew, the two of them glared at each other, swords in hand. The burnt remains of an old fire lay in the middle of the dry dirt; the lowest branches were so high there would have been no danger of them catching alight.

Rob suddenly launched at Tuck, swinging his sword hard at his older friend. Tuck blocked, the clash of metal on metal making me jump.

I joined John and Miller at the edge of the clearing. Miller watched with folded arms, while John leaned on his staff. "Training?" Hope and fear mingled in equal parts in my voice. I knew what the answer was, I just didn't want to hear it.

John shook his head.

"This is for real? They're trying to hurt each other?"

John didn't have to answer. There was murder in Rob's eyes, the same sentiment etched on Tuck's face.

"Why don't you stop them?" My voice rose in pitch as Tuck's sword struck Rob's.

"Won't do no good, milady. This has been building between them for a while now. Worse since Rob killed the deer." John ran a hand through his hair, making it stand on end. He didn't seem particularly worried.

"You're going to let them kill each other?"

John shook his head. "I shouldn't think it'll come to that."

I stared with my mouth open as the blades clashed again. "You shouldn't think? Are you watching the same thing I am?"

"Aye, milady, I am." John shrugged. "I've seen them do this before. Many times."

I let out a breath. I was worrying over nothing. "They won't hurt each other?"

"Of course they will. How else will they know who won?" Miller shook his head as if telling me what a stupid girl I was.

Rob and Tuck traded insults, their words coming between heavy breaths and clashing swords. The clang of metal on metal was loud, even over the howling of the wind. If Gisborne had followed us, we weren't going to be hard to find.

"Rob! Stop this. You don't really want to hurt him." Yelling hurt my head, but someone had to make him see sense.

The blades hit together twice more before Rob replied between gasps. "You're wrong, my lady. I very much want to hurt him. Badly."

I swallowed, unsure if he wanted Tuck to be badly hurt, or if he just really wanted to hurt him. "Tuck. Please stop. The soldiers might hear you."

Tuck didn't bother to reply.

John leaned against his staff, grinning at me. "Too late to talk sense into them, milady. You'll just have to wait until they're done." He winced as Tuck came within centimeters of striking Rob's shoulder.

I wasn't waiting for them to cut chunks out of each other. "Give me that," I demanded, pointing to John's staff.

John's eyebrows rose. Then he broke into a larger grin and passed it to me.

The staff was heavier than I expected, too heavy for me to easily swing in the air the way John did.

Rob and Tuck circled each other, their breathing ragged. "Rob, please stop."

"Can't, my lady. I'm about to win." His eyes were fixed on Tuck.

"Not likely." Lines of sweat ran down Tuck's hairline, dying the neck of his robe dark brown.

I crouched, laying the staff flat on the dry dirt. There wasn't much room here—enough for the old fire that the boys had kicked out of the way as they fought, and clearly just enough for a sword fight. But it wasn't as if they could get far from each other. Or from me. When Rob drew nearer, I pushed one end of the staff toward him. As he straddled it, getting his feet in position for another strike, I pulled my end toward John. The staff twisted between Rob's legs and tripped him.

"Ha! Well done, milady." John clapped his hands together and Miller grinned.

Tuck loomed over Rob, sword near his throat. "Yield?"

Rob shook his head. "Unfair. Let me up and we'll finish this properly."

"Until the next time your *lady* gets in the way."

Rob's eyes hardened and he pushed onto his elbows. "She has a name."

"And she's fighting your battles for you. Yield."

Rob licked his lips. "Some would say it's you whose battle she's fighting given I'm down here."

Tuck considered this, then slowly pulled his sword back. I stepped between them before they could start more of this foolishness. "Stop it, both of you. You're being ridiculous."

Tuck's lip curled. "Stay out of this, girl. You talk about things of which you know nothing."

I glared at him, my fingers curling around the staff. "I know if you two keep this up, one of you will end up hurt." I took a step forward, placing the end of the staff on his chest and shoving him. He took a surprised step back. "Or dead." Another shove. Another step back. "I know that, angry as you may be, neither of you actually want that." I gave him one more shove, just to make my point. "I know if there are any soldiers nearby right now, they'll hear your swords. I know if Gisborne finds Rob, it won't end well. Shall I go on?" I looked between the two of them. Neither met my eyes.

I dropped the staff on the ground and threw my hands in the air. "For goodness sake, you're acting like children. Perhaps you should be fighting with wooden swords."

John guffawed. "She might be right, boys."

Still neither Rob nor Tuck moved. "Fine, if you want to slice each other up, do it. Just don't expect me to sit around and watch it happen. And don't expect me to sew either of you back together afterwards, either." I glared at them both, hoping one of them would give in and put his weapon down. Neither did. Shaking my head, I stormed away, pushing through the undergrowth to the grassy area beside the tiny creek. Sitting among the long blades of grass, I placed the wet corner of Rob's cloak against my aching jaw, waiting for the sound of clashing blades to resume. In my mind, I could see Tuck's blade slicing into Rob the way the soldier's blades had at Edwinstowe. The way Edward's must have done when Rob was a child. It terrified me. Despite what I'd said, I would sew both of them up if I had to. And the way they were going, I probably would have to.

The undergrowth rustled and Rob pushed his way out. He gave me a sheepish grin and looked at his feet.

His lack of remorse lit something inside me. I jumped up, and shoved him with my hands, the same way I'd just shoved Tuck. "What was that about? You wanted to kill your friend? You wanted to lead Gisborne here with all your noise? You thought it might be a nice day to die?" I was so relieved he was no longer in a fight for his life that I was suddenly itching for a fight of my own, needing to yell at him to make myself feel better. It wasn't lost on me that this was exactly the same thing, albeit less physical, as Rob had been doing with Tuck.

I turned away, wondering if my anger was only about his recklessness, or whether there was something else involved. No, that was a lie. I knew where my anger came from, I just didn't want to acknowledge it.

I should be focusing on...on making him into Robin Hood so I could go home, back to my brother. Instead, I was angry because a guy I'd only known for a few days had somehow made me care that he could have been injured in a reckless argument.

As much as I didn't want to admit it, I liked being around Rob. And that was almost as scary as the point of Gisborne's sword pressing between my shoulder blades. The only other person I enjoyed spending time with was Josh. I used to spend every night in his room, talking until he was tired. Then I'd read to him and watch him fall asleep.

But this thing with Rob was different. So different. When Rob was around, it was as if there was a little less air to breathe. But it was the most delicious and intoxicating oxygen that had ever filled my lungs.

I shook my head, trying to clear it. I was being stupid. Soon, I would return home. There was no point letting myself care about him. Or anyone else I met while I was here.

"I'm sorry. For making you worry that Gisborne would find us." Rob's voice was soft, his eyes still on the ground.

I swallowed, matching his tone. "What about yourself? Are you sorry for almost getting yourself killed?"

Rob's head shot up and his mouth opened. He shrugged. "I was always going to beat Tuck." He threw me a grin that quickly disappeared when I didn't return it. "I was never in any danger of dying, Lady Maud. And the only way I would have been hurt was if I moved too slowly. And I'm not slow."

I scowled. He didn't get it. Accidents happened. Even when they weren't supposed to. Even when no one expected them to.

He sighed. "If I'd been killed today, what would it have mattered?"

How could he ask that? "People would have been upset. Your family——"

"Don't have any."

"Your friends, then."

"You're overthinking this. It was an argument that has been brewing between Tuck and me for weeks. Neither of us would ever have hurt the other. Not badly, at least."

"Me, then."

There it was. The reason for my anger. *I* would have been upset.

I stepped toward him. My heart stopped, then sped up, the intensity on his face sending tingles through my entire body. I couldn't move. Couldn't breathe. My voice wouldn't come, but it didn't matter. Rob understood. Something in his face changed.

He stepped closer, touching his fingers to my cheek. I shivered. His fingers were rough, and calloused yet gentle, and my skin danced beneath his touch. I leaned into his hand, and he drew his fingers slowly down my cheek and along my jaw. My earlier thought swayed at the edge of my consciousness, telling me I didn't want this because I wasn't staying here. But the progress of his fingers across my skin pushed all coherent thought away, nothing else mattered.

I placed my hand on his chest, savoring the way his heart hammered against it. My own heart was beating the same way. I wrapped my fingers in the rough wool of his tunic, wanting to pull him closer but not daring to.

He blinked and stepped away. "I'm sorry," he mumbled. "I shouldn't have done that. You're not…"

"Not what?"

His face hardened and he turned away.

Anger shot through me. Was I so starved of affection I'd take the first thing that came along? Twice now, he'd done the same. Made me think…no, it didn't matter. I wasn't attracted to him, I couldn't be. I wasn't staying here. I was going home. To the family who'd pushed me away for years, to the father who had forced me, against my will to do his bidding. I was going back to it all rather than stay here with people I didn't know. So it didn't matter. Nothing mattered.

I felt the tears coming and swallowed them back before they could escape down my face. Before *he* could see them and think they were all about him. Because they weren't. Not even a little bit.

Thirteen

MILLER charged from the undergrowth, almost running me down. "Lady Maud." He caught himself, stopping in front of me. "There you are. John wants to know if you want him to brew up some chamomile tea?"

I forced myself to focus on what he was asking rather than the thoughts about Rob that were spinning in my head. "I...um..."

Rob nodded toward my jaw, watching me carefully. "Is your head hurting? The tea will help."

"Yes. Thank you, Miller. Tea would be good." I started to follow him back to where the boys had been fighting.

Rob placed his hand on my arm, stopping me. "Can you just...could you wait. Here. For a moment. Let me explain."

Color rose in my cheeks. I didn't need to talk about this. We were friends and that was it. I already knew how his love story went, and it was with a girl called Marian. Not with a time-traveler from the future, no matter how similar our names might sound. I shook my head and forced a smile onto my lips. "John's going to show me how to make something delicious for dinner. I need to go and help him."

It was a lie and Rob knew it, but he let me go. I felt his eyes on my back as I followed Miller's path through the undergrowth.

Under the tree where Rob and Tuck had fought, the others had reset and lit the fire already, a small pile of wood sitting next to it. The pot John used to cook meals was sitting on the dirt, and a second, smaller pot dangled over the flames. I sank down beside him. "Can I help?"

He glanced at me with a raised eyebrow. "You sure you shouldn't be resting? I've got some tea brewing." His eyes went to my jaw, and I wished I had a mirror to see how bad it looked. And some ibuprofen.

I glanced behind, expecting Rob to have followed me out of the forest. He hadn't. Worry knotted my stomach. Had those couple of seconds of stupid ruined the friendship that had been growing between us? I hoped not, but the fact that Rob hadn't come back yet said otherwise.

John saw my look and interpreted it with a quiet, "Ah." He settled back on his hands. "Dinner just needs to cook, nothing more to do there. Miller, Lady Maud wants to be kept busy. Do you have anything for her to do?"

Miller looked up from his sword, which he'd been lovingly cleaning, and shook his head. "Sorry, milady. Maybe you should lie down and rest."

"That does seem to be the general consensus," I said dryly. I didn't want to lie down. I wanted to occupy my mind.

"Your head must be aching. He kicked you bloody hard." John looked me over and I shrugged. There wasn't much anyone could do about a headache. "I'd say he's damn lucky Rob didn't gut him, for hurting a woman that way...for hurting...you. Had he not been so worried about you, I dare say he would have."

I shrugged. "Rob doesn't need to get himself into trouble because of me. Just helping me back to the forest was more than adequate."

John opened his mouth to say something, then thought better of it. Pulling the pot out of the flames, he poured out some tea. "Think we might stop another carriage tomorrow."

Glad to change the subject, I said, "Perhaps some better planning might be in order."

"You have a squabble with our planning, milady?" Miller got to his feet and wandered over to the fire.

"She has a *problem* with everything." Tuck glanced at Miller, correcting his mistake. I hadn't noticed Tuck sitting at the edge of the undergrowth, but now he'd spoken, I could see him in the shadows, a mug of tea already in his hand.

I narrowed my eyes. "That's a little unfair, don't you think?" I was struggling to recall anything I'd objected to since I'd been here.

Tuck shrugged, his stare daring me to object further, but I wasn't in the mood. Half of me was listening for Rob's return, the other half was battling a headache.

"What would you do differently, Lady Maud?" John grinned.

I took a sip of my tea. "Perhaps be more certain there weren't soldiers following the carriage."

John rolled his eyes as if my idea was ridiculous. "Oh, yes. And how would you do that, exactly?"

I shrugged. It hurt to think. "Maybe choose a place where the trail is long and straight and stop the carriage right in the middle. Then you'll have plenty of warning of approaching soldiers. Or maybe have someone climb a tree so we can see them from farther away."

"Climb a tree?" I gripped my mug tighter at the sound of Tuck's mocking voice. "And get stuck up there when your *friends* find us stealing from them? Ha. Sounds like a trap to me."

"My *friends?* What does that mean?" I wasn't letting that go without a challenge. If my head wasn't hammering so badly, I'd have gotten to my feet.

"You're a smart girl. I'm sure you can figure it out."

"What is it you don't like about me exactly, Tuck?" I guessed it had something to do with the deer, but it seemed deeper than that.

"Girls like you don't belong out here in the forest. Not without a reason. I'm just trying to work out what your reason is. And whether it's going to end badly for us."

"I'm not here to hurt you." I looked at the others. There was nothing I could say to make him understand why I was here. What I did say was probably the worst thing I could have said. "Rob believes me."

"Then Rob's a fool!" Tuck shot back.

"Tuck!" John's voice was a low rumble, a warning. He said nothing more, but then, neither did Tuck.

"The middle of a long, straight trail, you say?" Miller bit on his lip as if neither Tuck nor John had spoken. "That might actually work."

I twisted my head, ignoring my rage. "You mean my idea has merry?"

Miller grinned at me. "That's exactly what I mean, milady."

I smiled, enjoying our private joke since most everyone else around here was being a giant jerk today.

Talk between the three of them continued around how and where they might be able to stop another carriage. I didn't join in. Tuck had made it quite clear he would disagree with whatever I said, anyway. As I listened to the rise and fall of their excited voices, I kept my ears and eyes open for Rob's return. I didn't want to watch out for him, but that's what I found myself doing.

It grew dark and we ate dinner. No one made comment about Rob's absence, and I wasn't going to be the one to bring it up. So, I ate my meal without tasting it and stopped listening as they spoke, casting my ear further afield. With each minute that went by, I grew more worried. There was a part of me that knew I was being silly, but I couldn't help it.

Just as I couldn't take it anymore and was about to ask John where he thought Rob might be, I saw him. He was leaning a shoulder casually against a tree in the place the light of the fire turned to shadow. He'd arrived silently, though I would have bet John knew he was there. I let out a deep breath, glad he was all right.

It was too dark to make out his face, but his eyes were on me. I could feel the weight of them, even as I tried to pretend I was interested in whatever it was John was explaining to Miller. A second glance at him and he beckoned. I got to my feet and walked to him without even excusing myself.

Rob took my hand, leading me away from the fire and into the darkness of the forest. The contact with him was soothing, easing away the worries I'd been feeling. About him. About us. About the soldiers.

Even once my eyes adjusted to the lack of light, I still managed to trip on every root on the trail, and I wished I had a flashlight. But Rob kept a tight grip of my hand, and I didn't once land on the ground.

He led me up a small hill, the path so narrow I had to walk behind him. Water gurgled nearby, and nocturnal bugs buzzed through the forest. It felt like we'd walked for hours when we stopped on top of a large rock.

The waning moonlight lit up Rob's face, but I couldn't gauge his mood. He'd not yet spoken. Rob tugged on my hand, pulling me toward the edge of the rock. "Come look."

The rock was smooth, but uneven, and I had no wish to fall to my death. Rob was sure-footed, and I trusted him. I inched out behind him, stopping a few steps from the edge. Here was the source of the running water. A little waterfall, burbling between the rocks to a stream below. Pretty and serene.

"I come here when I need to think." Rob's quiet voice cut through the night air. I thought he was watching me, but when I turned to look, his eyes were on the water. Perhaps it had been wishful thinking.

I nodded. "It would be the perfect place for alone time. Is this where you've been all evening?"

Rob dropped my hand and clasped his own behind his back. "Now, that would be telling."

The weight that had been locked inside my stomach since I'd last spoken to Rob, moved. He didn't sound angry. "I'll take that as a yes, then."

He sat, swinging his legs over the edge, then patted the place beside him. Sliding forward, I sat down.

"Did you get what you needed from Eliza?"

Okay. We weren't going to talk about what had or hadn't happened between us before. Fine by me. I shook my head. "She...wasn't who I thought she was. And she stole something of mine." My voice caught as I thought of how much I'd lost when she took my coin. Not only was it a link to my family in the nostalgic sense, but it was my way home. "I'm going to get it back. I just need to find her again. Any ideas?"

"On finding Eliza?" He shrugged. "She'll be wherever my brother is. He has land in Gisborne and Woodhurst, so they could be in either place. But with the Sheriff's tournament coming up, they'll be heading for Nottingham in the next week or so."

"That's perfect," I said, my voice soft. We were going to the tournament anyway. By the time we reached Nottingham, with any luck, Rob would be Robin Hood and I'd just have to retrieve my coin to go home.

"It means you have to spend three more weeks with us."

Three more weeks living in the danger of the forest, away from Josh. Three more weeks with

Rob. I wasn't sure whether to be disappointed or ecstatic.

Rob drew in a deep breath, his next words tumbling out in a rush. "I wanted to explain. About before." Rob glanced my way, then looked back at the flowing water below us. Tension made his shoulders rigid.

I shook my head. "There's nothing to explain. Nothing happened. Neither of us wanted anything to happen." I shrugged. "It's all good."

Something flickered across his face, gone before it was really there. Then he gave me a wide smile, a relieved smile perhaps. "Nonetheless, I would still like you to understand. About everything that happened today. About Gisborne."

"That he's your brother?"

Rob's voice was like steel. "Gisborne is the son of my mother and my uncle. He stopped being my brother the moment he shot an arrow into my back and left me for dead in the forest six years ago." He looked down, drawing a deep breath in before blowing it out, pushing all his anger away. When he met my eyes again, he was calm with the hint of a smile on his face. "Another scar I might show you one day, if you're lucky."

I shook my head. "I don't want to see your scar."

He raised an eyebrow, his gaze telling me he didn't believe me for a second.

Rather than admit he might be right, I changed the subject. "Why did he do it?"

The smiled disappeared from his eyes. "To get Woodhurst Manor. It was mine, but if I died, it reverted to my uncle, and then eventually to Gisborne."

"So, he just left you to die?"

"That's what he does, Maud. Whatever it takes to get what he wants. You might not have seen that side of him in the past, but something tells me you know it's there." He left the other words unspoken. *Otherwise, you would have gone to Nottingham with him today.*

It was better to stick with the story I'd given, than to pretend about something I couldn't know. "I don't remember. I barely remember *him*. I just knew I didn't want to go anywhere with someone using a weapon to bend me to their will." I watched him a moment, something clicking into place in my mind. "Is Gisborne the real reason you want to go to the tournament? To kill him?" I'd thought from the moment they invited me to travel with them that Rob's reason for attending the tournament was about more than the gold on offer. Suddenly it made sense.

He looked away.

"It is! Do the others know?" Because attacking Gisborne while so many others were around seemed dangerous.

Rob's shrug said, *of course they know.* "John always has my back. Miller too, although I think he secretly wants to win some of the gold on offer." He gave a wry smile. "And Tuck hopes he's going to be able to talk some sense into me before we get there."

"And will he?"

Rob shook his head. "I have to do this, Maryanne. Especially now he knows I'm alive. If I don't, he'll hunt me until he can kill me."

I didn't agree. I didn't like it, either. But something told me everyone else had tried, and failed, to talk him out of it, so I bit my tongue.

"It was brave of you, what you did to him today." He said the words quietly, and it was almost like he hadn't said them at all. Then he spoke louder, our eyes meeting in the moonlight. "Unfortunately, it only gets worse from here. After today, there are just two things Gisborne wants."

"A sense of morality and a new sword?"

Rob smiled, letting himself relax for a moment. It was something he didn't do often, I'd noticed. Not properly, anyway.

"If only. Morals and Gisborne don't mix. No. He wants you, perhaps only because you turned him down. And he wants me to suffer. There's a high likelihood he'll try to achieve the second by doing the first, and if he does, it won't be pleasant for you." He swallowed, looking into my eyes to make sure I understood.

I didn't. "You mean marrying Gisborne will be an unpleasant life for me?" Not that I intended to walk that particular path.

He shook his head. "I mean, if he captures us both together, he'll likely make me watch while he hurts you. And then..."

"And then what?"

The steel returned to Rob's voice. "He's already tried to kill me once, Maud. What do you think will happen?"

I stared at him. Rob's brother would use me to hurt him, and then kill Rob anyway. I licked my lips. "Are you asking me to leave?"

Rob closed his eyes. When he opened them the hatred for his brother was replaced by fragile gentleness. "I'm asking you to think carefully about what you want. I can find you somewhere safe to stay. Somewhere far from me, and from Gisborne. Or I can return you to Nottingham and help you get in touch with your father. But, Maud, while you're with us, know that I will not give Gisborne any reason to hurt you. Do you understand? And he may come looking for you anyway."

"That's very 'dashing hero' of you, but I can look after myself. Unless I've been kicked in the head." I grinned, attempting to lighten the mood.

I earned a weak smile in return. "Not against Gisborne, you can't. If you decide to stay with us, you'll be an acquaintance of mine, nothing more. There won't be any more river swims. He glanced at the bloody wounds on my hands from my fight with the tree this morning. "Or hand bandaging, or midnight walks. I'll be respectful of course, but there won't be...anything else. Not even friendship."

We couldn't be friends? "Surely Gisborne won't—"

"He will. Whatever you're thinking he won't do, he's capable of. Trust me. It's..." He swallowed. "It's better this way."

If this was what he wanted, I wouldn't fight him on it. In fact, I'd show him it was no big deal. "We didn't have anything different to that, anyway." Except a friendship better than any I'd known in years.

Something flashed in his eyes, and his gaze hardened. "Then I guess things won't change much while you're with us."

"I guess not." Making sure he became Robin Hood would be easier if I wasn't crushing on him, anyway. Not that I had been before, but just in case I ever did. "What if...Gisborne thinks we have a relationship anyway? I mean, you stormed out of the forest to save me. It might look, well...bad."

"If we come across him again, he'll think you're just traveling with us. We won't give him any reason to think otherwise."

Seemed he'd thought of everything.

Fourteen

THE next two weeks took a regular pattern, which included walking, stopping carriages for gold, and handing that gold to villages Gisborne's men had previously raided looking for unpaid taxes. Sometimes Rob took other things on the trail—like horses. He'd trade them for gold, or hand them straight to the people, never keeping a thing for himself. He was everything Dad suggested he might be, and watching him hand over gold he could have used himself made me proud.

As word of what we were doing spread, the moment we arrived in a new village people would come out with Rob's name on their lips. Sometimes they'd offer a couple of spare eggs, or a loaf of bread in thanks, but mostly, though they desperately wanted to, they had nothing to give in return. The women burst into tears when one of us pressed a gold coin into their hands, knowing they could now feed their children. Occasionally a man offered to join us, but Rob always refused that too, telling them their families needed them.

Rob was as good as his word. The two of us had stopped talking to each other from the moment he'd brought me back from the waterfall. In the two weeks since that night, he hadn't once looked at me, nor I at him—it just seemed easier for both of us to pretend the other didn't exist.

John and Miller had noticed our lack of conversation and kept trying to fill the silence as we traveled toward Nottingham.

Miller: *Want me to preach you how to use a sword, milady?*

John: *The word's teach, and she's got better things to do.*

Miller: *Like what?*

John: *She wants me to* teach *her how to cook.*

Miller: *Ha! What for? Cooking won't do her no good if she gets sliced up by a sword.*

John: *What do you think, milady?*

I'd roll my eyes and grin at them, to which Miller would say, "Want me to teach you to use a sword?" and the conversation would go around in a circle again. I didn't mind. They meant well, and listening to them stopped me worrying about what might happen if we met soldiers on the trail, or what would happen if I didn't find my coin.

Tuck seemed completely happy with the new situation, he and Rob spending almost all their time together. Tuck was even a little more tolerant of me. And though the new arrangement wasn't awful, it wasn't as good as it had been before.

As I hid at the edge of the trail wondering how much more Rob needed to do before he could be considered Robin Hood, a little wooden carriage with black wheels rumbled toward us, bumping loudly over the rough ground. John's bow rested in the leaves at my feet, the same as it did every day when there were carriages involved. I wasn't going to use it. I was sure they all knew it, yet Rob still insisted John leave it with me.

As the carriage drew closer, Rob stepped onto the trail, sword in hand, with John and Miller behind him. Miller's sword was sheathed but he was ready to draw it if he needed to, and John clutched his staff.

The carriage stopped in front of Rob, and the door opened almost immediately. A man in a bright purple tunic and matching hat stuck his head out. He looked at Rob, then held a little pouch out between his fingers. "Thought it might be you. I don't have much money and I don't want any trouble." He spoke quickly, perhaps trying to hide his fear.

Rob took the pouch, not bothering to look inside. He bowed his head. "The people of Blyth thank you, sir." With a nod, he indicated Miller and John should step aside.

Before they could move, six soldiers in Nottingham's colors rounded the corner on horseback. Coming our way. Fast.

I got to my feet. "Run!" I screamed, when no one moved.

The soldiers dug their heels into their horses. They sped toward us, hoof beats the only sound I could hear. "Rob! Run!" I clenched my fists tight, ready to sprint farther into the trees once I knew they were safe.

John moved first. He dropped his staff and dived through a bush ten steps away from me. I expected to see Miller right behind him. But when I looked back on the trail, he was standing where he'd always been, unmoving. His eyes were round, and he stared at a soldier mere seconds from slicing into him with his sword. Rob yelled, but his words were lost in the pounding of the hooves. He ran at Miller, grabbing the sleeve of the boy's tunic. But he wasn't fast enough. The soldier raised his sword.

"Rob!" I screamed.

The sword bit into Miller's arm. He screamed—I might have, too—and his legs crumpled.

Rob put an arm around Miller's waist and dragged him to his feet. They weren't far from safety, but Miller was slow. So very slow. A dark stain grew on the arm of his tunic.

Another soldier rode at them. Rob raised his sword to block his blow. Two more steps and they'd be at the forest on the other side of the trail. Two more steps and they'd be hidden from arrows among the dense foliage where a horse couldn't follow. Two more steps and they'd be safe for now.

There were too many soldiers, too close. I had to go, too. Didn't know where, just had to run. With a final glance at Rob, I sprinted deeper into the forest. Pushed through bracken, past ferns, dodged branches. Louder than my ragged breathing, footsteps pounded into the ground behind me. Someone was there, getting closer. I glanced behind and caught a flash of burgundy. A soldier's cloak. Faster, I had to run faster. I had no weapon. No way to defend myself. John's bow was on the ground where I'd left it, and the soldier was getting closer.

I jumped over a fallen log, fell, then scrambled to my feet. My chest was tight with panic. I couldn't let him catch me.

A hand closed on my arm, gripping tighter than a vise. I screamed and twisted, trying to wrench away. Almost succeeded. But the soldier clamped his other hand around my wrist so tightly I couldn't move.

"Lady Maud. I thought it was you." Gisborne was out of breath, his black hair stuck to his forehead with sweat.

"My lord." I went still, hoping he might loosen his grip.

He let one hand free, but not the other. "There's no need to run from me."

I pulled my lips into a tight smile and tried to keep my voice from shaking. "You and I will have to disagree on that count, due to the sword you pressed to my back the last time we saw each other."

I glanced at his fingers circling my wrist, the way his thumb and middle finger overlapped in the middle. Mom had made Carrie and I attend a self-defense class with her last year in case anyone ever grabbed us in the street. Lucky for me, the maneuver would work just as well in the forest.

Gisborne pouted. "Really, my lady. I would never hurt you. You must know a joke when you see one."

"Oh, believe me, I do. And that wasn't one." Twisting my arm, I pulled it up toward his thumb, using my other hand for extra leverage. Just like that, I was free. As Gisborne stared at his now empty hand in surprise, I aimed a kick between his legs. His chainmail rattled and he let out a howl and dropped to the ground. My foot throbbed from the metal of his suit, but not enough to stop me running.

I crashed through the forest, not caring how noisy I was, or how many branches scratched my face and arms. All I cared about was using the few extra minutes I'd gained to get as far from Gisborne as I could. There was no trail and I had no weapon. Running was my only defense.

I sprinted until I couldn't breathe, until the stitch in my side grew so bad I couldn't move any more. Then I stopped and listened for the footsteps of my pursuer. To my relief, there was nothing except the chirping of birds and a soft wind high in the trees. I was fairly sure Gisborne hadn't been in any condition to come after me, but still I couldn't relax. What if he could move silently through the forest, the same way Rob could? Perhaps he was waiting for me behind the next tree, ready to drag me to Nottingham so I could go and live Maud Fitzwalter's life. Or to torture me, the way Rob had suggested he might.

No. I would not think about that. I would not let myself become paralyzed by fears that were nothing but shadows. Gisborne hadn't followed me. He was probably curled on the forest floor, still trying to catch his breath. I picked up a heavy stick from the ground—it would do as a weapon for now, because...I had to go back. No matter how much it scared me, I had to find the others, to check if they were okay.

Rather than the mad panic of my run, my steps in the general direction of the main trail, became slow and deliberate. With every couple of paces, I stopped and listened. There was a chance, quite a high one, I was going in the wrong direction. The modern convention said don't move if you're lost in the forest, let rescuers come to you, and that thought was at the front of my mind with each step I took. I thought—hoped—Rob or one of the others would search for me as soon as they could. But since I had no clue if any of them were captured or injured, I couldn't sit around and hope they found me. I had to keep moving.

There was a rustle behind me, and my heart lurched. *Gisborne.* I'd been wrong about him. He *was* looking for me. A branch cracked. I raised my stick over my head, gripping it so tightly my fingers ached. As fast as I could, I turned around and swung it like a baseball bat.

The stick caught on the branches of a low hanging tree, taking some of the force from my swing.

But not all of it. My stick hit the raised forearm of my attacker.

He cried out and jumped back. "Lady Maud, it's me." He pulled off his hood.

I dropped the stick on the ground. "John! Why didn't you say so?" He rubbed his arm vigorously. "Oh, my gosh! I'm so sorry." I nodded to his arm. "I thought you were someone else."

He gave me a lopsided grin. "I should hope so, milady. Otherwise you and I have a serious problem with our friendship."

Tears pricked at my eyes. I was no longer being alone, but now I was worried about pointless things. "I left your bow behind."

"Ah, milady. No harm done. Was just a bow." He gave a shaky laugh.

"Did I injure you?" I reached out to look at his arm.

John shook his head. "Nothing more than a little bruise. Did Gisborne hurt you? I saw him chase after you, but I lost you both in the forest."

I winced. "Not as much as I hurt him."

"Good on you." John gave me a grin. "Come on. We have to get away from here."

"What about Rob, Tuck and Miller?"

The joviality immediately left John's face and he gave a slow shrug. "They're on the other side of the trail. They'll meet us at King's Cave as soon as they can; that's where you and I are going."

Despite his seriousness, he seemed certain and I felt better.

I followed John through the endless forest, over trails narrower than the width of my foot and through areas where there was no trail at all. Branches pulled at my face and cloak, scratching me and holding me back. Finally, we climbed a steep, shrub-covered hillside, and crawled through a small rocky opening. The cave—Kings Cave—opened up to an area big enough to seat fifteen people, but the ceiling sloped at the back until it was too low to stand up. Light fell across the center of the cave from an oculus above.

I searched the darkness for Rob and the others, but we were alone and I had the feeling I wasn't the only one disappointed. "Should they be here by now?"

John shook his head. "They'll get here when they get here." He sat down against the wall of the cave and fished in his bag, pulling out some sort of dried meat, broke it in half and handed a piece to me. "Plenty of things might have held them up."

"Yeah. And most of them are bad." I settled beside him and stared at the food in my fingers, too worried to eat.

He laughed as if I were joking, though there was tension around his lips. "No, milady. Some of them are bad. There are plenty of things that might have kept them away that are good."

I huffed out a breath. It felt as if a permanent frown was glued to my forehead, and I had the beginnings of a headache. Miller's arm had been bleeding, and Rob had half-carried him away from the soldiers. I couldn't think of a single positive reason for them not to be here yet. "Like what?"

John pressed his lips together, tapping them gently with his fingertips. "They came across someone they knew who asked them to stay for dinner."

I tilted my head to one side. "If you're trying to make me feel better, it's not working."

"Okay. Maybe they found a nice dark cave to hide in and then fell asleep. Once they wake up, they'll come here."

I pulled my knees up to my chest, my knuckles turning white as I held onto them. If these were the best reasons John could come up with, then something had to have gone very wrong.

John cleared his throat, suddenly interested in his hands resting on his lap. "Lady Maud. The very worst thing you could do to my friend is to make him think he has something with you, only to have you change your mind and go back to his brother."

"I...ah..." I blinked a couple of times trying to clear my head. John was the last person I expected to have this kind of conversation with; he didn't seem like the sort to talk about anything too serious. "You think, even knowing I've run from Gisborne twice, I'm still going to go off and marry him?" I was avoiding the real subject and hoping John wouldn't notice.

"I don't know. You do seem worried for Rob right now." He shook his head, looking up at the hole in the ceiling, and the grey sky beyond. "I guess I don't understand why you'd choose this." He swept his arm around him. "Over the grand life you could have if you returned to your home. Unless," he gave me a sideways glance. "You intend to stay in Nottingham after you've found Eliza?"

I shook my head. I didn't intend to spend much time in Nottingham at all, if I could help it.

John drew his hand down his face. "I like you, Lady Maud, but if you're going to hurt Rob, do it now before this thing between you goes any further."

I shook my head, bewildered. "The last thing I want is to hurt Rob; he's done more for me than anyone else that's been in my life these last few years. I have no intention of marrying Gisborne, either." I shrugged. "And for the record, there's nothing between Rob and me. We're not even talking anymore, so you have nothing to worry about there."

John grinned, the first proper smile I'd seen from him since the soldiers attacked. "Just you keep telling yourself that, milady. One day you might even believe it."

"But——"

He shook his head, his eyes still warm, and put up his hand to stop me talking. "I've seen what's between you and Rob. Neither of you could keep away from each other if you tried." He took a bite of his food. "Rob and the others will be here soon. They've probably stopped at Mansfield to hand out the gold."

I drew a deep breath then let it out slowly. Of course. That made complete sense. It had to be the reason they weren't here yet.

It was mid-morning the next day before they returned. John and I had silently decided to sit out the front of the cave in a small patch of sunlight, both too worried to speak. As we made ourselves comfortable, the three of them were suddenly there, standing in front of us.

I grinned and jumped up with a squeal. "You're all right!"

Miller's arm looked like it might need a new bandage, but other than that, they seemed no worse for wear.

Forgetting our new, Gisborne-proof arrangement, Rob engulfed me in a hug, holding me so tight I could feel his heart beating in his chest. I wrapped my arms around him and closed my eyes. I'd wondered if I'd see him again, and now that he was here, all I could do was smile. He was safe. They were all safe.

Pulling away, he held me at arm's length running his eyes over me. "Are you okay? Gisborne didn't hurt you?"

"I'm fine. We're both fine." I glanced at John who was patting Tuck on the back and laughing with Miller. "What about you?"

"Miller's arm has a nasty cut, but it could've been worse. We stopped off at the healer in Mansfield for a salve, so hopefully it'll be okay. Tuck and I are fine."

John clapped Rob on the back, and Rob smiled.

"Where have you been? The Lady's been beside herself with worry." John grinned at me.

I raised my eyebrows. "I wasn't the only one."

John turned his lips down at the edges. "What? Me? No, I wasn't worried, milady. Knew they'd turn up eventually. They always do."

I glanced at each of them in turn. "Well? Where else have you been? It doesn't take that long to get a salve."

"We were looking for you. Should have known John would find you first." Miller held his arm tightly against his body, but he wasn't pale, so I didn't think he was too badly injured.

"Shouldn't have bothered," muttered Tuck.

My lip curled, and words I hadn't wanted to snarl at Tuck for two weeks rose to the surface.

Before I could speak, Rob stepped between us. "Stayed at Mansfield for the night, handed out some of the gold we got yesterday."

John nudged me. "See. Told you."

"Then searched some more before coming here this morning." He looked at me, his forehead creased. "I thought Gisborne had you. I saw him chase after you, but I was on the other side of the trail, and Miller was bleeding..."

"He did. But a well-aimed kick was all it took to get away." I sounded braver than I'd felt.

Miller raised his eyebrows. "Whoa-ho! Very impressionable, milady."

I smiled, not having the heart to correct his mistake. Neither, it seemed, did anyone else.

John grinned. "Remind me never to make you angry. Or to keep my distance, if I do!"

I raised my chin, hoping to match John's jovial tone. "That's quite possibly something you all should remember."

John and Miller laughed, but Rob remained serious. "You need to get over your fear of the bow. It's too dangerous to be out here without a weapon."

Panic punched me in the chest. "I can't." I glanced at John and Miller, hoping for backup.

John nodded. "Rob's right."

"No." I shook my head again. Being in a high stress situation with a bow was only going to end badly. "A bow wouldn't have helped yesterday when Gisborne grabbed my wrist."

Rob shrugged. "Maybe not. But using it earlier could have stopped him from getting that close in the first place."

"It certainly wouldn't hurt to have another archer to rely on while we're stopping carriages." Tuck chewed on his bottom lip.

I glared at him. Out of everyone, I'd been certain he wouldn't want me to have a weapon. "Don't I get a say in this?"

Rob shook his head. "You'll say you don't want to, probably because you don't think you can do it. I, on the other hand, disagree. You might be one of the best archers in the forest, with a little practice." He grinned. "Behind me, of course." He held out his hand. "And I'll prove it to you." He looked at John. "Do you think it's safe to stay here another night?"

John nodded. "There's no one else nearby, from what I can tell."

"Lady Maud, come with me."

 FIFTEEN

I STARED at his offered hand feeling bullied, and thought about telling him to get stuffed. But he was staring at me with his eyebrows raised and the hint of a smile on his face. The smart-assed smile he hadn't shared with me since the day I met his brother. All I could do was take his hand.

We didn't go far, just a few minutes' walk around the base of the hill. The clearing Rob found was so small that the sunlight drifting down was mostly dappled by the leaves of the surrounding trees. Long, patchy grass covered the ground and a huge log spanned the entire width.

My mouth went dry and I thought I might faint. I pulled my hand from his grasp. "You're making me do something I don't want to do."

His grin was wide. I wanted to hit him. "You know, I do get that feeling." He held his bow out to me.

My heart was racing so hard I couldn't catch my breath. It was one thing to hold a bow. It was quite another to shoot it. "Then why are you forcing me?"

He sighed, running a hand down his face. "Because you're more than capable of taking care of yourself with a bow. You just need to believe you can do it."

I couldn't do it. But I could change the subject and hope he'd forget this stupidity. "Are we back to being friends again? Not worrying about what Gisborne might do if he finds us together?" I'd missed his friendship so much that if this was the price, I might just consider it.

He shook his head refusing to look at me. "Not friends. This is me making sure everyone in this group is safe, and that they can remain that way when there is no one else to rely on."

I set my jaw. Fine by me. I was here to do a job, and that was all. But I needed him to understand why I couldn't do what he was asking. "Can I tell you about it?"

His eyes went round.

"Strictly in a not-friends context, of course. Just so you know what this member of your group might be going through when you force her to pick up a bow."

He nodded slowly. "If you're sure?"

"I am." Because talking was better than doing. "Shall we sit?" My voice was clipped with stress. I indicated to the fallen log, then sat on it before he could answer. He sat beside me, twisted in so our knees almost touched, so he could see my face as I talked.

I swallowed hard, terrified of this conversation. Scared of what Rob would think of me once he knew. Although, if he decided I wasn't the sort of person he wanted to be around and left me here on my own, at least I wouldn't have to pick up the damn bow.

I thought back to the afternoon at the archery range, a memory that always lingered at the edge of my mind, waiting for an opportunity to assault me. There was a group of adults there that day, shut away in the meeting room discussing our up-coming trip to the National Championships. Me, Josh, Carrie and another boy were the only kids there. "I was stupid, cocky, thought I knew it all. When this boy, Liam, told me I was just a dumb girl and could never shoot as well as him for at least the hundredth time, I decided to prove him wrong." Liam Dawson had been the National Boys Archery Champion for three years running, so he had a pretty strong claim on being the best in the club. But I'd won at last year's championships and I knew—or thought—I was good. It was an old argument between the two of us, something Liam started almost every time he saw me. I glanced up at Rob. His leg was warm beside mine, and he was watching me intently. "We set up some targets and he shot first, got close to the center. I wasn't worried, knew I could do better, even told him to leave his arrow on the board, cocky enough to think I could hit it. Cocky about everything." I took a deep breath. Time to admit how stupid I'd been.

"My little brother was there." Unexpected tears sprang to my eyes at the thought of Josh. I missed him so much and I despised thinking about this day. "He used to look up to me, used to want to be just like me. And I didn't care enough to keep him safe." My voice wobbled, and a tear escaped down my cheek. I raked my hand down my face, swiping it away. "I let him stand to the right of the target, so he'd be the first to see up close what the result was. I wasn't even worried for him. There was no possible way I'd shoot so badly I'd miss the target completely. I'd made shots like this a hundred times before. Someone handed me my bow, I lined the shot up. And fired." Carrie had handed me my bow that day. And every day since then, she'd punished herself for that one small act by barely eating.

Rob started to speak, but I talked right over top of him. Now I'd started, I needed to finish.

"Everything happened really fast. My arrow hit the one that was already in the target, ricocheted off it and hit my brother just below the eye socket. Now he's blind in one eye. He should be able to see out of the other, but he can't. The doctors say it's psychological." I glanced at him, unsure if he'd understand. "You know, in his head, almost like he's pretending."

I stared at my feet, unable to face the look I knew I'd see on Rob's face. But I pre-empted his words, words I'd heard a thousand times already and knew I'd hear a thousand more. "I know it was stupid, I've known that since the second I hurt him. You can't tell me anything I haven't already told myself. If I had the choice, I'd take it back. There's no one I care more about in the world than my little brother."

The silence stretched out between us until I finally looked up. As our eyes met, he shook his head. There was no pity there, only sadness. "I've done some pretty reckless things, too. Only difference is, I got lucky. You already know how stupid it was, why would you need me to tell you?"

I blew a breath out my nose, a humorless almost-laugh. "Because most people feel the need to make it very clear."

"It's the guilt that gets you, isn't it?" He squeezed my shoulder, reminding me it was something he knew well.

I nodded. Guilt was my best friend. The one emotion I felt constantly. "How do you deal with it?"

Rob shrugged and I didn't think he'd answer in the silence that followed. But he did. "Eventually, I managed to forgive myself. I let myself think about Edward whenever he comes to mind, but I try never to remember that last day. Oh. And I hated my mother's husband to the day he died." He seemed to think better of his last words. "Sorry. That's not as helpful in your case, is it?"

"How can you think about Edward without remembering that last day?" I could barely think about Josh without seeing the arrow striking his face. Even if I managed to think about something else, that image would hit me unannounced.

"I don't know. A lot of practice. It's been almost eight years." He shifted slightly. "I think the real question is, what are we going to do about you?" Rob's smile was tentative. But it was a smile, and it was for me. I'd missed him more in these last two weeks than I wanted to admit, because how could I miss what I barely knew?

I shook my head. "It's done. There's nothing else to do." There was no fixing me. I'd been to so many health professionals, I'd lost count. The guilt was here to stay.

"I saw you shoot a deer through the forest and fog. I know you can use a bow and I know you're good. Seems like a waste that you won't believe it yourself." Rob held out his bow. "First, you're going to need to get used to holding it again." When I didn't take it, he pressed it into my hand and wrapped my fingers around it.

Without the pressure of having to shoot, holding the bow didn't feel so threatening. I wasn't even shaking.

He watched me carefully. "I never heard this had happened to your brother." It was a question, even if it didn't sound like one.

I'd forgotten for a moment he believed I was someone else. "It's not exactly something we're proud of, as I'm sure you can imagine." The condescension in my tone was something I recognized well. It was what I fell into when people asked too many questions about Josh's accident. But here I was using it with the only friend I'd known in a long time, because he was about to catch me in a lie.

"No," he said. "I don't imagine it would be." He met my eyes with a sad smile. My God, I hated lying to him.

He picked up a stick, weaving it through his fingers.

"Why did you come out of the forest and let Gisborne see your face at Edwinstowe?" *Why did you risk so much for someone you barely know?*

Brilliant green eyes drank me in. There was a war going on behind them, some internal battle that my question had brought on. He didn't want to tell me.

I shook my head. "Don't worry. I shouldn't have asked." I got to my feet.

He pulled me back down beside him. His hand on my wrist was warm, and sent goose bumps up to my shoulder. "You might not like the answer."

I nodded. It was a risk I was willing to take.

He drew a deep breath, letting the words fall from his mouth. "Because I couldn't leave you with him, knowing what a complete bastard he is. Because I could see how much you didn't want to be there. Because—" He looked at the grass beneath his feet, chewing on his words. "Because I wanted to get one up on him. I wanted to steal something he loved dearly, and I wanted him to

have to stand by and watch as it was taken away."
Six years of anger and hatred spilled from him
with those final words.

I sucked in a breath. None of that was what I'd
expected. And, I realized, it wasn't what I'd
wanted to hear. I schooled my face into something
neutral, hoping he couldn't see that those reasons
had hurt. I was used to being a means to an end.
That was exactly what I was for my father. And
that's what Rob was for me, so I couldn't blame
him for making me feel that way. Still, hearing it
was painful. "That must have felt good, even if
Gisborne didn't exactly watch us leave."

He shrugged. "Not as good as I'd hoped. But I
can't say I didn't enjoy it. There was another reason, too. but...given recent events, I don't think
it's important anymore." He watched me, and I
looked at my feet. I understood his reasons. Totally. There was nothing to be upset over.

Better to change the subject. To something
Gisborne had said. "There's a reward for...my return, right? Gisborne told me so."

His forehead creased and his eyes filled with
confusion, but I plowed on.

"And, we're going to Nottingham anyway.
What if John took me to collect it before the tournament? I need to spend time at the castle to get
my coin off Eliza anyway, and the four of you

would be able to buy clothing and food for yourselves for months with the reward." I grinned,
pleased with myself. If someone was going to receive gold from Maud's father, it might as well go
to people who needed it.

Rob remained serious. "What about you in this
amazing plan? You'd go back to your old life?
Marry Gisborne?"

"No. I'll never marry a person who uses a
weapon to force me to do something. I already told
you that." I shook my head. "I only want to go to
Nottingham to get my coin, but if Gisborne or
my...father won't let me leave..." My voice trailed
off. I guessed I'd figure that out if it happened.

"Perhaps..." He stretched the word out, a sparkle returning to his eyes. "...I could ride up to the
castle on horseback, kill everyone who gets in my
way and save you from my horrible brother." He
grinned.

"You make it sound so simple. If you're willing
to risk your life for a girl you just met, of course."
I smiled back. I'd missed this.

Rob lifted his chin. "I'd save you from him, if
you needed me to. But you seemed to do just fine
on your own last time."

Despite his smile, there was a seriousness at the
edge of his voice. I didn't want him to save me
from anything, especially if doing so gave his

brother an opportunity to kill him. "Don't be ridiculous. You need to keep as far from Gisborne as possible." To stay alive. To be Robin Hood.

"You don't know me very well if you think I'd leave a beautiful lady to be captured by my brother."

Still so serious. Perhaps he just needed a better reason to rethink what he was saying. "Yes, but if you're busy saving *this* beautiful lady, you might miss the opportunity to save *the* beautiful lady. The one you're going to fall madly in love with." *Marian.*

He leaned in, careful not to touch any part of me. "You're very good at deciding things, aren't you, Lady Maud. You decided we should go to the Big Tree, so we did. You decided you needed to see Eliza Thatcher, so you went. You decided Tuck and I should stop fighting, and we did." He licked his lips, though I tried not to notice. "This isn't one of those times. You don't get to make that decision for me, my lady." His breath touched my face and the inside of my stomach trembled. "If I want to risk my life for you, I will do it. Either with or without your permission."

He was playing with me again, trying to get a bite just so he could watch me squirm. The same as he always did. I closed my eyes. "Just as long as you know I'm not her. I'm not the one you should say that to." My voice wouldn't work the way I wanted it to. It was thin, quiet. Damn him for doing this to me. Damn me for letting him.

A grin grew on his face. "Again, not something you get to decide."

I swallowed, trying to regain control of the conversation. "Well, it should be." I was having trouble forming single words, let alone full sentences.

He leaned farther forward until our faces almost touched. "But. It's. Not."

Game or not, this was dangerous. If anyone heard him making declarations like that, he'd have a hard job ever convincing Gisborne that I meant nothing to him. Soon, it wouldn't matter. Soon, we'd be eight-hundred years apart, and he'd be free to say these things to the real Marian without risking Gisborne's ire, and everything would be right with the world.

His breath caressed my cheek and I forced myself to stand. "I think we've done enough training for today." I thrust his bow into his hand. 'We should collect some wood for the fire."

He chuckled and got to his feet, throwing his bow over his shoulder. "You know I'll take you to Eliza Thatcher in Nottingham before the tournament. But, if we ever claim a reward from Lord

Fitzwalter, it will go to the villagers and not to us." He started toward the trees in search of wood.

I watched his back.

I had no doubt he'd do exactly as he said.

Sixteen

"HOW'D it go?" Miller asked the moment Rob and I returned, our arms overflowing with wood.

I shrugged. We hadn't done anything except talk. I was no closer to feeling comfortable with a bow again than I'd been three hours ago.

John raised his eyebrows suggestively. "Well, now. I guess it can't be all work and no play."

I narrowed my eyes. "Believe me, John. There was no play whatsoever."

He grinned, clearly happy to get a rise from me. "Whatever you say, Lady Maud." He winked. "I'm surprised you didn't tell him what he could do with his bow and arrows."

Rob dropped his pile of wood loudly onto the ground. "Oh. She did. Many times. Just happens I'm not so good at taking instructions."

"That," I said, dropping my own wood onto Rob's pile, "would be the most honest thing you've ever said about yourself."

"Come now. I've told you plenty of honest things about myself." The light dancing in his eyes had been missing since Edwinstowe. I couldn't help but enjoy it.

I spoke without thinking. "Like how you think you're the most charming person in the forest?"

Our eyes met. He held my gaze, his smile growing wider the more I blushed. I waited for him to utter the words that would complete my embarrassment. Then, when he'd decided he'd made his point, he gave a tiny nod, and walked over to sit next to John. I crouched beside the firewood, busying myself with making a neat pile, while the words he didn't say rang in my ears.

I charmed you, didn't I?

He had. More than once. Pretty words were Rob's thing. Meaningful conversation, not so much.

While I made the best-looking pile of firewood known to man, Rob and the others decided we'd stay at Kings Cave for two more nights. To let

Miller's arm heal, they said. But I knew it was to give me time with the bow as well.

The following morning, Miller talked Rob into giving me a lesson with a sword, and me into having one. I enjoyed it more than I wanted to admit. When we were done, Rob took me back to the clearing where we'd spent the previous afternoon.

"I can't do this, Rob. Didn't you hear what I told you yesterday?" My hands were already slick with sweat, and I hadn't even touched his bow yet.

Rob moved in front of me. "You made one stupid mistake years ago. You can't spend the rest of your life beating yourself up over it."

I opened my mouth to speak, but he stepped closer, putting a finger up to quiet me.

"I know that's exactly what you planned to do. But that was before you met me." He grinned. "And I'm not going to let that happen." He handed me the bow. "Today, you start using it." He pointed at the undergrowth between two trees. "Aim over there."

I could stop this by throwing the bow on the ground and storming away. I didn't think Rob would force me if I showed him how upset I was. It's what I would have done at home. But then, at home, no one had bothered to help me through my misery. In the days after Josh's accident, where Mom and Dad had split their time between sleeping at home and sleeping in a chair beside Josh's hospital bed, I'd been desperate to have one of them wrap their arms around me while I cried. Neither of them had. Dad hadn't even been able to look at me, let alone help me deal, and he was still the same two years later. But Rob was trying to help. As much as I didn't want to touch that bow, I found myself wanting to see how far I could go.

He believed in me. Perhaps it was time to start believing in myself.

Taking an arrow from his quiver, I tried to nock it. But my hand shook so much, the two wouldn't go together.

"Do you hate your father?" Rob stood behind me to the right.

I didn't think so. Dad hated me, though. He might not have voiced the words, but I knew it anyway. He hadn't let me go with him and Mom to bring Josh home from hospital. Carrie went, but I had to stay behind. To make the house ready, they said. But there was nothing left to do. We'd already moved Josh's bed to the downstairs bedroom and decluttered so he could move around the house without tripping. When they returned, I hugged Josh, then asked if there was anything I could do to help him. Dad turned and said, "I think you've done enough." In the two years since, he'd spoken little more than single words to me, until the morning he sent me here.

I twisted to face Rob, but he indicated with his hand that I should face my target.

"You said something that day at the Big Tree, about blaming him," Rob continued.

I looked over my shoulder again. "He doesn't like me much. You can probably guess why." The accident. That was what everything always came back to. As far as Dad was concerned, Josh got a free pass to do whatever he wanted—because of what had happened to him that day. Carrie got Dad's time whenever she wanted it—because of what she'd witnessed that day. I got no kind words or loving glances, no attention at all—because of what I'd done that day.

"Well, he's a very stupid man." Rob cleared his throat. "I don't see any shooting going on, Lady Maud."

I let out a long sigh and heard that now familiar deep chuckle from behind me. I wished, pointlessly, that he wouldn't call me her name. That I could tell him who I was and have him believe me. "My father forced me to do something he knew I didn't want to do."

"I see." I could feel disapproval leaking from Rob. "Did this *thing* he made you do, hurt you?"

"No." I pulled the bowstring back against my cheek. "But there's a chance it still could." I still had to travel home yet which was dangerous in itself, and who knew what I might come up against before I finished making him Robin Hood, found my coin and left.

I fired, my body recalling the feel of the bow in my hand and making the movements of its own accord. The arrow barely flew three meters.

But it *had* flown.

I'd done it. I'd actually shot an arrow from my bow, thanks to Rob's distraction, something I'd never expected to do again. I turned to him, a grin splitting my face.

He grinned back. "Nice shot."

"It was a shot. But it wasn't even close to nice." The arrow hadn't flown fast enough to lodge in anything, instead skidding over the leaf mulch on the ground. I'd have got it farther if I'd thrown it. So no, it was not a nice shot.

His lips turned down. "Most beginners would be pleased with that on their second go."

"Yes, well. I'm hardly a beginner." I couldn't count the number of arrows I'd shot from a bow.

"Really? Because that shot..."

"Did you hear a thing I told you yesterday?"

He sauntered over to me, arms folded over his chest, dry leaves crackling beneath his feet. "I heard. You said you were good. I see an apprentice. Prove you're not."

I pointed an accusing finger at him. "I see what you're doing."

"Really?" he asked innocently. "And what's that?"

"You think I'll *want* to prove you wrong." I stepped closer and held out the bow. "I don't." I shook my head. "I can't." Not that I wasn't secretly pleased to have fired a shot, I was. But it was going to take more than a little goading to get a second shot out of me. And the way my hand was shaking, even if I could manage it, it wouldn't be any better than the first.

Rob surveyed me through heavy lids before leaning forward and whispering. "Prove you're not a beginner and we'll stop."

Stepping back, his voice resumed its normal volume as he said, "And even though he made you do this horrible thing, you still want to go back to the very place you hope he'll be?" He was talking about Nottingham. I wasn't. Yet the question still applied.

"I don't have a choice." Where else would I go once I was free of the twelfth century?

"There's always a choice, my lady."

Prove it. It might as well have been written across his face.

I can't. I was certain that was written on mine. The words formed in my head as my hands worked on their own. The arrow was already nocked before I could utter another word of protest. I didn't dare look at Rob. With the arrow ready to go, I couldn't risk hurting him. Instead, I pulled the string back and fired at the trunk of a tree just outside the clearing. This shot went a little farther, but not much.

I turned to find Rob smirking at me. Arrogant bastard. He'd distracted me. And I'd done something I hadn't been able to willingly do since I injured Josh. Twice.

He raised an eyebrow. "Well done, my lady. Still a beginner's shot. But getting better."

He took me back to the others after that and I spent the afternoon with John and Miller. They took over from Rob teaching me to use a bow again, while Tuck threw in the not-so-occasional comment. They didn't tell me anything I didn't already know, but still, keeping my hands from shaking and getting the arrow to fly more than a few meters was impossible.

When, by the third day, I still hadn't improved, I took my frustration out on Rob during our lesson. "Why are you even trying to help me?

You made it quite clear two weeks ago that you didn't like me." The last arrow I'd fired had been the worst in two days, and my hand still shook each time I picked one up. At least it was just the two of us. I didn't think I could deal with one of Tuck's jibes right now.

"Now, that's fishing for a compliment, if ever I heard it." He folded his arms across his chest and nodded at the gap between the trees. I tried not to notice the muscled forearms visible below his rolled-up sleeves. "Again." He waited in silence while I took another shot.

"I'm not fishing for a compliment. It was a valid question. You said you didn't want to spend time with me. And yet, here we are. Again." My shot was no better than the last, and when I turned to Rob, he was grinning. I nodded. "Unless you like watching me fail?"

His eyebrows rose and I was fairly sure his grin grew wider. "My, aren't you in a fine mood this morning?" He nodded for me to shoot again.

I shook my head. "And *you* are impossible to get a straight answer from."

He sighed. "Maud, you already know the answer to your question. I don't think you want to hear me say it again."

I did know. And I didn't want to hear him say it. But still I kept asking, hoping to hear something different. "We're still not friends?" Because it didn't feel that way. And I liked the way this whatever-it-was felt.

Something flashed across Rob's face, and for a moment I thought he was going to tell me I was wrong. But he closed his eyes and drew a deep breath, and when he looked at me again, whatever I'd seen was gone. "If you value your life, my lady, that's exactly what we should be."

I swallowed. *Should be.* We *should be* not-friends. Because it was safer.

"And seeing you fail is the last thing I want to watch." The sparkle returned to his eyes, making me dread whatever was coming next. "Unless you're not actually trying, because you want to spend time with me."

Cocky bastard. "Believe me, *if* I wanted to spend time with you, I have plenty of better ways to make that happen."

He sauntered across the rough ground toward me. It didn't seem to matter what he said, the way he watched me made my heart pound. "Oh, really? Like what?"

I tried not to smile. If this was being not-friends, maybe I could deal. "That's something I only share with the people I want to be around. Usually people a lot less arrogant than yourself."

His grin was wide as he nodded at the trees. "Again."

We spent a week at Kings Cave in the end. Miller's arm was healing nicely, and Rob was certain rest would help. I improved slowly. No one would ever confuse me with the archer I used to be, but as each day passed, and Rob continued to distract my mind during our lessons, I got better. By the end of the week, I could hit a target on a tree. And even more surprising, doing so made me smile.

Tomorrow we would leave here and begin our trek to Nottingham, for the tournament and my coin. The boys were determined to have fun along the way. And their source of entertainment had become robbing carriages.

"What about Hidden Bend?" Miller's question was met with silence around the fire, each of the others considering the suggestion. When John had ventured into Mansfield yesterday for supplies, he'd heard rumors of a carriage that would be traveling through the forest tomorrow, owned by a very rich lord. The boys wanted to take advantage of the advance notice.

Tuck's lips turned down and I waited for him to reject the idea, as he'd done with every other. "That could work."

Rob nodded. "The road's straight and long. If anything goes wrong, we'd have plenty of warning." Unlike last time. He didn't need to say it. We were all thinking the same thing. "We could hide Maud beside Little Rise. That way she'd have a perfect view in both directions."

My eyebrows rose. "For what, exactly?"

Rob pressed his lips together, considering his words. "Lookout. Actual lookout. With a bow in your hands, ready to use."

I caught a worried stare from John, and realized they'd already discussed what my role might be this time. The fact they hadn't bothered to include me in their conversation and were now telling me what to do, made a flash of heat shoot through me. I folded my arms across my chest. If they thought they could tell me what to do without including me in the conversation, they had another thing coming.

"But only if you want to," John added in a rush.

I looked at Rob for confirmation. He nodded and I let out my breath. They weren't going to force me into anything.

"You'd watch for anyone coming in either direction and if you saw someone, you'd fire an arrow onto the trail as a warning. There's a chance the trail might be busier than usual with the Sheriff's tournament drawing nearer."

"And if I don't want to do it?" I wasn't sure I did.

"We'll put Tuck there instead. And hope we get no resistance from inside the carriage, since he'll be too far away to shoot them."

I considered what they were asking as each of them stared at me, waiting for my answer. If I did this, I had to be prepared to shoot. Their lives were at risk if I said I'd help then didn't do what they were expecting. Perhaps it was time to give something back to this group of friends who'd taken me in since I arrived. My shooting had improved this week and what they were asking was no longer outside the realm of possibility. Plus, this could be the carriage that would finally make Rob a legend and let me go home.

With a deep breath, I nodded. It was about time I earned my keep around here. "I'll do it."

Rob gave me a half-smile that made my heart stop, a smile that said he was proud of me. A smile I was going to miss like crazy when I went home. I was happy here, most of the time. "I could stay here." Aside from missing Josh like crazy, I suddenly realized I'd be okay if I never found a way back home. Life here might be more dangerous every day than an entire year was in my own time, but I'd never felt as alive as I did when I was around Rob and the others.

Rob spoke in my ear as the others continued talking. "For as long as you wish, Lady Maud."

I'd spoken out loud?

Something in my gut went hard, as it always did when he called me *her* name. I wished, just once, he'd call me Maryanne. "You should be careful to whom you make an offer like that."

His brow furrowed.

"With all that charm you ooze, you might have every Lady in the vicinity coming to dwell in the forest with you."

He shrugged playfully. "I'm failing to see how that could be a bad thing, my lady."

I laughed quietly. "None of them would be anywhere near as acquiescent as myself."

The corners of his lips flickered. "Acquiescent? How so?"

"None would be as willing to bow to your demands about arming themselves as I have been."

"Funny," he said. "I've seen no willingness to bow whatsoever." He tilted his head. "Of course, should you wish to get down on your knees and bow for me now, I wouldn't say no."

Color crept up my cheeks. How did I always talk myself into a corner with him? I dropped my head as he chuckled beside me. Then I realized the talk around the fire had stopped. My God. Had they heard that? I sincerely hoped not.

Attempting to hide my embarrassment and fill the silence, I looked at John. "How is it you all know each other?" I'd wondered many times since I'd met them, but there'd never been a good time to ask until now. John and Rob were of similar age, but Tuck was older by quite a few years. And Miller much younger. They seemed such an odd mix.

Three sets of eyes went to Rob, and I found myself following their gaze to stare at him, too. He was as relaxed as I'd ever seen him, the frown lines on his forehead completely gone and his hands resting lightly on his knees. The stop at Kings Cave had done more than just Miller some good.

"Tuck," he said with a shrug.

I frowned. "You all know each other because of Tuck?" Maybe I didn't want to know this story. At least, I didn't want to have to ask Tuck to share it.

Rob nodded, glancing at his friend with raised eyebrows. "You want to tell her?"

Tuck shook his head. "Not my story to tell."

Rob took a deep breath. "Tuck found me after...after Gisborne tried to kill me. I was cold and wet, and fire raged inside my chest every time I

took a breath. I was waiting for everything to stop
hurting. When I opened my eyes, I thought I must
have died because why else would Edward be looking down at me." He shrugged at Tuck. "But, no.
It was his big brother, back from religious training
at St Mary's in York, and somehow able to forgive
me for what I'd done to his family two years earlier. He nursed me back to health out here in the
forest and has been looking after me ever since."

When I was younger, before I hurt Josh, I often
woke at night, screaming. Mostly, I didn't remember what had woken me, or if I did, I only recalled
fragmented images like blood, missing limbs, red
swords—which, now I thought of it, was a lot like
the things I now saw on a daily basis. But there
had been a couple of recurring dreams that had
stuck with me. They'd felt so real at the time, and
they were a complete story, not a fragment. One
of them went a lot like the story Rob had just
shared: fire raging with every breath, waiting to
die, a savior arriving just in time. Except in my
dream, I couldn't trust my savior. Because he'd
been the one to put me there.

A shudder ran down my back. I hadn't thought
of that nightmare in the longest time, but even
now, all these years after I'd dreamed it, it still
terrified me. Better to think of other things completely. "Tuck is Edward's brother?" Rob nodded.

"And you're...?" I wasn't sure what I was asking. Of either of them. How was it they didn't hate each other? I doubted I could have been so forgiving. Suddenly Tuck's protectiveness of Rob made sense. He'd saved his life, then taken care of him, raised him to be someone with high morals and a sense of right and wrong.

I licked my lips, directing my question at Tuck. "Is that why you're running around in Sherwood Forest rather than living in a monastery? Because you decided to nurse Rob back to health?"

Tuck shrugged. "I'm not so good at staying in one place for long."

Rob gave a gentle smile. "Plus, you have a soft spot for kids who can't look after themselves." He looked at me. "Tuck supported John and Miller after each of their parents died."

Tuck sat across the fire, his eyes on his feet. He didn't seem used to having people talk about him. We hadn't seen eye-to-eye since I arrived, but maybe I could understand it now. Tuck had done a good job with these boys. They could all have had completely different lives if it hadn't been for him. "You're a good man, Tuck."

For once, he met my eyes without hatred. "Thank you," he said quietly.

Seventeen

THE boys were buzzing as we began our trek toward the main trail the next morning. "You're all excited to steal more gold, aren't you?" I spoke to no one in particular as we walked single file along the grassy riverbank.

"Steal's rather a harsh word, don't you think?" John turned and walked backwards, grinning as he spoke.

I pursed my lips as a smile tried to form. "What would you call it?"

"Redistribution of funds." Miller nodded, pleased with himself.

I gaped at him. Of all the words I expected him to get right, it wasn't that one. Clearly, he'd heard it used a few times in the past. "Really, Miller," I said dryly. "And who told you that?" As if I couldn't guess.

"Rob, of course."

Rob glanced around innocently. "You don't approve of us doing this again?"

Actually, I *did* approve. And not just because it would help their legend. Before I came to their time, I hadn't approved. Back then, I'd thought them nothing more than thieves and murderers. The movies in my time portrayed a ruthless group of men who did anything to increase the weight of coin in their pocket. *That* Robin Hood had only wanted to benefit himself. He hadn't cared how hard life was for the people he stole from.

These boys couldn't have been more different. They were exactly like Dad's version of the legend. They knew the villagers needed help, and they were doing something about it. But, now I knew them, there was more at stake than simply doing what was right. Stopping carriages was so very dangerous. "Just...be careful." I looked at Rob as I said it, but I meant everyone.

Rob stopped me with a hand on my forearm, letting the others go ahead of us. "You be careful, too."

"The first sign of trouble, and I'm gone." My voice was small, even as I tried to grin. Not so much because of the danger. Because he was standing too close. I closed my eyes, trying to get it together, then opened them to find him staring down at me, his eyes the same color as the forest. I should step away, we were not-friends. I forced a grin onto my face. "After I fire that warning arrow, of course."

"Yes, well, we'd be most grateful if you'd remember to do that first."

"Are you worried I won't be able to shoot if I have to?" They'd given me a huge responsibility without questioning my suitability. If I had to shoot a warning arrow and got it wrong, I could hurt someone. If I was too petrified to make the shot, they could all be hurt—or worse—by whoever was coming up the trail. There was a hollowness in my gut just thinking about all the ways I could screw this up.

"Not in the slightest." He met my eyes, and I could see he meant it. "Are you?"

I shook my head. A lie, but if he could say he believed in me, then I would tell him I believed in myself.

"Good," he said quietly. Anticipation sparked off his body. I'd never seen him quite so edgy. He turned to follow the others.

"You're nervous."

His eyes slid across my face. "You think I shouldn't be?"

I shook my head. "No. You should be. Especially after what happened to Miller last time. I'm just...surprised." He was usually so good at hiding his nerves.

A lazy, almost predatory smile spread across his face. "Surprised by my reaction? Or surprised by your own reaction to it? No, don't answer. I already know."

Games.

Again.

"Of course you already know," I snapped, trying to hide the color that rose up my cheeks. "Because one of those suggestions is ridiculous. You know very well I meant I'm surprised to see you wearing your nerves." He was right, damn him. I wasn't admitting it because he'd twist it into something else, but I was totally attracted to the way he worried for his friends.

He stepped toward me with assurance, his head tilted to one side. "See, I don't think that's what surprised you at all."

He was standing too close, sucking all the air from the small space between us. I stepped away. "That's not what I meant, and you know it." My traitorous voice didn't sound like my own. "Perhaps you should go back to ignoring me. Then there wouldn't be these mix ups." Another step back.

He paused, seeming to consider. "I could. But where's the fun in that? Besides, you enjoy this as much as I do."

True as it might be, I wasn't picking up that particular thread of conversation. The smart thing would be to walk away. Clearly, I wasn't smart. "What is it you want, Rob?"

His grin widened and he stepped forward again, a branch cracking beneath his foot. "That's something you already know."

I shook my head, unable to breathe. He'd stop soon. Laugh and walk away. That was what he did. What *we* did. Because it was fun. Because neither of us could go where all this teasing might end. "To be not-friends," I whispered, backing up again and finding the rough bark of a large tree at my back. Not-friends was what we both wanted. It was.

"Not-friends. Yes. That *was* what I said, wasn't it?" He gave his head a twist. "Pity you're not so good at listening."

"Me?" Indignation filled my chest and I straightened. "You're blaming this," I indicated between us, "on me? Because you——"

He closed the gap, his hands going to either side of my head against the tree, his breath touching my face. "I told you it couldn't happen. But you had to challenge everything I said." He took a breath. "And care about the poor. And stand up to Gisborne." He closed his eyes. "And that damned soap you use makes you smell so good. And in this entire forest, there's no one more beautiful."

I wanted to show him I was in control, but that breathlessness returned to my voice. He'd called me beautiful. "I never challenged you on us. I think you'll find I agreed with you."

"Saying it and meaning it are two completely different things, my lady."

I narrowed my eyes. "Right back at you, my lord."

Rob stilled and his pupils dilated. He'd liked that I'd called him that. I guessed he never heard it these days. If Gisborne and his father hadn't been so power hungry, that would have been Rob's title.

He moved toward me, his gaze dropping to my lips. He was going to kiss me. *This* was exactly where all that teasing was always going to end. *This* was exactly where I'd wanted it to go, if I was honest with myself.

But was it what he wanted? I put my hands on his chest to stop him. I didn't need to hear him laugh in my ear because this was all some stupid game to him. Somewhere along the way, it had stopped being a game to me.

He didn't stop. And I didn't even try to make him.

Our lips brushed, the lightest of touches, and the world dimmed to that place where our bodies met. His lips were soft, warm, welcoming. And though I wanted more than that fleeting touch, I didn't dare move for fear he would stop.

"Maud," he whispered.

Maud.

That's who I was to him. Not Maryanne. Everything he thought he knew about me was a lie. This kiss was a lie. I forced my hands into his muscled chest.

He blinked, soft, hazy eyes fully focusing on me.

"This...us..." I shook my head, indicating between us. "If you're going to laugh at me and walk away, do it now, because that's as close as you're getting to me." Now there was some space between us again and I could breathe, I couldn't believe I'd put myself into a situation where he might say something to hurt me. And I was taking my anger at myself out on him.

"Laugh at you?" He frowned. "I would never."

"What?" I narrowed my eyes. "You laugh at me all the time. You say things to me, and when I start to believe you, you laugh. Besides, this," I indicated between us again, "isn't how not-friends behave." I pushed past him and stormed up the trail.

He caught me in two steps, taking hold of my hand. I refused to look at him, color flooding my cheeks and anger filling my chest. I didn't need anyone but myself. I especially didn't need a guy who couldn't even become the legend he was supposed to be, without someone helping him.

He waited, probably for me to look up. When I didn't, he sighed. "I was trying to protect you."

My head flew up. "I don't need protecting." I spat the words at him, knowing if I really wanted to, I could rip my hand from his grasp, and storm away.

He blinked once, his face pained. "I know," he whispered. "But..." He dropped my hand and ran his palms down his face. "When I saw you with my brother, smiling at him, it crushed me. It shouldn't have, you two have history, everyone knows that. Yet it did. In three short days, you'd done something to me no one else has ever been able to. You'd made me care about something other than revenge." He looked at the ground, then back to me, his eyes full of sorrow. "So, when I saw him draw his sword on you, I acted without thinking."

"Because you wanted to piss him off." That's what he'd told me.

Rob shook his head. "That's not why I came down there. It was..." He licked his lips. "I can't say seeing him angry didn't please me. But it wasn't the reason." He looked over my shoulder at the bubbling river. "When I got you back to camp and Tuck yelled at me, I fought with him because I knew he was right. I'd put everyone else at risk by letting my brother see my face. He'll hurt anyone he thinks I care for, just to get at me."

"So, you made a mistake, then took it out on me because you felt guilty?" He'd decided the two of us couldn't be friends that night.

Rob nodded. "I'm not sorry I came out of the forest for you. But I am sorry I stormed down there angry and wasn't careful enough to keep my identity a secret. I'm sorry I let Gisborne know I was alive. I thought if you could make me act that way after just a few days, what would you do to me after a couple of weeks? That's why I said we shouldn't be friends."

"Not because of what Gisborne might do to me?"

"Because of that, too. It's complicated. But, Maud..." He shrugged. "Those two weeks of not talking to you were horrible. And I might *say* we're not friends, but meaning it..." He shrugged again. "I thought you already knew I didn't." The shadow of a grin flickered up his face, gone again a second later.

On some level, I guess I'd known. I'd told him so, right before he'd wanted to kiss me.

Maud. The name played over in my head. That's who I was to him, who I'd always be, unless I told him the truth. "We need to talk. There are some things you need to know about me."

He blinked slowly. "That doesn't sound good."

"It's not."

He nodded. "Now?"

"After."

He reached for my hand and held it tightly. "If you need to talk, we can do it now."

I didn't want them to miss this opportunity. But I also wasn't ready to have this conversation. "But the carriage——"

"There'll be others."

"But none as rich as Lord Sutherland."

He shrugged. "Then we stop an extra three carriages to make up for it."

I squeezed his hand. He was telling me he was here for me. That I was more important than this thing he desperately wanted to do. He was doing for me what no one in my life had done in years. And I was about to make him hate me. "We'll talk after."

He eyed me with caution, before finally nodding. "After."

Rob placed me on the opposite side of the muddy trail from Tuck, at the top of a small rise. Tuck was a little farther down the hill, at the point they hoped to stop the carriage. The thick canopy of trees was dead still, not a breath of air moving. The stillness made me jumpy. I didn't want this to go the same way our last carriage robbery had gone. But then, this time they were relying on me to warn them of any imminent danger, so perhaps it wouldn't be an issue.

Tuck stiffened. With his focus farther along the trail, he slowly raised his bow. Looking in the same direction, I saw nothing, heard nothing. Yet still, Tuck remained on edge. I readied my bow.

Then finally, I saw it too. A slight movement, a singing voice weaving between the trees. And coming around the corner, far in the distance, a carriage. I held my breath, waiting for the soldiers I was certain would follow, but there were none.

As the carriage made its slow progress down the rough trail, the coachman ducking time and again for the low branches that threatened to sweep him from his seat, Tuck flexed his hand on his bow.

This carriage was far more ornate than any we'd stopped before. Decorations carved into the wood were painted white and edged with gilt. The bottom of the carriage was splattered brown with mud, and it was pulled by two white horses. When it was perhaps ten meters away from them—far closer than I would have liked—Miller and John stepped out from opposite sides of the trail, their hoods drawn over their heads. The horses jolted.

"Halt," called John, his voice echoing in the trees as he held up his hand. His other hand clenched his staff.

The coachman shook his head. "Get off the trail or I'll run you down." The horses had slowed and were barely moving, so it seemed an empty threat.

"Certainly," said John. "Once you pay the tax."

The coachman scoffed, his horses still walking slowly toward Miller and John. "Tax? I know of no tax."

Miller stepped forward. His arm was almost healed, and he could hold his sword again. "Surely you've heard of the nobility traveling tax. It endures safe passage through Sherwood Forest."

John cleared his throat. "What my friend here means is, pay the tax and you'll pass through safely."

"Ha! I've heard nothing of a tax, and I drive through here often. Now, move and let me pass."

Rob stepped from the trees, the fur-lined hood of his dark brown cloak covering his head. His sword hung from a belt at his waist, plainly visible though not drawn. He cut a magnificent figure, his stance commanding. The boy that stepped out on the trail at that moment was exactly how Dad had presented him every time he told us a story when we were kids.

Taking hold of the bridle of one of the horses, he pulled it to a stop. He spoke softly into the horse's ear and patted her nose. Then he looked up at the coachman. "You've not heard of the tax?" His voice was filled with mock surprise. "No matter. I'm sure you've heard of us?"

The coachman shook his head, lips turning down at the edges. "N-no. Never."

Rob gave a nod. "Ah, well, that explains it. Let me introduce myself." He planted his hand upon his chest. "I am Rob. And these," he indicated toward John and Miller, his eyes never leaving the coachman. "These are my friends. You owe a tax for using this road, and we are the tax collectors."

As he spoke, Miller made a great show of admiring his sword, while John calmly pounded his staff against the dirt. Threatening, but not.

The coachman shook his head. "No." He gave a flick of the reins, urging his horses forward, but with John and Miller in the way, there was nowhere for them to go.

Slowly, Rob drew his sword. "Drop the reins." His voice was calm and almost cajoling.

The coachman set his jaw. A small red circle had appeared on each of his cheeks. "No."

At that moment, Tuck let his arrow fly. It whistled through the air and embedded itself in the carriage, not far from the coachman's head. He jumped, dropping the reins immediately.

Rob nodded, then went around the side of the carriage. "Did I forget to mention the rest of my men?" He shrugged. "Probably best you leave those reins at your feet if you don't want an arrow through your heart. Do as we ask, and no one will get hurt." Though Rob spoke softly, there was no doubt who was in charge.

He walked up to the carriage and pulled open the door, and a girl, maybe a year or two older than me, stuck her head outside. She was wearing the most beautiful rich-blue dress I had ever seen, and had a large necklace encrusted with jewels decorating the pale skin of her neck. She glanced between Rob and her coachman.

Rob bowed his head "Lady Sutherland. How lovely to see you."

Lady Sutherland blinked, her eyebrows rising.

Rob kept hold of the door. "There's no need to be frightened. I'm here to collect a tax, not to hurt you."

Lady Sutherland didn't look the least bit frightened. Surprised, yes. Satisfied, perhaps. But not scared. "Robin Hood, I presume?"

Rob inclined his head. "I believe some people call me that. My friends call me Rob."

"What have you done to Matthew? My coachman."

Rob glanced up at the coachman. "Nothing. He's sitting up there on his seat as good as new." He used the heel of his hand to bang on the side of the carriage. "All right, Matthew?"

Matthew, who had been staring straight ahead with his hands clasped in his lap, jumped. His voice shook as he answered. "Yes, sir. I'm fine, my lady."

Lady Sutherland's chin tilted in defiance. "There is no tax to pay. This is the King's road and he is the only one who can collect taxes."

"The King's taxes are too high in this part of the forest and the people can't afford to pay. I'm sure someone as compassionate and graceful as yourself will understand and be more than willing to help the poor."

Lady Sutherland's face lit at Rob's compliment. I groaned under my breath, loud enough to draw a loathing look from Tuck down the trail. Easily impressed as she may be, I couldn't take my eyes off her. Her brown hair was plaited intricately off her face, held in place with jeweled combs. Her fingers were laden with shiny gems and the fabric of her dress shimmered. She was so different to the women of my own time. Graceful, like Rob had said.

I smoothed my dirty pants. Although I'd managed a quick wash in the creek this morning, it was many days since I'd had anything resembling a bath. Looking at Lady Sutherland, the contrast between the two of us couldn't have been more obvious.

"That's what you're doing? Helping the poor?" She batted her eyelashes as she spoke.

Rob sheathed his sword and raised his hand palm up. "Of course. What else would we do with it?"

"Use it for yourselves."

Rob turned to John and Miller. Very deliberately, he ran his eyes over their faded tunics and tatty cloaks. Then he glanced down at himself. Although his green tunic and pants were tidy, it was clear they were not made from expensive fabric like the silk Lady Sutherland wore. There was a smile in Rob's voice when he spoke. A charming smile. "Now, I know you're far too bright to believe that. Our clothing is humble. We have no horses. Plus," he took a step closer to her, his voice growing quieter. "You've heard about us. You know who we are. And what we do. You knew before you came into the forest today that you might meet us."

Her cheeks colored and she flashed him a smile, clearly not immune to flattery from a stranger. Without turning away from Rob, she reached into the carriage, feeling around on the seat. When her hand appeared again, it was gripping a small leather pouch. "The poor need all the help they can get." She dropped the pouch into Rob's hand, smiling so wide, dimples appeared on her cheeks.

Rob inclined his head in thanks but remained standing beside the carriage. "Your generosity comes second only to your beauty, my lady."

Lady Sutherland leaned forward, speaking quietly in Rob's ear. He laughed, clearly enjoying himself, and said something equally quiet to her. My fingers tightened on the bow.

She reached inside the carriage again, this time pulling out a larger leather pouch. "Will this do it?" Her smile was wide, and her lashes fluttered as she searched for Rob's face beneath the shadow of his hood.

Rob opened the pouch and glanced inside. The smile in his voice was enough to tell me how much he was relishing this exchange. Which was the direct opposite to how I felt. Just moments ago, he'd been making me blush, telling me...what exactly? He hadn't actually said how he felt about me. I didn't want to be just another girl, charmed by his pretty words and smiles again, but perhaps that's exactly what I was.

He shook his head. "It's not nearly enough to allow you to see my face, my lady."

She pulled a large gold ring from her finger, a sapphire sparkling in the center, and dangled it in front of him. In my time, a ring like that would have been worth some serious money. "This is all I have." She pouted. When Rob moved to take it from her, she pulled her hand away. "Nah-ah. I've heard you're a gentleman, Robin Hood. I don't believe you'll hurt a lady just to get her jewels." She stared at him, waiting for an answer, but she didn't get one.

Probably because she was right. Despite the weapons he carried, I also doubted he had any intention of hurting her.

Narrowing her eyes, she gave him another huge smile. "We understand each other, then. You may have this ring if I can see your face."

Tuck moved, drawing my eye to him. He met my glance with a glare, pressing a finger to his lips. His eyes demanded my silence, even though I didn't think I'd made a sound.

Rob hesitated. He couldn't be considering her offer; the price she asked was high. If she saw his face, he would never be able to go anywhere without his hood for fear of being recognized and brought before the King.

Personally, I'd have told her to piss off, that sultry smiles and sapphires couldn't always buy everything she desired. And for a moment I thought Rob was about to say that exact thing.

Then he took a single step forward and pulled his hood so it sat on the back of his head, his face visible to Lady Sutherland.

Her smile grew wider. "Oh. You're even better looking than I imagined." She giggled.

Giggled! My fingers closed of their own accord around the bow, squeezing tight. He'd shown her his face! How could he? He'd put himself in danger all because of a pretty smile. He wasn't the person I'd thought him to be.

Taking the ring and stuffing it inside one of the coin pouches, Rob smiled at her. "You are lovelier than any of your jewels, my lady. You don't need to wear them; they detract from your beauty." He took Lady Sutherland's fingers in his. Slowly he raised her hand, pressing it to his lips. Then he said something I didn't hear.

The edges of my vision flashed red and I fired an arrow at the center of the trail.

Eighteen

MY hand didn't shake, not even a little. The arrow landed exactly where I'd aimed. I didn't celebrate.

Rob turned his head slowly toward it, before looking back at Lady Sutherland. "Seems our time together is up, my lady. Thank you for your generosity. I hope we'll meet again someday."

He let go of her hand and turned abruptly. In five steps, he'd disappeared into the concealing arms of the forest. When I looked back at the trail again, John and Miller were gone too, already making their way back to the tiny grassed area far from the main trail that we'd agreed would be our meeting point. I shuffled back into the trees, not ready to leave yet.

Lady Sutherland watched the place Rob had last been, a stupid smile on her face. Then she looked down at the fingers he'd kissed, cradling them gently in her other hand, and sank back into the carriage. Before shutting the door, she called, "Matthew. Let's be off." The carriage rolled slowly away, narrowly avoiding the arrow in the middle of the trail and bumping up the hill past me.

Tuck called from where he'd hidden. "Let's go."

I shook my head.

He shrugged. "Your choice." He strode off, toward our meeting place.

I closed my eyes and forced myself to say his name. "Tuck." Disappointed with myself didn't even begin to cover the way I was feeling. I should never have let my emotions take charge of my actions; firing that arrow had been petty and dangerous. But then, I should never have let myself feel anything for Rob, either.

Slowly, Tuck turned to face me.

I walked along the trail to where he waited. "I know you don't want me here, and I understand why." I licked my lips. "You don't know me. You blame me for Rob becoming an outlaw. I just wondered——"

The muscles in Tuck's jaw tightened. "I've known Rob for many years, and in that time, he's always been careful with how he acted. *If* he broke the law, it was always for a good reason and he did it when no one was watching. Always had his eye on the bigger picture, knew what he wanted and what he needed to do to get it. You turn up and within an hour, he's an outlaw." Tuck narrowed his eyes. "Seems to me you're exactly the person to blame."

I swallowed. Put that way, it was a fair assessment. "But Rob doesn't think——"

He leaned toward me, his face pinched. His voice was quiet and accusing. "Don't tell me what Rob thinks. I can see it written over his face every time he looks at you. But I know you too, even if you pretend not to remember me. And I know you're exactly like every other wealthy person he's ever met. Once you have what you want from him, you'll hurt him."

I squared my shoulders. This man did not know me. He might think he knew Maud, but I wasn't her. "I don't think you know him half as well as you think you do. He doesn't want me any more than he wants Lady Sutherland. Or Eliza Thatcher." It was all a game to him. I'd known that all along, even if I'd forgotten for a few moments. But, God, I sounded petty.

Tuck's eyes flashed. He leaned close. "Believe me, I know both of you. He's given up everything he ever wanted. Because of you. And you, you're about to repay him by storming off in a fit of jealousy." He stepped back, his lips tight. "Am I right?"

I shook my head.

"Oh? So where are the approaching soldiers? The ones you heard before you fired your arrow?"

He might be close to the mark about how I was feeling. There had been no soldiers, just a childish need to get Rob away from Lady Sutherland. But he couldn't pin all Rob's choices on me. "I know about Rob. I know Gisborne left him for dead in the forest when he was a child. So, don't try to make me think Rob gave up his wealthy lifestyle by choice three weeks ago when he met me."

The muscles in Tuck's jaw tensed again. "Did he tell you where he was going on the day you met? Did you ever think to ask him why he was passing Edwinstowe that day?"

"No. But..." I'd been about to say that if he'd been going somewhere important, he would have told me in the days since, that we'd grown close. Instead, I saw his lips pressed to Lady Sutherland's fingertips while he stared into her eyes. I shook my head. "Where?" My voice was tiny.

Tuck pushed his lips tight as if he was trying to stop words flying out. "Not my story to tell."

He turned and walked into the forest. "You coming?"

I was so tempted not to go. The words were on the tip of my tongue. But I didn't want to prove Tuck right. I didn't want to storm off in a fit of jealousy the way he'd said I was going to. so I followed along behind him.

Suddenly, Tuck stopped and took a deep breath, his back to me. "For the last six years, the only thing Rob's been interested in is revenge." His words were forced, like he didn't want to say them. "Until you. Since then, some of the Rob I used to know has returned. He's smiling again and the frown lines on his forehead aren't there permanently anymore. As much as I hate to admit it, it's because of you. He wants you around. Not Lady Sutherland. You. And though I might not trust you, I want Rob to be happy." He took a step, then paused, still not looking my way. "Glad to see your archery lessons are helping. That was a decent shot."

He walked away. I followed sullenly behind wondering when I'd turned into a jealous shrew. A few minutes ago, I'd fired an arrow that had landed exactly where I aimed. I should be celebrating, yet I couldn't. The reason I'd been able to shoot so well was because I was consumed with emotion. Today it had been jealousy, weeks ago when I shot the deer, terror. I wasn't improving with a bow; I was responding to my emotions in a way I should never do with a weapon in my hand.

I followed Tuck into the clearing. Miller was pacing up and down one side, his eyes on Rob; John was checking his bow, and Rob was pacing around the other side of the small area, flattening the grass.

"Did you hide the gold?" Tuck had barely stopped walking before he spoke.

"What do you think?" Rob asked, an edge to his voice. He sent a smile my way, but I couldn't return it. Even so, his eyes meeting mine made my heart jump. I could still feel the softness of his lips brushing mine.

"With you, lately, I have no idea." Tuck shook off his quiver and sank to the ground, removing his boot and shaking a stone from it.

John looked up from his bow. "Of course we did, Tuck."

"Don't want to be hanged for having stolen goods." Miller's eyes rarely left Rob, always checking what he was doing then adjusting his behavior.

"Did you hide it away from here? Or were you too busy thinking about other things?" Tuck was looking at Rob, who sat down on the ground, drew his sword and began to clean it.

"Leave him be." John got to his feet. "You took so long to get back here that he was worried for Lady Maud. The gold's hidden. You're back. Everything's good." He turned to me, flashing a grin. "Unless there's soldier's coming that the rest of us didn't hear?"

"I...ah. It must have been the wind I heard." My cheeks reddened.

John raised his chin. "The wind. Of course it was."

Miller stopped pacing and turned slowly toward me, all thoughts of being like Rob forgotten. "Your eyes are very green today, Lady Maud." He grinned.

John laughed out loud, not looking my way. I glanced at Rob in confusion. He was smiling into his chest as he worked on his sword. There was even a slight grin on Tuck's face.

"My eyes are brown. Not green. And you'll need to brush up on your flattery if you're going to be a match for Romeo over there." The words came out harsher than I intended. Even after what Tuck had said, I was still annoyed with Rob. Even more annoyed with myself.

"I don't know who Romeo is, milady, but believe me, I wasn't trying to flatter you."

"Then, what...? Oh." I looked at my feet. "I'm not jealous." I couldn't even make it sound like I meant it. Probably because I didn't. I had been stupid and petty. And most of all, it had been dangerous to alert the party we were robbing of my presence in the trees. All because I'd had to watch the one person in the world who might actually have understood me, while he flirted with another woman. And even after all of that, I still found myself going mushy inside when he smiled at me.

I dug my fingernails into the palms of my hands, telling myself to toughen up. Rob was easy to talk to, yes. Good-looking, hell, yes. And he knew how to make me feel better. But he was also eight hundred years older than me. I was going back to my own time as soon as I could. There was no point to this jealousy.

Making everyone else believe that was a different story. "Why would I care about someone who clearly prefers women draped in gold and silver?"

"Ooooh." Miller and John spoke at the same time, then looked at each other and burst into a fit of giggles.

John glanced over at Rob. "Don't get on the wrong side of this one, Rob. You might end up with an arrow in your head."

The world slowed and I went still. I saw my arrow fly into my little brother's face. No matter where I was in the world, or in time, Josh's accident was always going to be there, waiting to pop up when I least expected it.

Rob jumped to his feet, his sword falling onto the dry dirt. "Enough." His voice was just loud enough to hear over John and Miller's continued laughter.

"Careful, Robbie. I can see you're shaking in your boots." John dropped his voice to a mock whisper. "She'll be able to see it too, and you should never let them know you're scared."

The two of them bent over with laughter again.

"I said enough." The edge in Rob's voice dared anyone to argue.

John let out another peal of laughter before meeting Rob's eyes. His laughter cut off immediately, leaving the clearing in silence.

Swallowing, John looked at the ground. "Sorry. I was only kidding."

Needing some space, I turned to leave, but before I could, Rob strode over and placed a hand gently on my forearm. "It's not me you should be apologizing to." His voice was soft, but only a stupid person would have dared argue with him. I wanted to hate him for the way he'd acted with Lady Sutherland, but no one had stood up for me this way in the two years since I'd shot Josh. All I could do was hate how easy it had become for me to feel safe and happy around him, no matter what he did.

John glanced between Rob and me. "But she's just...a girl."

"Yes. And while she's our guest, you'll treat her with the same courtesy you give the rest of us." He looked at Miller. "Both of you."

"It's fine. No harm done," I mumbled.

Rob folded his arms, tilted his head back and watched me. I felt like I couldn't breathe, like my world was spiraling out of control, like I didn't know what was happening around me. We needed to talk. Once we had, he'd never look at me this way again.

I shook my head. "I just need a few minutes to myself." To compose my thoughts and stop the fluttering in my stomach.

I pushed my way down a trail that led from the clearing, taking no notice of where I was going. Fog had started to roll through the forest, blocking out the sun and sending a shiver up my back.

"Maud. Where are you going? Do you *want* Gisborne to find you?" Rob was suddenly in front of me, his voice making me jump. "You're heading toward the main trail."

I clenched my jaw. I hadn't thought about that. Or to be more exact, I'd ignored it because, really, what were the chances of Gisborne finding

me in this huge forest? I shook my head, trying to
step around him without meeting his eyes, because
I knew what they would do to me. But he folded
his arms across his chest and blocked my path
with his body.

I stared at his boots and listened to his silence
for a long moment before he finally spoke. "I
didn't tell them, you know."

I drew a deep breath, trying to calm my rapid
heartbeat. He thought I was upset because he'd
shared my secret and now he was trying to do
something about it. I couldn't remember the last
time someone had worried about the way I was
feeling—except Josh. Not that it mattered.
"Whatever."

"What does that mean? You don't believe me?
Or you don't care?" His forehead was creased and
covered with the two locks of blond hair that fell
into his eyes.

"Take your pick." I hated that I was being so
mean, but I was confused. About everything.

Rob stepped closer, ducking until I met his
eyes. "What is it you're annoyed about, Maud?
What John said, or something else?"

"You showed her your face!" My words surprised me. I thought I was upset about the comment John had made, or about the way Rob had
acted with Lady Sutherland. Not about this.

He went still, his words deliberate. "I did."

I shook my head. "I can't believe your ego needed such a boost. She'll go back and tell everyone what you look like. She wasn't even that beautiful." I mumbled the last words. God, I *was* jealous. Still, I couldn't keep the edge from my voice, wasn't even sure I wanted to. "If you're caught and captured, what will the villagers do? Starve? Live without shelter? Without food? What, Rob? Did you stop to think about any of that, or were you so enamored by her you just had to let her see your face?"

He blew a breath out his lips. "I thought you knew me better than that."

I stared at him. "Seems like I don't know you half as well as you think."

He folded his arms across his chest and watched me with hooded eyes.

Waiting.

I stared back at him, defiant. And slow to understand. Eventually I got there. "You did it *because* of them." He really was the Robin Hood of Dad's tales. He cared more for the poor than he cared about what might happen to him if he was caught.

Rob nodded. "A gold ring like that will fix up an entire village. They'll be able to buy food, rebuild homes, fix animal pens. They'll be able to do everything they need with the proceeds from that single ring."

"What if she tells the Sheriff who you are?"

Shaking his head, Rob met my eyes again. "She won't. I doubt she even remembers the color of my cloak, let alone the color of my hair."

"You're wrong. I saw the way she watched you. She'll remember everything about you, Rob. And she'll tell the Sheriff."

He shrugged. "There's a small group of women from Nottingham, of which Lady Bridgette Sutherland is one, who spend their time searching for ways to impress each other. They are young women with very old, very rich husbands, and plenty of time on their hands. Bridgette Sutherland probably came out here today on the strength of rumors, hoping to find us just so she could tell her friends she was attacked in the forest. She has no interest in seeing me caught, it'll ruin her story. And her husband is so rich he won't even miss the gold she gave us today."

I wasn't so sure.

He took a step closer, brushing a piece of hair from my face. His fingers against my skin sent a shiver up my spine.

"That was a great shot, Maud."

I shook my head. So long as my shots were controlled by my emotions, they weren't good.

He raised his eyebrows, almost smiling. "Unless you were aiming for something else? Like the back of my head, maybe?"

"No. I just..." *Maud.* There it was again. I had to tell him. "Rob. We have to talk."

"Ah," he said. "That."

"Yes. That."

He indicated to a rotting log at the side of the trail. I sat, pulling my cloak around me against the cold and pushing a low branch out of the small of my back. He lowered himself beside me, his leg a breadth away from mine, feet buried in a mire of dead leaves. He didn't look at me, but his leg jiggled up and down.

I took a deep breath and let the words tumble out. "I'm not Maud Fitzwalter."

Silence. He'd heard because the jiggling had stopped. He watched me a moment, then looked away and gave no other response.

I plowed on. "My name is Maryanne Warren. And I'm from eight-hundred-years in the future. Remember I told you my father made me do something I didn't want to do?"

Rob's eyes were fixed on the other side of the trail, on a branch partially broken long ago and now growing at an odd angle. He gave the smallest nod of his head.

"Well, he forced me to come here. He paid Eliza Thatcher's sister for my safe passage. Told me to fix the mistake he made when he lived in this time, and that I couldn't return home until the job was done. I'm not Maud. But I am her many-times-great-granddaughter. And you're famous, in my time."

He glanced my way, eyebrows lifting. "I'm famous? In eight hundred years? What did I do to achieve that honor?"

I shrugged. "Pretty much what you're doing now, from what I can tell. Taking from the rich, giving to the poor." A petty thief, I once called him. He was so much more than that. He was Dad's version of the legend and not a thing like the legend my friends knew.

Rob's lips turned down at the edges. "Doesn't take much to be famous in your time, does it?"

"I guess not." I thought of all the internet stars, famous for doing far less than Rob had ever done. "You, your legend, there's a woman in it." I waved my hand between us. "This...me....I'm not part of your legend."

Fog crept in thickly around us. He blew out a breath and his shoulders sagged. "You've told me that before. Do you remember what I told you?"

Of course I remembered, and it wasn't what I wanted to talk about now. How had this conversation gone so far off track so fast?

He leaned forward until his breath touched my cheek. His voice was a whisper. "I told you the choice is entirely mine. And, in case you've forgotten..." He waved his hand between us, copying me. "I'm fine with this, whatever it is."

I was fine with whatever it was, too. More than fine. He probably wouldn't be once he knew all the facts. "I don't think you're hearing me, Rob. I'm not Maud Fitzwalter. I'm Maryanne Warren, and I'm from the future."

I waited for him to speak. "Aren't you going to say something?" His silence scared me. I'd expected something else from him. Anger. Or hatred.

A muscle in his jaw moved, but the rest of him was still. "Are you serious?"

I nodded.

"What do you want me to say?"

I pulled my lips into a smile, trying to lighten the mood. "That you're good with it. That it doesn't bother you. That you'll still be my not-friend."

He turned to me. Slowly. So slowly, like every movement was an effort. "Can you hear yourself? You sound insane. If you don't want anything to do with me, at least have the decency to say so." He spat the words, and it wasn't anger or hatred on his face. It was disgust.

"Rob, no." I shook my head. This wasn't about him and me. "It sounds insane to me, too. Why do you think I haven't told you until now?" My voice was quiet, perhaps too quiet for him to hear.

He shook his head, his jaw taut. "Oh, I can think of plenty of reasons, and none of them have you coming here from another time. You were always close to my brother. My guess is that he's had you searching the forest for me for two years, and now you've found me, you're going to hand me over to him. In fact, I wouldn't be surprised if he were lurking in the trees, waiting, right now." He turned to the thick foliage behind us, yelling. "Gisborne! We're over here!"

I put a hand on the corded muscle in his forearm, squeezing to quiet him. As his voice rose in pitch, mine grew quieter. "You know I wouldn't do that."

He ran his eyes over me, his lip curling, and shook his head. "No. I don't. It would appear I don't know a single thing about you."

"Will you...will you at least let me explain?" I almost couldn't say the next words. "Or do you want me to go? Because...I will." If that was what he wanted.

"Go where, exactly?" He didn't need to say the next words. The pain was written across every centimeter of his face. *To Gisborne?*

"Who I am is the only thing I lied about, Rob. Everything else I said, how I feel about Gisborne, that's all true! I won't go to him. Ever."

"Who you are is a pretty big thing to lie about, don't you think?" His voice was rough and angry. He shook his head, his lip curling. "For weeks, I've wondered why I sometimes have to say your name two or three times before you hear me." He smiled tightly. "Now I know."

I raised my eyebrows. "So, you believe me?"

"No!" He jumped to his feet. "I'm not that stupid."

I stood up, right in front of him, hoping he would see by looking at me that I wasn't making this up. "Remember what I was wearing before you found me these clothes? That was what we wear in my time. No dresses or tunics. Just shorts and T-shirts."

He blew a disgusted breath out his nose and shook his head.

I wracked my brains for further proof, something else that might make him believe the unbelievable.

The white soles of my Converse were now a dirty brown from traipsing through the mud these last few weeks. I held my foot out. "Everyone wears them. In my time."

Rob turned away, massaging his temples.

I had no idea what he was thinking. "Rob? You understand I'm not Maud Fitzwalter, don't you?"

"No, damn it! I don't. You look exactly like her." He twisted to face me, his eyes cold.

"I'm not her, Rob." My voice was soft as I begged him to understand the impossible.

He pointed a finger at my chest. "You're insane. Tuck warned me not to trust you. I should have listened." He shook his head, nostrils flaring. "I should never have let myself care."

Something sparked inside me at the derision in his voice. "I told you on the night we met that my name was Maryanne, and you wouldn't listen. Now you're upset I didn't tell you sooner? I'm sorry for the lies, but don't act like you're the injured party when this," I indicated between us, "has been nothing but a game for you. You never cared about me. Not like that." He'd tried to tell me otherwise earlier, but when I thought back to the words he'd used, he'd said nothing. He hadn't said how he felt about me, only how much he cared for his friends. Only how much he hated his brother. All these emotions, and not one of them was for me.

For a second, his expression was pained. Then he blinked it away, and his face became unreadable.

That spark inside me grew. A reaction, that was what I'd been after. For Rob to tell me I was wrong. Less than an hour ago, he'd almost kissed me. Then he'd kissed Lady Sutherland, and that hurt. Sometime in these past weeks, I'd started caring for him, and I wanted him to feel the same about me.

I should have let him walk away right then, but I had to have the final word. "You're only upset because when I leave you don't have a bargaining chip with your brother."

"What. Does that. Mean?" His voice was venomous.

Even as I told myself to let it go, I couldn't stop. "It means you only let me stay with you as a safety net. If Gisborne had captured one of your friends, you were going to give him me in exchange for them." I raised my chin. "Tell me it's not true." I didn't mean it. Not even a little bit. I just wanted to hear him deny it. Hear that there was something, no matter how small, between us.

But he didn't. The guilt on Rob's face told me I was right.

I felt like I'd been punched in the gut. I shook my head, unsure if I could breathe. Fine, I'd survive without air, because damned if I was going to let him see how much that admission hurt. "Guess that makes us even. I'll find my own way to Nottingham from here."

A stick cracked in the bushes behind me and Rob's body stilled, his hand going to his waist. He slowly drew his sword.

My heart kicked into high gear. Rob stepped in front of me and I squinted past him through the fog off the trail, trying to see whatever he'd seen. Three soldiers appeared suddenly, stepping out from the surrounding forest. They pounced on Rob, two of them grabbing his arms while the third removed the sword from his hand.

"Maud, run!" Rob's voice seemed overly loud in the quiet forest. He twisted and bucked, trying to get away, but three on one wasn't a fair fight. "Run!" He yelled again, his voice breaking with the effort. "Tuck! John!" A soldier punched him in the stomach, and he hunched forward.

"No!" I grabbed a soldier's arm, pulling him off Rob. He pushed me away and I stumbled backward onto the ground. His laugh mingled with my frustrated cry. They dragged Rob away down the trail before I could get back to my feet.

It was from the ground that I saw the fourth soldier.

His boots came into view first; dark brown and laced up to the knee. Later, I wondered if I should have recognized them immediately, and sprinted in the other direction. But I neither recognized nor ran. Instead, I drew my eyes slowly up his legs and body. Over the burgundy and gold cloak that was just millimeters from dragging on the leaf-covered ground. Over his black tunic, ornately decorated with grey embroidery around the cuffs and hem. And over the black wavy hair that curled into ice blue eyes.

The eyes of Sir Guy of Gisborne.

Nineteen

I STUMBLED to my feet to run but he was faster, grabbing my arm before I'd taken a step. Dear God. Rob would think he'd been right, that I was working with Gisborne against him.

"My lady. It seems Lady Sutherland's coachman was correct when he suggested we'd find Robin Hood on this trail." He spoke into my ear and I suppressed a shudder, his hands on my body reminding me how casually he'd pointed his sword at my back when we met.

A slight smile crossed his lips as he let his eyes wander over my face and down my body. "Where are you off to in such a hurry?"

I searched for Rob and the soldiers on the trail, but they were gone, disappeared into the thick fog. I wrestled to get free. "John! Miller! Help me!" My voice cracked with the strength of my scream.

Gisborne raised his eyebrows. "There's nothing your friends can do to help you, my lady."

"Why? What have you done to them?" There was a tremor in my voice I wished I'd been able to hide.

He placed his hand on my shoulder and turned me in the direction the soldiers dragged Rob. "Lady Maud, I believe we have a marriage ceremony that's long overdue. Surely you're not going to walk away from me again?"

"Are you giving me a choice?" I'd felt Gisborne's sword on my back and knew what he'd done to his own brother. Going with him wasn't an option. I wondered if I was brave enough to run.

He sneered. "Not at all." He slid his hand from my shoulder to my elbow and guided me along the trail beside him, his fingers tightening on my arm so I could go only where he guided me.

At the clearing, he pushed me ahead, and in that moment, I was glad his hands were no longer on my body. Until I noticed the smirk on his face. Then I followed his gaze. Tuck, John and Miller were all on their knees in the grass, disarmed and each with a soldier holding a sword at their throats. Rob was also on his knees and surrounded by the three soldiers who'd captured him. There was a dark bruise rising on his cheek.

I was the only one not held by a weapon. "Rob." He didn't look at me, wouldn't. He thought I'd done this. Brought Gisborne here to kill him. "This wasn't me. I didn't tell Gisborne where to find us." My voice was thick with stupid tears that wanted to spill over. Thick with the need for him to believe me.

Gisborne rubbed his hands together. "What's this? A lover's tiff?"

"Rob. Please. I didn't do this. I would never."

A muscle in Rob's jaw moved.

"The lady has spoken." Gisborne strolled over to Rob, his hands clasped behind his back. He crouched in front of him. "But you know better than to believe her, don't you, brother? You know I've done everything in my power to find you. Including sending my very own Lady Maud out here to seduce you. And she did a good job, I think."

Rob lifted his chin, his beautiful face twisted with hatred. As his eyes met Gisborne's, he blinked slowly. Then he spat in Gisborne's face.

Gisborne's fist shot out immediately, hitting Rob square in the stomach. Rob doubled over, gasping.

"Rob!" My scream split the forest. I ran to him, dropping to my knees. "It's lies, Rob. None of it's true." As if he'd believe me now. I didn't even think he'd heard me.

"Get away from him," Gisborne bellowed, wiping away the glob of spittle that ran slowly down his face. When I didn't move, he picked me up and dragged me away.

I kicked out at him, missing completely. "Let go of me." My voice was shrill, the sound echoing around the forest. I had to help Rob.

"Quiet," he snarled.

"No! Put me down!"

Gisborne did exactly that, placing me on my feet beside him. Without a moment's pause, he pulled his arm back and hit me in the stomach. All the air raced from my lungs. I tried to gasp in a breath but couldn't. Couldn't breathe at all. Couldn't make a sound. Could only see the brown leather of Gisborne's boots beside my head—when had I fallen to the ground? I heard someone speaking. Or yelling. I wasn't sure. It was so far in the distance.

As my vision began to go black around the edges, I managed to draw the smallest breath. Then another. Then a loud, wheezing gasp. The sweet smell of grass filled my nostrils as I gasped again, and again.

Asshole.

How dare he hit me.

Gisborne's hands were on me. I tried to break his grasp, but he dragged me to my feet. "Ah, my lady. I'm so sorry. But your voice. It was getting on my nerves. Next time, it might pay to listen when I tell you to be quiet." The temptation to spit at him as Rob had was overwhelming.

Something had changed in the clearing. I glanced from John, to Miller, to Tuck. All of them were still on their knees. So was Rob. But two soldiers lay on the ground near him, groaning quietly. Blood ran in a thin line from Rob's nose, over his lips and down his chin. His left fist was grazed. He'd fought. Even knowing it was hopeless, he'd fought.

For me?

I felt him watching me and met his eyes. Worry, anger and something else filled them. Respect? Trust? I hoped it was both but couldn't be sure. He twisted his head in silent question, the same way he'd done at Edwinstowe. *Are you all right?*

I nodded, giving him the same questioning look—*was he?*—to which he gave me the same answer.

He'd fought for me. I knew it with every part of my body. When he should've given up on me for lying, for hurting him with my words, he hadn't. He wasn't like anyone I'd ever met. He was strong, and honorable, and caring. Meeting Rob was the best thing that had ever happened to me. And it was because of that, rather than because of Dad's task, that I made my decision.

I would not let Gisborne destroy Rob.

Gisborne's men were going through their belongings and I still wasn't clear what they wanted. "What are you doing?" I asked. There were so many weapons in this small area, all held against us.

Gisborne grinned as if he'd been waiting for that exact question. "We came across Lady Bridgette Sutherland on the trail to Nottingham. Her coachman told us she'd been accosted today in her carriage, not far from here. The robbers relieved her of a substantial portion of her fortune. I have reason to believe the gold is here. With your *friends.*" He spat the final word at me.

My heart sank. "Lady Sutherland gave you a description of her attackers?" Rob had been wrong about her. He should never have shown his face.

Gisborne shook his head. "Lady Sutherland was too distraught to speak with us. She kept insisting they take their leave—probably too scared to stay in the forest a moment longer."

"Her coachman then?" If Lady Sutherland hadn't given a description, then it had to have been him. If they'd given one at all.

"He saw a number of hooded men."

"But not their faces? If so, you have no evidence. Why would you think you'd find the gold here?"

He gave me a dismissive smile and waved a hand in the air as if that was answer enough.

Rob stared at the ground. Though his jaw was rigid, his shoulders seemed relaxed—I had no idea how, with a sword pointing at his body. Tuck also looked serene, although his hands and body were hidden in his robes, so it was difficult to tell. Miller's face was red with agitation and John looked like he could jump up and thump someone any moment.

"The ring's not here, my lord." One of the soldiers called to Gisborne from across the clearing.

"It has to be." Gisborne barely looked at the soldier as he spoke. His eyes were filled with loathing and fixed on Rob.

Another soldier walked up beside Gisborne, his voice quiet. "With respect, my lord, these aren't the ones. The reports said there were more of them than this. And that Hood's cloak was red. None of these have a red cloak."

"With respect, Sir Kerrington, the Lady Sutherland was so scared, or perhaps besotted, by this robber, she could barely remember her own name."

"But the cloak——"

"Today it was red. Last week's victim said gold. Someone else said black. None of them know what they're talking about." Gisborne's voice grew louder with each word, and his cheeks redder.

"We have no gold, my lord." I met his eyes, hoping doing so would convince Gisborne I was speaking the truth, even as I attempted to lie our way out of this. "We're heading south, to Nottingham. I couldn't live in the filth of the forest another day longer and was coming to find you, hoping you'd take me back. The others were coming for work." Something told me to keep quiet about our real reasons for visiting Nottingham.

Gisborne didn't answer, just tapped his foot impatiently on the grass waiting for me to continue. "We did pass a group of men, earlier today. They were better dressed than us and without horses. In fine spirits and heading north. Perhaps they were the people you're searching for? One of them even wore a red cloak."

Gisborne stepped toward me, a forced smile on his lips. "How many?"

"Sorry, my lord?" I'd heard the question but needed to buy some time. I couldn't throw any old number at him; it needed to be close to the number Lady Sutherland's coachman had given.

"How many people were in the group you saw?" He enunciated every word, making sure I had no reason to question him further.

I clasped my hands sedately to stop them shaking. Lady Sutherland had seen three of us. Plus, an arrow had come from Tuck's bow, and another from mine—two different directions. She knew there were at least five of us. But other than the arrows, there was no struggle; she'd handed over most of her gold without being asked. Of course, she'd never admit that. She'd make it sound terrifying. So, ten men? Twenty?

"Ah, I'm not so good with detail, you might want to check with one of the others, but there might have been fifteen of them."

Kerrington marched over to Tuck. "How many men did you see?"

Tuck drew himself up, his brown robe bunched around his knees. The rope he tied around his waist had come loose and lay on the ground beside him. "I'd say fifteen to twenty, easily. Didn't think to count them, my lord." There wasn't a hint of the terror I was feeling in his voice.

Kerrington strode back to Gisborne. "He's a man of God. Wouldn't lie. Sounds like the people we're after."

A flush of red rose up Gisborne's face. His grip on my arm tightened painfully and he glared at Rob. "Kill them."

"No! You can't!" I twisted to face Gisborne. "They're good people. You can't kill them!"

Gisborne's eyebrows rose. "That's where you're mistaken, Lady Maud. *I* can do whatever I wish."

I looked at my friends, but none of them had reacted to Gisborne's words. They all kneeled calmly as if their lives weren't in danger. Why weren't they fighting? It was almost as if Rob and the others *expected* Gisborne to kill them.

Gisborne smirked. "Oh, don't worry, my lady. You're quite safe. You'll be returning to Nottingham with me."

Blood thrummed in my ears. It was true I wanted to go to Nottingham. But I wanted to go on my terms, so I could find Eliza, get my coin back and leave. Not like this.

Drawing myself up, I met his eyes. "Do you want to marry me, my lord?"

"Of course. You know that." He broke our stare to watch Rob.

"For my dowry?" My voice shook and I prayed he wouldn't call my bluff. Lord Fitzwalter was a powerful man with a lot of money. He probably had some sway with the Sheriff, too. At least, that was the theory I was working off.

"No, for love." Gisborne's sarcasm made the back of my neck prickle.

"For money, then. I'm guessing you don't want to do anything to upset that."

"I'm not sure I follow." His brow creased, but his eyes, for once, were on me, waiting.

In another time and place, I might have found Gisborne good-looking. Carrie certainly would have. He was exactly her type with the jet-black hair that curled across his face, brilliant blue eyes and full lips. Yet, those eyes were icy and his lips mocking. This man knew he was far more powerful than any of us. And he reveled in that knowledge.

I raised my chin. "Imagine if I'm reunited with my father for the first time in two years, and I can't even talk to him because I'm so upset. Imagine what he'll think when I tell him the man I'm supposed to marry, killed the people who were kind enough to free me from my prison deep in the forest."

"Oh, I'm not going to make you watch, my lady." His lips curled at the corners as he spoke. Perhaps he thought he was smiling, but it certainly didn't look that way.

"I believe you are missing the point. My lord." I folded my arms across my chest. I wasn't scared of him. He needed me. He wouldn't kill me.

Gisborne's stare grew distant for a moment and I could almost see him calculating what it would mean to be out of favor with Lord Fitzwalter. At least, I hoped that was what he was considering. Finally, he narrowed his eyes. "I spoke in jest, my lady. You and I clearly need some time to reintroduce ourselves so you understand me again. We are, of course, grateful to your *friends*." He spoke the word like it was poison on his tongue. "We would not want the people who returned you to us, to be punished."

Something about the way he spoke put me on edge. I lifted my chin, unable to break his gaze. I wasn't backing down. "Since we are so grateful to them, we shouldn't delay them in their travels any longer."

Color rose on Gisborne's cheeks. He might have said the words, but it seemed he didn't mean them. The only way Rob and the others would be safe, or at least safe-for-now, was if Gisborne allowed them to leave.

I took a step forward, close enough I could feel the heat radiating off Gisborne's skin. My voice was steel. "I don't believe you're taking me seriously, my lord. I *will* tell Father what you've done if you hurt any of these men. After two years thinking me dead, do you really think he's going to force me to marry someone so cruel as to kill my rescuers? Especially when I tell him I'm scared to be near my fiancé."

A thin layer of sweat broke out on my forehead. I was playing with fire, but I was also desperate. I had to take this risk, to pretend I knew the man everyone thought was my father. I had to hope Gisborne would assume I knew him better than anyone, knew exactly what he was likely to do.

Gisborne pursed his lips with barely concealed anger. "Just so you know, Lord Fitzwalter is currently residing in France. Once we get you safely back to Nottingham, we'll send word. But you know how long that is likely to take."

I didn't. But it didn't matter where that man was, so long as Gisborne was terrified enough of him to let my friends walk away from here. He stared at me for what felt like an age, then gave a slow deliberate blink and turned to his men. "Drop your weapons. Let them go." As if it hurt him to say the words, he focused on Rob. "For now."

Rob's jaw was clenched, and his nostrils flared. He was the boy Tuck had spoken of, the one who had been filled with the need for revenge for a third of his life, and he was kneeling in the dirt in front of me with a snarl on his face. That same anger had been there when I first met him. Perhaps not as concentrated, but there. Slowly over these past few weeks, it had diminished, just as

Tuck had said. As his hands clenched and un-clenched, I willed him not to do anything stupid.

Gisborne's men did as they were asked, stepping away from each of their prisoners. None of them sheathed their swords, but neither were they holding them with menace any longer.

John and Miller climbed to their feet, dazed, as if they couldn't quite believe they were free.

"Go." My voice was a croak and only just audible. I couldn't have spoken any louder if I'd tried.

"But——" John was torn. He understood his life was at risk if he didn't leave, but it wasn't in his nature to leave anyone behind.

I tried to smile. I didn't want to go with Gisborne, but if that was what it took to save four lives, I would do it. "I'm fine, John. Going back where I'm supposed to be. And happy about it." I forced some lightness into my voice and put my hand on Gisborne's forearm, the same way Maud would have, I hoped.

John gave a quick nod. I wasn't sure he be-lieved me, but that was all it took for him and Miller to turn and run into the forest. I just hoped they kept running.

Tuck hadn't yet moved. Nor had Rob. A part of me had known it would be difficult to get Rob to leave while Gisborne stood in front of him.

Perhaps I'd hoped it would be difficult for him to leave me, too.

I had expected Tuck to be gone without a second thought.

As I considered how to make them leave, it was Rob who spoke. He glared at Gisborne with undisguised hatred. "Go, Tuck. This isn't your fight."

"It became my fight on a stormy night six years ago."

Rob shook his head. "Stay and you'll die." When Tuck didn't move, Rob added, "I'll be along soon."

Tuck glared my way, still on his knees. I don't know what else he expected from me. I was trying my hardest to save them all.

"Tuck. Please." Rob's voice broke in his desperation to save his friend. With worried eyes and slow movements, Tuck sighed, stood and quietly left before Gisborne could change his mind.

"Don't test me, Woodhurst." Gisborne's voice was pure hatred. "I won't give you another chance to leave with your life. You're only getting this one because of her." He motioned in my direction.

A muscle in the side of Rob's jaw worked. A lock of hair had fallen forward onto his face, but he didn't bother to brush it away, maybe he didn't even realize it was there. The bruise on his cheek had already turned a deep purple. Knowing it would never happen, I itched to be the one to hold a cold cloth to it, to take away Rob's pain.

He tore his eyes from Gisborne to look at me. "Lady Maud, I don't need you to look out for me. You don't have to go with him." There was a pleading note in his voice. Not begging me to stay with him but telling me not to go with Gisborne. Perhaps there was a little part of him that believed I wasn't Maud. Or maybe he just knew me well enough to know I hated the idea of going anywhere with this man.

I shook my head. "Yes. I do." *For you.*

"You don't belong there. I'll take you wherever you need to go. I'll get you home. You have...other options."

I didn't. There was no other option available if I wanted to save them. Him. I did what I hoped was a good impression of Lady Maud, aloof and proud, praying it was enough to make him leave. "I belong in Nottingham. Gisborne will take me."

Still Rob didn't move, torn between saving himself and leaving me with his enemy.

I squared my jaw. He had to go. Going to Nottingham to find Eliza had always been my plan—he knew that. All that had changed was who took me there, and the fact that I no longer planned on hanging around to watch the tournament—the sooner I could give Gisborne the slip, the better. In the meantime, so long as Gisborne wanted to marry me, my life was not in danger. I sidled closer to Gisborne and swallowed down the bile in my throat as I took his hand. "I appreciate everything you've done for me, but I need to go back where I belong."

"Woodhurst..." There was a warning in Gisborne's voice. If Rob didn't go soon, it would be too late.

"Go," I whispered, blinking away the tears that wanted to slip down my cheeks. He had to go. He had to live. People needed him. He was going to make a girl with a familiar name very happy one day.

With a final torn gaze in my direction, he strode away, fists clenched. Gone because I'd asked. The complete opposite of the other man in my life, my father, who'd forced me into a trip back in time that I hadn't wanted to take.

I watched Rob's back as he disappeared into the forest, telling myself it didn't matter that I'd never see him again. Telling myself I should think myself lucky to have met a legend in real life. Telling myself I'd said everything I wanted to say to him.

I barely noticed the commotion in the clearing until one of the soldiers bumped my shoulder and sent me sprawling onto the ground. I picked my-self up as the last of the soldiers disappeared into the forest in the same place Rob had gone moments before, leaving Gisborne and me alone.

"You broke your promise." Red flashed across my vision, but I kept my voice even.

Gisborne turned his lips down at the edges. "I don't think so. You asked me not to kill them in front of you and to let them go. I did both those things. But now I have prisoners escaping, so I've sent my men after them."

There was a shout from the direction they'd run, followed by the cracking of branches.

"You're going to kill them anyway." My voice was flat.

He raised his hands palm up. "Not me. I'm right here with you. Unfortunately, I can't control what my men do in the heat of battle."

I put my hand over my mouth as a wave of nausea rose inside me. "Call them back." I was light-headed. It could have been because of the punch to my stomach, but I didn't think so.

Gisborne shrugged, smiling. Enjoying this. "I can't."

I stepped toward him. "Do it. Or you can forget about marrying me."

"Ha." Gisborne had been looking at the place Rob had gone moments before, but now he turned to me. "It's funny you even think that's an option. Your father would disagree, I'm sure."

I spoke through my teeth. "My father will want me to be happy."

"And you will be. With me."

I sank to the ground, long blades of grass dampening my pants. Those men were not supposed to die today; the legend of Robin Hood lasted longer than a handful of raids on the wealthy.

"On your feet, my lady. We have a long ride ahead of us." He held out his hand, the grey embroidery of his tunic the same color as the fog swirling at his ankles and pulled me up. I didn't have the energy to protest.

Another yell came from the trees, farther away this time, but I was certain it was Rob. Or perhaps Miller. I was rooted to the spot, listening to them die as penance for not saving them.

Taking hold of my shoulders, Gisborne turned me away and dragged me to his horse.

Twenty

I COULDN'T stop thinking about them. No matter how far away we rode, their yells still filled my ears. I went over everything in my head, wondering what I could have done differently. Wondering if I could have saved them.

And while thinking about them was difficult, it was easier than constantly noticing how close I had to sit to Gisborne on the back of his horse. I didn't want to touch the man who had killed my friends, but I had to wrap my arms around his vile body and hold on tight.

He talked constantly, excitedly. I had to keep reminding myself it was Maud he was seeing, not me; and he probably *was* pleased to have her back after all this time.

"Do you remember the rose you gave me for my birthday the week before you...disappeared, Lady Maud?" He twisted in the saddle, waiting for my response.

I made an affirmative sound in my throat, unable and unwilling to engage fully with him.

"It was a deep red, the most beautiful color—reminded me of your hair in the sunlight. After you...left, I had the gardener at Nottingham plant a bush beneath the window of my chamber there. I also had him send another of the same bushes to my home at Woodhurst Manor." He twisted around again, giving me a smile. For a second, I saw him as someone else—a boy who'd had his heart broken when his girlfriend disappeared. Then I thought about how he'd come to be living at Woodhurst Manor, remembered the cruelty in his eyes as he'd told me his soldiers were hunting Rob down, and I shuffled backwards, eager to put some distance between our bodies.

Gisborne didn't seem to notice. "No one is allowed to pick the flowers from those bushes. Except on my birthday. Then I have the gardener pick a single rose to bring to my chamber. I like to pretend it came from you."

He was silent and I wasn't sure if he was awaiting my reaction to his somewhat creepy admission or collecting his thoughts. It seemed he'd been a very different person when Maud was alive.

It was almost dark when we arrived in Nottingham, and though I could make out the looming silhouette of the castle, the light of the full moon showed me little more. The street was cobbled, candle-lit homes on either side, the smell of cooking meat wafting out to the street.

The sound of a second pair of hooves against the cobblestones didn't register in my mind until the rider was beside us. His face was impossible to see in the darkness, his hood drawn high, but he wore the burgundy riding cape of Nottingham's men.

"My lord," he said as his horse fell into step beside us. For a moment, my heart stopped. The soldier sounded like Rob.

Gisborne looked the soldier up and down before giving him permission to talk. "Flemington."

My heart dropped. Not Rob. Of course not. Couldn't possibly be.

"We got them."

Gisborne twisted in the saddle to face him. "You're sure? Did you see it?"

Flemington nodded. "All but one. The monk. He got away."

My chest tightened and I didn't think I could take another breath. "Friar," I mumbled, but neither took any notice. My hands were suddenly cold and clammy, and a dagger pierced my heart.

"And the others?" Gisborne almost leaned toward the rider, his voice eager. I swallowed down the bile that rose in my throat. This man was despicable; excited by the death of others.

"The skinny one got Faulkner's sword through his stomach and the tall one took an arrow in his back. The other one, the leader—"

Now Gisborne really did lean forward. "Yes?"

"I saw him in the distance. He was running like a coward. Took three arrows to bring him down."

That was it then. Rob really was dead; I could no longer hope otherwise. The dagger twisted inside me.

Gisborne moved under my arms and I realized I'd clenched my fists around his chainmail and was pinching the skin on his stomach. Good. I hope it hurt.

He broke my grip and nodded slowly. "You're sure of this?"

"Aye, my lord. The roads of Sherwood Forest are safe again, for sure."

"Ha." I couldn't keep myself quiet. Safe was a relative term, so long as the Sheriff's men were around.

"Did you have something to add, my lady?" Gisborne pulled the horse to a stop and dismounted, offering his hand up to me.

"How can Sherwood Forest be safe when your soldiers are killing people every day?"

I couldn't see Gisborne's face; the shadows were too long. But I imagined a benign smile upon it. "You've been gone a long time, my lady. You speak of things you simply can't understand."

I took his hand and slid awkwardly from the horse, landing on his foot. He yelped but I wouldn't let him step away, talking through my teeth. "You'd be surprised the things I understand, my lord. I understand that the rich are getting richer by making the poor work harder and pay more tax. I understand that you and your soldiers are trained fighters, preying on farmers and people who've never had the privilege of being taught to use a weapon. I understand that your men killed the four people I owe my life to today because of a personal quarrel. If you think I'm going to marry a man like that, you're sadly mistaken."

I was surprised to find I meant it all. I wasn't just spouting propaganda for the sake of achieving Dad's task. Rob's was a cause I believed in. I'd seen the rich folk in their fancy dresses and expensive carriages with gold and jewels dripping from their bodies, and I'd seen the poor living with their entire family in a one room hut and working day after day just to have it all taken away from them by the whim of someone more powerful. By Gisborne. I would not be part of it. Gisborne might think I was with him for good, but he was wrong.

My legs began to shake. Where would I go if I did manage to escape? Rob and the others were dead. The people I'd spent the last few weeks with, the people who had taken me in and kept me alive, were gone. And the only reason I wasn't dead with them was because a stroke of luck made me look like a missing girl. I was very close to bending over and emptying the contents of my stomach onto the ground.

"My lady? Are you all right?" Gisborne reached out and took my hand.

I pulled out of his grasp. "No. I'm very much not all right. Friends of mine are dead. And you seem excited by it. It makes me sick. *You* make me sick."

Gisborne called over his shoulder to Flemington. "See to my horse, will you? The stable boy should be around somewhere."

"I'm sure you're too busy to deal with women's problems, my lord. I could show Lady Maud to her chamber, if you like?" Flemington's voice drifted down from where he sat on his horse.

"Lady Maud has an appointment to keep. She'll come with me. See to my horse." Placing his arm around my waist, he marched me across the stone courtyard, lit only by the brightness of the moon, and toward the towering castle. "It's been a long day. One more quick stop and then we'll find you a place to sleep. You'll feel better about all this in the morning." His voice was cajoling and crept up my spine in a way that made me want to scratch his face.

I would not feel better in the morning, but at least if I was shown to a room, I would be away from Gisborne. Right now, that seemed like a major bonus.

The air inside the castle was colder than outside had been, and I pulled my cloak tightly around my body. Gisborne located and lit a candle, then led me through narrow hallways that twisted and turned, always keeping one hand upon me. Other people, servants perhaps, stepped aside as Gisborne neared, letting us pass. He walked purposefully, his shoes making a hollow tapping sound against the stone floor. My modern rubber soles were silent as I struggled to keep up with his long strides. He led us up a spiral staircase with steps so small and tight I was certain my foot would slip, and I'd tumble to the bottom. I had no idea how Gisborne managed with his large feet.

Gisborne finally stopped outside a closed door guarded by two soldiers. "Sheriff in there?"

"Having his supper, my lord. And he's not to be disturbed." The soldier looked over Gisborne's shoulder.

"He'll want to be disturbed for this." Gisborne's smile didn't reach his eyes.

"But he said——"

"I don't care what you think he said. I have a matter of urgency to discuss with him and I suggest you step aside." His voice was low, the words enunciated. A man used to getting his way. I hated him more with every second I spent in his company.

The guard swallowed and glanced at his mate before reluctantly doing as he'd been asked.

Gisborne barreled through the door, dragging me behind. I tried to pull away, but he held me tight.

At first, I thought we'd entered the wrong room. Apart from a servant standing quietly among the shadows at the far end, I could see no one. It appeared to be a bedroom, a huge bed with a heavy wooden frame taking up a large portion of the area. At the far end though, was a table piled high with platters of all manner of food—fruit, vegetables, meat and the most delicious smelling bread. And sitting alone at the table by the light of two candles, was a small man with a large gut. He was stuffing food into his mouth as if he hadn't eaten in a month.

"I said no interruptions." The Sheriff forced a chunk of white meat into his mouth, his eyes focused on the huge plate in front of him. His voice was deep and rich, like the burgundy of his tunic.

"This is important, my lord." Gisborne and I came to a stop three steps from him.

"Ah, Gisborne." I waited for the Sheriff to say more, but he continued to chew loudly without speaking.

Gisborne apparently knew better than to interrupt further, standing to attention and watching as the Sheriff mopped up gravy with a piece of bread. Finally, the Sheriff looked up, wiping his face and hands on a burgundy napkin.

The Sheriff of Nottingham was older than I'd imagined, probably in his late forties. A scar ran from the corner of his left eye down under his full-face grey beard. His eyes were hard as he watched Gisborne. He didn't seem to have noticed me. "Am I right to believe Lady Sutherland was set upon today, in Sherwood Forest?"

"Yes, but—"

"And, am I right to understand she's a very substantially poorer now? That she lost a considerable amount of her fortune to the bandit they call Robin Hood? Money that was promised to the King in taxes and gifts?"

I blew a quiet breath out my nose. Rob had said Lady Sutherland's husband was very rich; if he was right, I doubted she was going to be living in the poorhouse after today. Besides, she'd as good as given it willingly.

Gisborne swallowed. "With a cut going to yourself too, no doubt my lord."

The Sheriff raised his chin. "What benefits me, benefits you, Gisborne."

Gisborne glanced at his feet, shifting uncomfortably.

"Remind me, Gisborne. What exactly do I pay you to do?"

"Collect taxes and keep the forest safe, my lord."

The Sheriff raised his eyebrows.

"The forest is safe again, my lord. My soldiers killed Robin Hood and his men earlier today."

The Sheriff nodded. "Go on."

As Gisborne spoke, I saw it happening: John falling in the middle of the road, an arrow in his back. Miller slashed with a sword. And Rob.

No.

I would not think about this.

"My lady, are you all right?"

I blinked twice and suddenly Gisborne was standing over me, looking down as I lay on the ground. Even the Sheriff was on his feet. What the heck?

"My lady?" Gisborne crouched, seeming uncertain what to do.

"I'm fine." As I tried to sit up the room began to spin. I lay back down. "What happened?"

"It appears you fainted, my lady." The Sheriff stood over me, his tone dry and slightly bemused.

I was already embarrassed to have fainted; I didn't need anyone laughing at me. "Do I amuse you, sir?" I glared up at him, unsure where *that* vocabulary had come from. I'd never called a person *sir* in my life.

The Sheriff checked his grin. "No." He swallowed. "No, my lady, you do not." He looked past me to the door. "Guard."

Gisborne stiffened and his eyes swung from me up to the Sheriff.

Looking at the guard standing to attention on the far side of the room, the Sheriff said, "Take her to the guest suite in the south quarter. Wait outside, and don't let her out."

"My lord?" Gisborne pushed himself to his feet, moving between me and the advancing guard. "What are you doing?"

The Sheriff rested his hands on his belly before turning slowly to face Gisborne. "Locking her up."

"Why?" He shuffled a little closer to me.

Locking me up? Oh, no he wasn't. I sat up, waiting for the spinning to stop so I could stand.

The Sheriff gave a single shoulder shrug and stared at Gisborne as if he thought the answer should be obvious. "Because I don't believe this is Maud Fitzwalter."

Two guards lifted me from the cold floor, one on either side guiding me away to the sound of Gisborne arguing with the Sheriff about who I was. They deposited me in a room far from where I'd met the Sheriff, then left me in the hands of a servant girl who helped me into bed. My brain told me to fight her. She was so little that I could easily overpower her and escape, but my body lacked the energy to fight. Instead, I lay my head on the pillow and thought of Rob while the moon made its slow progress across the sky.

All night long, I told myself they were dead because they'd had the misfortune to meet me. For six years, they'd kept away from Gisborne. He'd never have known about Rob if I hadn't insisted on searching for Eliza.

And even when I reminded myself that, according to Dad, Rob would have been heading for a life of villainy by now had I not come to this time, I still couldn't stop the ache in my chest from the tears I choked back. I wished I was still in the forest with him. Green eyes and blond hair were all I could see in my mind. The only place I'd ever see them again.

I swiped away the tears dribbling down my cheeks, and opened my eyes, surprised to find I must have, at some point, slept. Dust motes danced in a beam of bright sunlight that fell across the room.

I sat up, letting the soft linen bedding fall around my waist. It had been almost four weeks since I'd had the luxury of sleeping in a bed, but all I wanted was to be back in the forest sleeping on the ground with my cloak, rather than sheets and blankets, wrapped around me for warmth. With Rob snoring softly nearby.

Someone, probably the servant girl, had placed a tray of food at the end of the bed. My stomach rumbled just looking at it. I didn't recall when I'd last eaten, and I fell on the tray, barely chewing and definitely not tasting before swallowing the selection of fruit and bread upon it.

With food in my stomach and a small amount of sleep, life didn't seem quite so desperate. I glanced around the sparsely furnished room. There was just the canopied bed I'd slept in, a chair and small table beside the window, a large tapestry in the Sheriff's colors on the stone wall, and another on the floor. A huge vase of deep red roses rested on the table—from Gisborne, I guessed. A shiver of revulsion ran up my spine.

The coals in the fireplace glowed red. I was tempted to throw the flowers into the embers, but I held my pettiness in focusing instead on the best way to get out of here.

The Sheriff *thought* I might not be Maud, but he wasn't certain. If he was, I'd be in far worse lodgings than this room, possibly the dungeons after all those carriage robberies. With any luck, he'd had a change of heart overnight. Maybe Gisborne had convinced him I was Maud and my room was now unguarded. Maybe I could walk out that door and not stop until I found Eliza and my coin.

After that, I'd go to the forest and search for Tuck. The soldier had said he was still alive. He'd know where Rob was buried so I could say good-bye. After that, I wasn't certain. Hopefully, he'd been successful enough as Robin Hood already and I'd be able to go home. If not, maybe I'd finish what he started, become Robin Hood for him.

I searched for my clothes, throwing back the blankets on the bed, lifting the cushion on the chair, getting down on my hands and knees and looking under the bed. Everything I'd worn yesterday was gone, leaving me with just the long nightgown the servant had helped me change into last night.

Well, fine. I'd wear my nightgown out into the castle to search for Eliza. I wore less than this when I went out at home anyway.

I walked over to the door, turned the handle and stepped out.

A guard stood on either side, just like the Sheriff had promised. Gisborne clearly hadn't had any luck in getting him to change his mind about me. Both of them stared straight ahead, unflinching even when I opened the door.

I stepped into the corridor, the floor icy beneath my bare feet. Both guards moved with me, blocking the way in either direction. "Excuse me." My voice sounded small, lost among the high ceilings and stone walls.

Neither guard moved. I glanced in both directions, then made my decision. With quick feet, I stepped behind one, but he was faster, blocking my exit. "Go back to your chamber," he growled. "Someone will be along soon to help you dress." The guard refused to meet my eyes, probably due to my state of undress.

I glanced between them, searching for a way past. There was none; not at the moment, anyway. With a sigh, I retreated into my room and shut the door.

Of all the people I'd met since I came to this time, the Sheriff of Nottingham was the only one I'd really needed to believe I was Maud Fitzwalter. He was the person powerful enough to make life difficult if he thought I was an imposter. If I couldn't escape, or if I couldn't find a way to convince him I was her, he'd keep me locked up. I wasn't having that.

I marched over to the only window in the room, opened the latch and leaned out. I was on the second level, too high to jump. If I'd been one or two rooms over, I'd have been able to jump from the window to the large oak that grew there, but only the very ends of the branches touched my window, too thin to hold my weight.

"What are you doing, milady?" The servant girl from last night pushed through the door and into my room. A bucket of steaming water sloshed in her arms, a few drops spilling over the deep burgundy apron tied around her waist. She lowered the bucket to the floor and smoothed out her matching burgundy dress before pushing a stray strand of hair beneath her bonnet.

"Where are my clothes?" I was in no mood for niceties, hadn't been since I'd learned Rob was dead.

"Oh no, milady!" The girl's eyes went wide. "You need to wait for your bath to be ready."

I shook my head. Bathing implied I was staying here at the castle for a time. I wasn't. I was leaving as soon as I could, hopefully today. "I don't need a bath, just my clothes." My words came out with a bite I hadn't intended.

"Y-your old clothes have been taken away to be burned. Aggie's searching for a dress that might fit right now." The girl looked at the ground, too timid to meet my eyes.

"Burned? What do you mean?" They couldn't burn them. Rob had found those clothes for me. They were all I had to remember him by.

"Well, they're not..."

I stared at her, waiting for her to finish whatever she was trying to say.

She swallowed. "They're not exactly appropriate for wearing around the castle. You'll be needing a dress." Because I'd been wearing pants.

"I don't want a dress. I just want my old clothing back." And to get out of here.

She shook her head frantically. "The Earl of Woodhurst. H-he said you'd be h-happier with pretty clothes."

"The Earl of Woodhurst?" That was how Gisborne was known around here? It had never occurred to me that Gisborne might have some other fancy title; a title that probably should have been Rob's. Hearing the servant girl speak of Gisborne that way made me realize what an impossible fight we'd been in. He had wealth, power and prestige—and he'd used all three against us—while we had nothing. I wasn't letting him think he'd won so easily. I leaned toward the girl. "Let's get this straight right now. Gisborne is not in charge of me. *I* am in charge of me. If you receive instructions from him that involve me, from now on check with me first. Is that clear?"

She nodded, shrinking into herself.

I sighed, sorry for yelling. None of this was her fault. Gisborne had flipped my bitch-switch, and she was the one picking up the pieces. "What is your name?"

"Xanthe Mason, milady."

"It's lovely to meet you, Xanthe." I eyed the door through which she'd come, then glanced at the bucket at her feet. If she thought I was having a bath, there were likely more servants on their way with water and a tub. A plan was beginning to form in my mind, but I had to act fast. "Are the guards still outside my door?"

She nodded.

"I'm going to need your dress." I waved at her head. "And your bonnet."

Xanthe touched her hat, then glanced at the ground shaking her head. "I don't understand."

"I need to get out of here. Dressed like you, those guards out the door might let me pass."

Her eyes rounded. "Oh, no, milady. I couldn't do that."

I drew in a deep breath, smiling sweetly. There was no other way to get out of this room, which left me with no choice but to convince her it was the right thing to do. "You're worried you'll get in trouble? Tell the Sheriff I threatened you with a knife."

She shook her head. "I couldn't."

"Please, Xanthe. I'm not supposed to be locked up this way."

"Lord Woodhurst says it's for your own good." She tried to smile.

"You don't believe that." At least, her attempted smile suggested she didn't. "I can't stay in here. Please help me."

She shook her head. "I'm sorry, but I can't."

She could. She just needed the right motivation. I climbed up onto the sill of the open window. "Either I go out the door. Or the window." I held her shocked stare, hoping she wouldn't call my bluff. "And don't even think about calling the guards, or I'll jump."

Xanthe ran her hands over her skirt, her eyes flitting from the door to the window.

I inched forward, trying not to look at the distance to the ground. I'd never been great with heights. "Come on, Xanthe. Would you prefer the Sheriff find me half-dead at the bottom of this window, or not find me at all after I escape in your clothing?" Actually, if I were in her shoes, I'd go with the first option. At least finding me injured would mean she wouldn't get in trouble for helping me escape.

She licked her lips. "Rumor has it, you've been living with Robin Hood since you disappeared."

Her question took me off guard. Both because of the mention of Rob stole my breath and because she clearly thought I was Maud. "I am. Was."

She nodded once, then untied the laces on her apron and lay it on the bed. "He helped my mother. Gave her gold when she couldn't afford to eat." She pulled the bonnet from her head then threw that beside the apron. "Don't jump. You can have my clothes. But, I will still tell them you attacked me with a knife."

I climbed from the sill and pulled the shutters closed, hoping my relief didn't show on my face. "Thank you."

I pulled on Xanthe's clothes—which mostly fit, except the sleeves and hem, which were a little short—leaving the nightdress for Xanthe, and started for the door with the bonnet in my hand. Maybe she would help me one last time, in gratitude for her mother. I turned to her. "Xanthe. Could you tell me where to find Eliza Thatcher?"

Xanthe's eyes went round. She ran to the door and leaned against it, refusing to let me past. "Oh, no, milady. You don't want to see her. You never used to want to go near her, before you...disappeared."

I tilted my head, trying to gauge what her startled reaction was about, and spoke carefully. "Well, I want to see her now. Is she here?"

"Ah..." Xanthe licked her lips, twirling the end of her long ponytail around one finger. "Yes, but...going to her chamber would be unwise."

"Why?" I fought to recall whether I knew anything about Eliza that meant I shouldn't go and see her. "Because she's a witch?"

Xanthe's eyebrows rose even higher. "Yes. But, well, I wouldn't like you to do anything that might put yourself in danger."

I pulled on the bonnet, twisting my long hair up beneath it and tying it beneath my chin. "I'll be fine, Xanthe. No one will be in any danger." So long as I got that coin back. I bared my teeth, knowing I wasn't smiling, and hating the person I was this morning. Rob's death was all on Gisborne, yet I was taking it out on Xanthe. "Please give me directions to her room."

She licked her lips again. "Lord Woodhurst is waiting for you. With the Sheriff."

My stomach clenched. With any luck, I'd be gone before they sent someone to get me. "The longer I spend trying to find Eliza Thatcher within the castle, the more likely they are to find me, and all this will be in vain."

Xanthe licked her lips again, then with a deep sigh, gave me the directions I needed to find my coin.

When she was finished, I opened the door just enough to slide out—I couldn't risk the guards seeing Xanthe sitting quietly on the bed. She could call them the moment I left, but I didn't think she would since she was repaying me for Robin Hood's generosity.

My heart pounded in my ears as I ducked my head and walked quickly past the guards. Neither looked twice at me, and I turned right and started along the dark, cold hallway. With each step, my shoulders relaxed a little more. If they were going to call me back, they'd have done so by now.

The dimness in the corridor was occasionally interrupted by narrow shafts of light falling from high windows. I passed servants in burgundy dresses like mine, and guards wearing burgundy and gold capes. I kept my eyes down, and no one bothered me, but I found my heart beating fast, both with the prospect of getting my coin back, and with knowing how upset Gisborne would be when he found me gone.

I found the staircase Xanthe had directed me to, and tip-toed down a narrow twisting staircase to another corridor, counting the doors until I came to the one I was searching for.

It was silent down here. No servants, no soldiers. No one around. I stepped up to the door and knocked. Something about Eliza had creeped me out that day at Edwinstowe. It might have been the vibe she gave off. Or that John called her a witch. Or perhaps I was channeling Maud—I had the distinct impression the two hated each other.

There was no answer. I knocked again then tried the handle. The door opened. For a second, I stood on the threshold gathering my courage, then I stepped inside.

Her room was dark and tiny, lit only by the light from the hallway. There was a narrow bed, a cluttered desk, and hundreds of jars filled with herbs and other things I didn't want to contemplate, lining the walls. If Eliza went wherever Gisborne went, it would seem the two of them spent a lot of time here at the castle and this was her permanent room.

Her messy desk seemed as good a place as any to start. Gingerly, I rifled through the mess of herbs in jars, parchment, ink, a mortar and pestle, branches and leaves set out to dry.

No coin.

No damn coin.

I could have thrown one of those jars across the room just to see it shatter into a thousand pieces the same way I was about to. I had no clue what to do next.

As I adjusted the bonnet on my head, my scalp itching beneath it, Eliza Thatcher stepped soundlessly into her chamber.

Her hair was wound neatly at the back of her neck, the deep blue of her dress bringing out the blue of her eyes. She was a tiny little thing compared to me, but when she looked at me, it took all my resolve not to step backwards. I would not show her I was scared.

Her eyes roamed over me. Then she placed her candle onto the desk, and slowly shut the door.

"Well, well. I heard you'd finally returned to the castle. Expected you might want to see me. Just didn't expect it would be so soon." She narrowed her eyes. "Nice dress."

I raised my chin, ignoring her words and my racing pulse. "You stole my coin."

She shrugged. "Borrowed, would be a more accurate term, I believe."

"It's only borrowed if you give it back."

She took a step farther into the room. "Or if you intend to. I was going to give it back once I was finished with it."

Eliza was playing this cool. I could do the same. "What do you want with it?"

She sized me up, speaking in that deep, melodic voice. "Same thing as you, I imagine."

"It's a family keepsake, that's all." Or all she needed to know. Her searching stare made me clasp my hands together to keep from shaking.

She tapped her long fingernails against her lips. "I'm not stupid, Lady Maud. You were gone. Now you're back. You claim to have seen my sister, and you have with you a token." She produced my coin from somewhere in her layers of clothing, making it appear like magic between her thumb and forefinger. "I only want two things in this world, and one is to see my sister again. If that means I must time travel, so be it. So, how about you tell me how you did it? How did you manage to travel through time, Lady Maud?"

I shook my head, clamping my lips shut. I wasn't telling her anything until I had my coin back.

Her hand closed around the coin. "Are you back here for good, Lady Maud? Or do you plan to go back to wherever you came from?"

I stared at her, unmoving. She wasn't getting anything else from me without giving first.

Her tone grew condescending. "The way I see it, there are two options. We both want the same thing. You want to go back to whatever hole you just climbed out of; I want to find my sister and bring her home. Both of us know what we want is possible. Neither of us know how to achieve it."

"You have no idea what I do or don't know."

She stepped forward; her face close enough that her breath pushed at the few wisps of hair I hadn't managed to cover with the bonnet. "You're back from the dead. I think you time traveled back here by accident. If you knew how to go back, you wouldn't still be here, would you?" She didn't wait for my answer. Already knew she was right. "Tell me what you know, and between us we'll find a way to make it happen again."

Pushing away the temptation to do as she suggested, I shook my head. I didn't trust her and had the distinct feeling she'd never share anything she knew with me. "Give me back my coin and figure the rest out yourself."

Her eyes narrowed and nostrils flared, but when she spoke her voice was even and calm. "I can see on your face you still hate me as much as you did when you left. Well, the feeling's mutual, darling. But let me tell you this. If you decide not to travel again and instead stay here and live your old life, know that Gisborne doesn't love you anymore. He loves me, now."

My mouth dropped open. "But...you're cousins!" That was just plain wrong.

"Second cousins. And plenty of people far richer than me have married their cousin and been happy." She leaned toward me, speaking in a conspiratorial whisper. "That kiss you saw between us the day you disappeared? That was nothing compared with what the two of us do together now." With folded arms, she waited for my reaction.

Gisborne and Eliza? If Maud had discovered them together, it was no wonder she ran into the forest, not caring about the danger that would eventually kill her. Sudden anger welled up inside me for Maud. How dare they do that to her? How dare Eliza throw it back in my face as if it were a game? I clenched my fists so tightly my nails dug into my palms.

She flashed the coin at me, the sneer on her lips suggesting she had everything while I had nothing. Well, she could have Gisborne, I certainly didn't want him. But she wasn't getting my coin. With a growl from the back of my throat, I launched at her.

She was going to give me my coin, even if I had

to force her. I grabbed her hand, trying to wrench open her fingers, but she was strong. She pushed me away, tripping me with her foot behind my ankle. I fell, and my head slammed into her desk. Everything spun, but I didn't care. I was not leaving here without that coin. I struggled to my feet and dived at her.

The door to the room flew open with a bang.

Before I could reach Eliza, Gisborne's hands clamped around my waist.

Twenty-One

ELIZA turned slowly toward Gisborne and curtsied. "My lord. How nice to see you all the way down here."

Gisborne's fingers dug into my waist. "Lady Maud. What are you doing in here? Are you all right?"

I glared at Eliza, shaking off his hands. Refusing to let him touch me. "Eliza and I had unfinished business."

Gisborne's face turned pale in the low light and he swallowed. "I'm aware of that, my lady. But I had hoped you would speak to me before you took matters into your own hands." He held out his hand again. "Come. You have a nasty bruise on your head. Let's get you back to your chamber."

"No." My voice was louder than I'd intended, and Gisborne jumped. "Eliza has something of mine, which she refuses to return. I'm not going anywhere until I get it back."

A frown formed between Gisborne's eyebrows, and he turned to Eliza. She stared defiantly back. Her chin jutted, then she gave in and threw the coin in my direction. "Fine. Have it. Doesn't work anyway." She smirked at me. "I tried."

The coin clattered on the stone floor and I scrambled to pick it up before it was lost in the mess of her chamber. The moment I closed my hand around that little piece of copper, something shifted in the air, like the click that happens when two Lego bricks fit together. Gisborne didn't seem to notice, but Eliza felt it. Her eyes narrowed and fingers curled as she watched me, but she said nothing.

As the air shifted, voices came at me. Dad's voice. Tabitha's. They spoke over top of each other, their words jumbled and senseless.

Gisborne touched my arm. "Lady Maud."

I forced the voices inside my head away and focused on Gisborne. He gestured to the door. In the corridor, Xanthe—wearing a new dress identical to her old one—was nervously wringing her hands.

I marched past them both, and Eliza's melodic voice floated out to us. "Offer's still open, my lady. We can help each other." I continued to walk away. I had no time for her.

Xanthe ran to catch up to me. "I'm sorry, milady. I thought you were set on revenge. I was worried for you, had to tell Lord Woodhurst."

"It's okay, Xanthe." I had my coin back. Now, the next moment I got an opportunity, I could run without needing to stop anywhere along the way.

Gisborne fell into step beside me. "I trust you have that out of your system?"

I didn't have the energy or the will to answer.

He shook his head. "What you saw the day you disappeared, it wasn't what it looked like."

Anger for what he and Eliza had done to Maud filled me. I wanted to stand up for her since she was no longer around to do it. "It wasn't a kiss?"

He swallowed, refusing to meet my eyes.

I shook my head, hoping I sounded like Maud. "Thought so."

As I walked away, he grabbed my arm, spinning me to face him. "It was a kiss; you know it was. And I'm sorry. I didn't want to kiss her, don't know what came over me. I told you weeks ago in Edwinstowe I would do as you once asked and make her leave. I'm sorry I didn't do it on the day it happened." Tears pooled in his eyes and I wondered again if Gisborne really had loved

Maud. "I don't want it to be like this between us, Maud. I want to fix it."

Getting into this conversation would only show him how much I didn't know about his fiancé. I wasn't going there. I placed my fingers to my temples and feigned a headache. I didn't have to try hard, the voices I'd heard on constant repeat since I got my coin back made it difficult to concentrate.

Suddenly, I felt drained. Returning to my chamber and blocking everything else out except thoughts of Rob was like the only thing I had the energy to do. The tears I'd cried last night weren't nearly enough. "I need to return to my chamber."

Gisborne looked torn. He pressed his lips together. "I'm sorry, my lady, but the Sheriff is waiting."

"I'm feeling unwell. I'm not going to see him." Didn't have the strength to deal with him right now.

Gisborne took my arm, squeezing tightly so all I could do was stop walking and look up at him. His black hair framed his face and rested on the shoulders of his burgundy cloak. His eyes were soft. "I hate to have to remind you that you stay here under the Sheriff's hospitality, my lady. That he has given you a bed, food and clothing, which puts you in his debt."

"He's also given me guards on my door."

Gisborne shrugged. "Maybe so. But until your father returns from France and confirms your identity, you'll have to get used to the guards. And after what you've done this morning, you'll be lucky if the Sheriff doesn't banish you to somewhere with less comfort and more guards." He tried to smile, his demeanor when no one else was around was far from that of the killer I'd seen in the forest yesterday. "I have orders to drag you to him by your hair, if I need to. Do you understand?"

I tried to pull loose, but his fingers dug into the flesh on my arm.

His voice hardened. "Do. You. Understand me?"

I bit down on my lip and nodded. It wasn't like I had a choice.

Gisborne held my arm tightly and guided me back up two flights of the narrow stairs to the room I'd met the Sheriff in last night. He was sitting at a desk, his back to us with rolls of parchment spread out in front of him, but he wasn't working. He was staring out the window. Outside the inner castle walls were tents as far as the eye could see, and then more tents outside the outer walls; people setting up for his tournament.

"How are the preparations going, Gisborne?" The Sheriff spoke to the window.

"Excellent, my lord. There looks to be an exceptional turn out." As we entered the Sheriff's rooms, Gisborne pulled his shoulders back and lifted his chin, his business face back on.

"It's lucky you no longer have to patrol the forest searching for that band of thieves." The Sheriff's voice was dry. "You might actually be able to watch."

Gisborne clenched his jaw.

The Sheriff twisted to face us, running his hand across his greying beard. "That will be all, Gisborne."

"You wanted to see Lady Maud?"

The Sheriff looked me over, head to foot. Then he twisted his face into something close to a smile. "I did. But I will speak to her alone." He got to his feet. "That will be all, Gisborne."

I took a shuffling step back, suddenly terrified of the man in charge in the King's absence. Gisborne gave my arm a squeeze, stopping me. A scowl crossed his face. "My lord, Lady Maud is feeling quite unwell. I think it would be best if I remain with her."

The Sheriff blinked slowly. "That will be all, Gisborne."

Squaring his jaw, Gisborne squeezed my arm again, as if telling me everything would be all right. He bowed his head and walked from the room.

The Sheriff waited until the door clicked behind him before looking at me again. "I see my servants found you something to wear, my lady. Perhaps tomorrow they'll find something that doesn't make you look like you're on my pay roll." His voice was dry.

I met his eyes, trying to work out how angry he was at what I'd made Xanthe do, but I had no clue. "Thank you, my lord."

"I trust your chamber was suitable."

I nodded. "Yes, my lord." Without knowing what he wanted from me, it seemed best to answer his questions as briefly as possible. I assumed he was going to give me a telling off for trying to escape this morning, but this conversation didn't seem to be heading in that direction.

He stared at me a moment, the scar on his face even more prominent in the morning light. "You've been gone a long time."

I nodded, my movements careful. "You believe I'm Lady Fitzwalter, then?"

He watched me for a long time before answering. "I believe, given the reason she left, Lady Maud would have made Eliza Thatcher's chamber her first visit, no matter what she had to do to get there."

I met his eyes, unsure how to respond. He hadn't answered my question, and he'd spoken as if Maud was someone other than me.

He sighed. "Yes. Given the way you acted this morning, I think you could be her." He turned to look out the window again. "Gisborne is pleased to have you back."

I tilted my head to one side, knowing he was watching me out the corner of his eye. "Gisborne is probably just pleased to receive the reward my father offered."

The Sheriff glanced my way, trying to hide his smile. "He said you're more inclined to speak your mind since your return."

I raised my eyebrows. "You disagree about Gisborne?"

"Not entirely. I'm just a little surprised to hear you say it. You know, he's still a good man. And it seems clear he still loves you very much."

I wasn't sure what to make of the Sheriff. This was small talk, but I doubted he'd brought me here to pass the time of day.

"You know your parents are away in France?" He ran his hand over his beard.

I gave him a benign smile. Where Maud's parents were, didn't concern me.

"I'm writing to your father, telling him of your return." He nodded at the parchment on his desk. "I'll send it with a rider shortly. In the meantime, you will remain at the castle under my hospitality." He paused, awaiting my reaction.

I bowed my head. "Thank you, my lord." I couldn't quite bring myself to ask if the guards on my door would be removed.

The Sheriff stepped up beside me. A long lock of my hair had come loose from my bonnet and fell beside my face. The Sheriff reached out and took it between his fingers, pulling gently. "Of course, if I find you have deceived me, your lodgings will become far less desirable." His voice was slightly husky. "I may even require some sort of...payment, to ensure your safety."

I swallowed, meeting his gaze, disgusted. *This* was more like what I expected from him. "I'm not sure I understand, my lord?"

The Sheriff dropped my hair and stepped away, a small smile on his lips. "No. I'm sure you don't." His tone was dry. "Gisborne will no doubt be happy to show you around the preparations for the tournament."

Looking at the tournament preparations was the last thing I wanted, but looking at them with Gisborne, never in a million years. "I'm not feeling so well, my lord. I think I might lie down for a while."

"As you wish."

I turned to leave, my relief at walking away from this man also loosening my hold on the voices that had been mumbling inside my head since I got my coin back.

...moon...

...don't come here...

"Oh, Lady Maud, I almost forgot. You'll be my personal guest at the tournament tomorrow. You and Gisborne will sit in the gallery with me."

If he decided to remove the guards from my door, I had no intention of being here tomorrow. "Thank you, my lord. It would be an honor."

The Sheriff nodded and went back to his desk, leaving me to let myself out.

A guard met me at his door, escorting me back to my room—chamber, I had to remember to call it a chamber. The guards would remain, then.

At least, with a few quiet moments to myself, I might be able to think of a way to escape, plus, I could listen to whatever Dad was saying in my mind. Throwing open my door, I rushed inside, and stopped dead.

Sprawled on my bed was Eliza Thatcher, her smile shark-like. "Can I help you, Lady Maud?"

"Get out," I hissed. "You're not welcome in my chamber."

She blinked slowly. "And you were not welcome in mine. Yet that didn't stop you."

Tabitha's voice filled my mind again, louder this time. *Tell my sister to stay away from the tree, or she swaps one problem for another.* Then Dad's voice came straight after. *...full moon...*

"Are you ill, Lady Maud?" Eliza watched me from my bed, lying on her stomach with a hand propped under her chin.

I had, at some point, sat on the only chair in the room, the voices suddenly overwhelming me. *Tell my sister to stay away from the tree, or she swaps one problem for another.* I pressed my fingers to my temples, trying to get rid of them. I did not trust Eliza Thatcher. I needed my full concentration when she was around, and I couldn't concentrate at all with the voices repeating in my head. Especially now, when they might as well have been yelling.

They'd started in Eliza's chamber. The moment my hand had clamped around my coin.

Could that be the way to get rid of them?

I twisted in my chair, so my arm was hidden from Eliza by the vase of flowers Gisborne had left. Hesitating a moment, I slipped the coin off my wrist and dropped it onto the table in front of me, behind the vase. The voices stopped.

Silence.

I could think again.

With a clear head, I looked at Eliza. Now, I could concentrate on removing her from my chamber. Once she was gone, I'd deal with those voices. She was sitting on my bed, her legs dangling over the side and her mouth slightly open. Her eyes moved between my face and my coin, which clearly wasn't as hidden as I'd hoped.

I scooped it up. She was not getting her hands on it again.

I was suddenly back at the Major Oak with Dad. Tabitha was there, too. I was already leaving, getting farther from Dad with each second that passed. His mouth was moving, but the words were jumbled. There were only two I heard: full moon. Then he was gone, and I was back in the room with Eliza standing directly in front of me and the coin laying in the middle of the table between us.

"What's happening, Lady Maud? Is the coin talking to you?"

I shook my head. I didn't know what was going on, but whatever it was, I wasn't sharing it with her.

Her eyes narrowed, moving from me to the coin between us. "Very well. If you don't want it, perhaps I'll take it again." She reached for it. I could see she was moving slowly, bluffing about picking it up, but my hand moved on its own and I scooped it up before she could get close.

I found myself in a white room, Tabitha in her russet-colored gown standing in front of me. *Tell my sister to stay away from the tree, or she swaps one problem for another.* She reached out to pat my shoulder, but I skittered away. And backed into the cold stone wall of my chamber.

The coin was at my feet, and from across the room, Eliza watched, her face thoughtful. "What did you see?"

I lifted my chin, trying to keep from panting. The visions were so real, it was as if I was traveling back through time again. Not that I'd tell her so. "What do you care?"

One shoulder lifted then dropped. "I don't. I just thought you might want to know what was happening."

I glared at her, reluctant to ask for her help. I didn't trust her and didn't know why she'd want to help me.

She shrugged again and started for the door.

"Wait!" The word was out of my mouth before I could stop it.

She turned, smiling sweetly. "Yes?"

"I saw Tabitha. And my father."

"Memories?"

I shook my head. "It was the day I came back in time, but...not." I couldn't explain it any other way. What I was seeing had never happened, yet it felt real.

Eliza's eyes rolled over my face. "I've been trying to work it out. Since you came back, you're not quite so angry, so does that mean you've forgiven me? Or perhaps it means you no longer care for Gisborne and don't want to fight for him? You don't even seem that annoyed I sent you through time. So maybe the memory loss associated with time travel didn't go away and you don't remember me. She turned her lips down at the corners and gave a quick shrug.

I tried not to let my surprise show. I'd thought Maud was dead. Rob told me he thought she'd drowned, and I'd never considered there might be another option. My heart constricted at the thought of him, but I wouldn't dissolve into a puddle of tears in front of Eliza Thatcher. I pushed thoughts of him away, considering Maud instead. Had she survived the trip through time? Where was she now? Was she trying to get back to her home? I fought to keep my questions to myself. It was safer if she continued to think I was Maud. But I would have given my left arm to know where Maud Fitzwalter had gone.

"Or perhaps it means you aren't Maud? Could you possibly be some sort of imposter, sent from another time?"

"You're out of your mind." *Deny, deny, deny,* because I wasn't answering that question.

But, since she seemed to know what was happening to me, perhaps we could help each other, then get out of each other's way. "Tell me what's happening when I touch my coin, and I'll give you the message your sister asked me to give you." She'd asked me for it at Edwinstowe. That day, I'd only had a vague recollection of Tabitha telling me anything. Today, I was certain I knew what she wanted to tell Eliza.

She watched me a moment, making some calculation in her head before turning to the door again. "No deal."

I glanced at the coin Dad had given me to return home—that I currently couldn't pick up— then at Eliza's hand on the door. If she knew something that could help, I had to get her to share. "Fine. What do you want from me?"

Eliza's hand remained on the handle, her back to me. "Tell me how to call her, at the Big Tree. *And* give me her message. Then we'll have a deal."

Calling Tabitha was something I hadn't managed to do, but I'd seen Dad do it, and I could see no reason not to share with Eliza. "Fine." I waited until she faced me before speaking again. "You call Tabitha by tapping on the tree in this rhythm." I clapped my hands to the beat Dad had used.

She grimaced, then let out a deep sigh.

"You knew that?"

She nodded. "I saw someone do it once, but I can never get Tabitha to turn up when I try it."

That made two of us. "Why am I hearing voices and seeing visions? And how do you even know any of this?"

"Time travel sometimes causes temporary memory loss. Usually the memories come back slowly over the first few days in a new time. But since you *lost* your key, there was no link between you and your memories until you got the key back. Once all the memories return, I think the visions and voices will settle." She folded her arms over her chest, looking smug.

I raised an eyebrow, waiting for her to answer my second question.

With a shrug, she said, "I know this because I've spent the four years since Tabitha was tricked into that portal learning everything I can about time travel. I've talked to old witches, who told me what they knew, and to people who claim they've traveled. I'm learning everything I can because I'm going to find a way to get her out of there." She put her hands on her hips. "Now, her message?"

A deal was a deal. Anyway, the message meant nothing to me. "Tabitha said you must stay away or swap one problem for another."

She blew out her breath. "I'm not staying away. And I'll deal with any problems going to the tree creates once I get her back. Did she say anything else?"

I shook my head. Tabitha hadn't. But Dad had. I needed Eliza to leave so I could consider what he'd said. I didn't trust her enough to share.

I must have given her what she came for, because she nodded and walked to the door, letting herself out without another word.

I crawled over to where my coin lay in the middle of the floor, my hand hovering over it a moment before I closed my fingers around it.

Dad was in front of me again, the Major Oak behind him. His lips moved, and his voice floated to me. *Full moon is the only time you can return to us. Avenge Avery Woodhurst's death for me, Maryanne. Take any opportunity you get.*

Full moon. *That* was why I hadn't been able to go home last time I tried.

Tomorrow was full moon. *And* the Sheriff's tournament. I was his personal guest tomorrow. Getting lost among the hundreds at the tournament would be far easier, than slipping out of my guarded chamber tonight.

I sank onto the bed, feeling like finally, something was going my way, just as a quiet knock sounded. "Come in," I sighed.

The door cracked open and Xanthe crept in. She crouched in front of the fire, drawing life from the embers. "Cold in here, milady. You should've called for me to set your fire." She added some small pieces of wood to the embers.

"Why did you tell me I shouldn't go to see Eliza this morning? Why were you so sure I'd do something wrong that you summoned Gisborne?" Now I'd heard a little about Maud Fitzwalter, I want to know it all. If the servants had talked, maybe I could get Xanthe to share what she knew.

She busied herself in getting the wood to catch. "Well...because, well, you know, milady."

I shook my head, pressing my fingers to my temples. There was so much going on inside my mind, I thought my head might explode. "Please, Xanthe, could you pretend I don't. Pretend you're telling a stranger."

She climbed to her feet. Her eyes darted from the fireplace, to Gisborne's roses, to the canopied bed where I sat. There was a bruise on her cheek I hadn't noticed earlier. I wasn't sure if I'd been too wrapped up in myself, or if it was new.

"Well, because...you weren't happy they kissed the last time, and not much has changed between them since that day."

I took the lock of hair that had escaped from my bonnet and wound it around my fingers, trying to work out what she wasn't saying. "You thought I'd hurt her?"

Xanthe swallowed. "On account of what you did last time, milady."

"Again, would you mind telling me as if I were a stranger?"

Her eyes darted. She was clearly uncomfortable. "You understand I wasn't there, milady? I don't like to gossip."

"Just tell me what you heard."

"You caught the two of them together...kissing, and demanded Lord Woodhurst send her away. When he refused, you attacked Lady Eliza." She drew three fingers across her cheek. "Here."

"*I* caused those scars?" They must have been deep gouges to still be visible two years later. I smiled on the inside, proud of Maud for standing up for herself. "You were worried for her?"

"Oh no, milady." A smile crossed Xanthe's face, the first I'd seen from her. "That one can look after herself. I was worried for you because of everything that happened after."

"Tell me." I patted the edge of the bed, hoping she'd sit down. I needed to know about Maud.

Xanthe clasped her hands together. "I can't. You'll think I'm out of my mind, milady. It doesn't make any sense." Her eyes were large, imploring me not to make her speak.

"I won't." I tried to keep my tone gentle, hoping to coax the words from her. "And you won't get into trouble. I won't ever mention it again. Please tell me what you know."

She took a deep breath and as she let it out, she forced the words from her mouth. "You were staying at Lord Woodhurst's manor when you caught them together. You ran into the forest, to the Big Tree. The moon was full, like daylight and Lady Eliza could easily follow you." She glanced at me, hoping, perhaps, that I'd ask her to stop. "The two of you argued and Lady Eliza pushed you. And then..." She shrugged.

"And then what?" I walked over to her, impatient to hear the story I already knew.

"You, well, you just disappeared. Your father sent out huge search parties, but no one could find you."

"How is it you know any of this, Xanthe?"

"My cousin, Aggie works for Lady Eliza. She went with Eliza that day but was sworn to secrecy. Eliza didn't want anyone to know they'd been there. But Aggie told me."

Full moon. That's when Maud had traveled.

It was when I would travel, too. Tomorrow night.

Twenty-Two

THE tournament field was a long and narrow patch of dry grass outside the outer castle walls that had been roped off so only contestants could enter. Nobles sat in a tiered gallery along one side, everyone else pushed for the best spot to stand around the other sides. The gallery backed onto the castle wall and looked out across the competition field to the forest in the distance. By the time I arrived on Gisborne's arm, the area was a hive of noise and movement as everyone searched for the best vantage point.

He'd given me an appreciative smile as he collected me from my chamber, mumbling something about how stunning I looked. I'd smiled and blushed because I felt beautiful. My hair was pulled off my face and delicately French braided around a bun that sat high on my head, and Xanthe had woven tiny blue and white flowers through the braid. My dress—which fitted perfectly—was gorgeous. Navy blue with a white panel down the front, it was laced tightly from the neck to just above my waist. The embroidered sleeves were long and wide, hiding the coin tied around my wrist, and I wore a matching blue cloak. My outfit was the most spectacular thing I'd ever owned, and coupled with my elegant hairstyle, I hardly recognized myself. At home these past two years, I hadn't worn any color but black. Like this, I almost felt as if I belonged here.

Today was the first time I'd seen Gisborne wearing anything other than chainmail and a riding cloak, and I hated to admit how handsome he looked. His tunic was grey-blue and made his blue eyes bright. His black hair fell softly against his shoulders, fanning his face. He seemed relaxed, almost happy.

He leaned over to whisper in my ear as the archers walked out single file onto the trampled brown grass of the tournament field. "The one in the middle, in the red tunic, that's Sean McKenzie. He'll win today." Our cushioned seating had an unobstructed view of the competition, the awning above the gallery shielding us from the midday sun. The Sheriff sat on the other side of Gisborne, his hands resting on his giant belly. Eliza was seated beside me.

As the contestants took the field, the villagers cheered. Many of them wore colors to support their favorite knight, much like a football match. Behind us, the finely dressed nobles clapped sedately, their gold or silver jewelry jingling as they moved.

Sean McKenzie was in his thirties, not the oldest competitor, but close to it. His brown hair was plaited down his back, and his beard was clipped short. He held his head high and somewhat arrogantly, reminding me of Gisborne, which made me dislike him instantly.

Gisborne leaned over again and I forced myself not to recoil. "Do you remember the rules?"

I shook my head, wondering if he'd explain or whether I'd be able to work them out without help.

"All the entrants shoot from this distance. The one with the worst shot is dropped and the targets are moved back ten paces. Then they do it all over again until there's a winner."

I nodded, looking from the tiny straw-filled targets to the contestants as they lined up for their first shot. "And you're a supporter of McKenzie?"

Gisborne grinned, showing off dimples I hadn't known he possessed. "I am while he's winning."

McKenzie's stance was wrong, and he didn't look relaxed with his bow. I was certain he wouldn't be here after the first few rounds. But Gisborne must have known something I didn't, because with the first shot, McKenzie's arrow landed closest to the center out of any of the twenty-plus competitors.

As they moved the targets back, Gisborne turned to me. "Isn't he brilliant?"

I shrugged. I wasn't convinced it hadn't just been a lucky shot.

"Very well then, my lady. Who would you choose to win?" Gisborne was grinning in a way that made me want to punch him, even if he was attempting to tease me. I guessed Maud hadn't known a thing about archery. The Maud from two years ago hadn't, anyway.

I looked along the line of entrants, a rag-tag bunch of various ages, heights, and wealth—the archery contest being the only one of the day where anyone could enter, not just knights. I nodded to a man three along from McKenzie. A peasant wearing a long brown cloak. I couldn't see his face since his hood was up and his back was to us, but I liked the way he held his bow. "I choose him."

Gisborne laughed. "The one with the fifty-year-old bow?" He straightened his face. "If *he* wins, my lady, I'll give you anything you wish for."

I smiled benignly, wondering if there was any way Gisborne would honor that promise and allow me to go to the forest unopposed tonight, should my archer win. I doubted it. But I would play his game anyway. "I'll start putting a wish list together, then."

Gisborne gave a twist of his head, raising his eyebrows deliberately. "Certainly, my lady." He glanced at the archers before returning his gaze to me. "But I wouldn't get my hopes up, if I were you."

I was anything but confident. I'd chosen the archer solely because of his stance, but now Gisborne had pointed out the age of his bow, I could see he was right. There was no chance of my man winning. But still, there was something about him that made me lean forward in my seat.

The archers lined up for their next shots. McKenzie stood confidently on his mark, barely taking a moment to aim. The raucous crowd burst into cheers as his arrow hit the center of his target.

By comparison, my archer was slower, spending time to line up the shot. Still, my archer's arrow also hit the center of the target. And round after round, he shot as well as McKenzie.

Eliza tapped me on the shoulder and leaned over to whisper in my ear. Graceful as always, her silver dress rustled as she moved. "Did you recall any other memories over night? Anything that might help me get my sister out of that portal?"

"Shhh!" I glanced at Gisborne, but he was watching McKenzie, a smile on his face.

Eliza gave a slow blink. "Give me some credit, Lady Maud." She glanced Gisborne's way, her eyes lingering a moment longer than necessary. "He's engrossed in the games. Hasn't heard a word I've said. The memories often come back one at a time. So, did you remember anything else?"

I had remembered Dad telling me that the portal only opened at full moon, but I couldn't forget that Eliza had taken my coin. I was keeping that piece of information to myself. I shook my head.

Her shoulders slumped.

"How is it," I asked, "that you're here, and your sister is...there?"

She glanced out at the contest as another cheer went up, but her stare was distant. "My sister was tricked by a witch she met at the Big Tree." Her bottom lip wobbled, and her voice grew soft. "Tabitha was only trying to secure a future for me."

She went quiet, and I thought that was all she was going to say, but as another cheer came from the villagers for another good shot, she spoke again. "The witch promised her the only thing she'd ever wanted; a safe and secure future for the both of us. Ever since our mother died, we'd had nowhere to live, no money." She shrugged. "All she had to do was tell ten people that witch's name, then return to the tree at the next full moon. If she did as the witch asked, she'd get her wish.

"I laughed and told her she was being stupid, no one would grant her a wish like that in return for something so easy. When she didn't come home, I went looking for her. I found a letter tacked to the Big Tree. It said she was now the Keeper of the Portal, and she'd come back to me when she could." Eliza glanced at me. "That was four years ago. If my uncle hadn't taken me in and treated me like I was his own, I would have had nowhere to live."

"I'm sorry," I mumbled.

Eliza's nostril's flared, and her voice hardened. "Don't be. I've made it my mission to learn any-thing I can about the portal, so I can get her back. Once I do, I'm going to find that witch and make her pay for trapping Tabitha." She turned back to the competition and clamped her lips shut as if she hadn't just shared such an intimate secret.

One by one, the archers dropped out of the contest until there was just my brown-cloaked archer and McKenzie. Their targets were so far down the field that the dot in the center was impossible to see. The distance was difficult already, but the angle of the sun and the slight breeze made it an even harder task.

Gisborne sat forward in his seat, his knee bobbing in anticipation. Even I found myself sitting straighter, watching and waiting as the calls of the crowd grew ever louder.

McKenzie seemed confident, talking to the crowd and laughing with them when they answered. By contrast, the brown-cloaked archer stood perfectly still, his hood drawn high as he focused on the far away targets.

"Remove your hood!" The call came from somewhere inside the crowd, just as there was a moment of quiet.

Beside me, Gisborne nodded, a growl of agreement coming from his throat. Raising his chin, he called down to the archer. "Sir. Remove your hood and allow us the opportunity to see your face."

The Sheriff murmured his agreement.

The archer turned to us, making no move to do as he'd been asked. He bowed deeply then called in a clear voice. "I'm sorry, I must decline. The sun is so bright today and my hood is the only thing keeping it from my eyes. I'm sure you understand, my lord, being such a brilliant archer yourself."

The crowd erupted into cheers and the archer turned back to take his shot.

I leaned farther forward. That voice. The stance.

It couldn't be.

Gisborne sat back into his seat. I didn't dare to look at him, unsure what he might see on my face.

My archer lined up his shot, and the crowd went quiet. A gust of wind blew across the field and he waited for it to pass before drawing the bowstring back against his cheek. One of these men was about to walk away with a gold trophy worth so much, they could feed an entire village for the next year. He fired, landing his arrow in the very center of the target.

A cheer went up and I found myself raising my arms in triumph. I grinned at Gisborne.

He lifted an eyebrow, not ready to concede defeat. "Still one shot to come."

As the crowd quieted, a deep voice called through the near silence. "Outlaw!" No one moved. and the voice came again. "Stop him. That man is an outlaw!" The owner of the voice, a soldier, pushed through the people and onto the field. His black hair was slicked neatly back and his beard full. He pointed at my archer but looked from the Sheriff to Gisborne.

Gisborne stood and stepped forward to lean on the gallery railing. Remaining seated, the Sheriff steepled his fingers beneath his chin, watching.

Gisborne spoke as if it were an effort to remain civil. "Which man are you talking about, Blackwood? As you can see, there are hundreds of men here today."

Standing, I gripped the rail beside Gisborne and squinted at Blackwood. He looked familiar, but I couldn't place him. A voice in the back of my mind told me to sit down, this was none of my business. But I couldn't.

Blackwood raised his arm and, looking down his nose, pointed to my archer.

I remembered.

The last time I'd seen him, he'd been running away. Moments before that, he was fighting with Rob beside the Big Tree on my first day here. I clutched the rail so hard the rough wood cut into my palms. My chest went tight. I'd dismissed the thought before because it wasn't possible.

Yet, somehow, it was.

Gisborne made a circular motion with his hand, and down below us, everything happened at once. Two more soldiers sprang from the crowd, pulling the bow from my archer and taking hold of each of his arms. Then they drew the hood back from his head.

Gisborne let out a loud gasp, seeing what I'd realized moments ago.

The archer was Rob.

Twenty-Three

ROB wasn't dead. He was standing in the field looking up. At me. I put a hand over my mouth to hide my grin.

He was alive!

As our eyes met, his lips stretched into the smallest of hidden smiles before he locked glares with Gisborne. Other than the bruise on his cheek, he didn't seem to have any injuries from his run-in with Gisborne's men. Not any I could see, anyway. His blond hair was tied neatly at the back of his neck, but for a lock that had fallen free. I itched to reach out and brush it from his face.

The kick of ecstatic joy was quickly followed with a flash of anger. He was flanked by three soldiers; two were holding his arms. Coming here had been stupid and dangerous, and would probably end up getting him killed. Whether he'd come to help me or kill his brother, he should have stayed in the forest.

But he didn't, a voice whispered inside my head, and I held back the smile that wanted to form. Because in my heart, I knew he was here for me, not for Gisborne.

"Hello, brother." Rob lifted his head as he called up to Gisborne, smug satisfaction on his face despite his predicament.

Gisborne glanced at the Sheriff.

Both down in the crowd and up here in the gallery, shocked exclamations were overtaken by pushing and shoving as everyone, villagers and nobles alike, jostled to get a better look at the outlaw who had called himself Gisborne's brother.

I waited for people to call him a liar. But through the shocked conversation, I instead heard his name, Robin of Woodhurst, repeated again and again.

Gisborne gestured to the soldiers still holding Rob's arms and it was enough to quiet the crowd. "You were right, Blackwood. The man *is* an outlaw. Take him away and ready the gallows. Looks like we'll finish the day's events with a hanging."

He turned to the Sheriff. "What do you think, my lord?"

The Sheriff pushed to his feet and stepped up to the rail on Gisborne's right, resting his gut on top of it. He gave Gisborne a quizzical look, then addressed the crowd. "If you're certain this man is an outlaw, Gisborne, then a hanging we shall have."

The command drew an excited cheer from the crowd.

This was ridiculous. Surely Gisborne couldn't order a hanging. And even if he could, shouldn't there be a trial first? Witnesses called, all of that.

Grabbing his arm, I attempted to drag his eyes from Rob, to make him look at me. "What are you accusing him of? Where is your proof?" My voice rang out across the field, the villagers suddenly silent.

Gisborne blinked then raised his eyebrows. "What charges?" He seemed confused by my question.

"You can't hang him without telling him why "

"Here, here," called someone from the crowd.

Gisborne's gaze went to the ground, torn. To admit he thought Rob was Robin Hood was admitting he hadn't killed him two days ago like he'd claimed. But he was nothing if not a quick thinker He nodded at the soldier. "Very well, Blackwood. What is he charged with?"

"Killing the King's deer in Sherwood Forest, my lord. First, he drew his sword on me, then as I retreated, he shot the deer."

A slow smile spread across Gisborne's face. Relief, perhaps, that he didn't have to admit his men were incompetent. Perhaps he couldn't prove the Robin Hood connection, and now it didn't matter. He had a charge against Rob, and a credible witness.

I dug my fingers into Gisborne's arm, desperate to stop this. "Don't you have to give him a trial or something?"

Gisborne blinked as if he couldn't believe I'd asked that question. He sighed loudly and turned to Rob. "Do you have anything to say for yourself?"

Rob shook his head, his jaw clenched as he stubbornly refused to show even a flicker of emotion. I wanted to slap his face. He could stop this. Didn't he realize Gisborne would hang him today if he didn't speak up?

"Did you kill one of the King's deer?" Gisborne spoke slowly, making sure there could be no misunderstanding.

Rob tilted his head to one side. "If your man says he saw me do it, then it must be so."

Gisborne narrowed his eyes as if trying to figure Rob out, then he gave a nod. "Very well. Take him away and prepare the gallows."

"No!" The strength of my voice surprised me. There was a flash of fear in Rob's eyes, but it was gone faster than it had appeared. He tore his gaze from Gisborne and gave a small shake of his head, telling me to keep quiet, the way he'd asked the day I shot the deer.

I couldn't. This was my fault and I wouldn't let him take the blame. I wouldn't let him die for something I'd done. "Stop!"

This time Gisborne didn't bother to conceal his anger. His eyes remained firmly on Rob. "There is no reason to draw this out, my lady. Sit down."

His tone was threatening, and his knuckles white as he gripped the wooden rail in front, but I didn't care. It suddenly made sense. This was how I was supposed to save the legend of Robin Hood. This was the reason I was here.

I turned to Gisborne. "It wasn't Rob who shot the deer."

Gisborne's shoulders were stiff with anger. He opened his mouth, but I didn't give him the chance to speak.

"It was...me."

Gisborne stared at me. "You? Lady Maud Fitzwalter, you picked up a bow and used it to kill a deer?" He burst into a fit of cruel laughter, and was joined by some of the nobles behind us.

The man was an asshat. If anyone had bothered to show Maud Fitzwalter how to use a bow,
she would have been able to do it. Maybe she'd
even have pointed it at him for cheating on her.
"Yes. It was me."

Gisborne laughed again then signaled to his soldiers. "What are you waiting for? Take him
away."

"Stop! I did it." I gripped Gisborne's arm. "And
I can prove it." A hundred different scenarios
raced through my head on how exactly I might be
able to prove it, ranging from taking Gisborne and
the Sheriff out to the place I'd killed the deer, to
asking Blackwood if he remembered me.

The Sheriff cleared his throat and called down
to the soldier. "Who shot the deer, Blackwood?"

The soldier opened his mouth to speak, then
closed it again. He hadn't seen the arrow leave the
bow; he'd been too busy fighting with Rob. "I
don't know, my lord. But I didn't see Lady Maud
holding a bow."

"I'll show you." I stepped around Gisborne to
plead directly with the Sheriff. "I'll shoot at the
target and when I hit it, you'll see I know how to
use a bow." If they didn't think I could do it, I'd
prove them wrong.

The Sheriff regarded me a moment, then gave
a single nod, the smile on his face far from happy.

He called to Blackwood. "What distance was the deer shot from?"

Blackwood couldn't possibly know the answer to that question, but it didn't stop him. "A little less than the distance the targets are currently set."

The Sheriff nodded. "Release him."

The soldiers let Rob go, but continued to flank him on either side.

The Sheriff turned to him. "My soldiers will escort you over to the targets. When you get there, you will pick up the target holding your arrow and hold it to your chest." The Sheriff turned to me, running his fingers over his beard. "Because I'm feeling generous, you, Lady Maud, will have five shots to hit that target. With each miss, he will move ten paces closer to you. If you're unable to hit it, I'll know you lied and will think up some sort of fitting punishment for interrupting my tournament. If you hit the target within the center two circles, we'll believe you shot the deer, and it will be you heading for the gallows." He pursed his lips. "On second thoughts, perhaps the dungeons—don't want to upset your father by killing you. If you hit him—" He nodded toward Rob, a small smirk forming on the edge of his lips. "Well, I guess all discussions here will be null and void."

My heart pounded so loudly in my ears it obstructed every other sound. Surely he hadn't just suggested I shoot my arrow at a target Rob held to his chest? "I...I..." I shook my head. "I can't. Please don't make me shoot at him." I hated that I was begging, yet it was all I could do. Shooting while Rob stood behind the target was my worst nightmare.

The Sheriff gave a long, slow blink. "I'm not making you do anything, my dear girl. You're the one who seems desperate for us to understand how a well-bred lady like yourself can use a weapon of war. If you don't want to show us, then this man will be taken away. The choice is completely yours."

I swallowed. There was no possible way I could shoot an arrow directly at anyone, let alone Rob. There was also no way I *couldn't* do this. *I* had shot that deer, *I* should take the punishment. I couldn't let him die. I nodded.

With terrifying speed, two soldiers dragged me down from the gallery and into the center of the competition field.

Hundreds of sets of eyes stared hungrily at me, yet the crowd remained silent. They'd come from far away for action and drama. Maybe even death. I glanced at Rob. There was a very real chance that was exactly how this would end.

Two years ago, I wouldn't have thought twice about hitting the center of that small target. Two years ago, it would have been well within my range. Right now, it looked impossible, like I was about to hurt someone I cared about. Again. Because whether I admitted it to myself or not, I did care for him.

The soldiers led me to Rob, to receive his bow. This wasn't one of the bows I'd borrowed in the forest for training; it was completely different. I had no idea how much force I should use when I pulled the string back.

Behind me, from his place in the gallery, Gisborne began to speak, his voice ringing out across the field. "That man is not my brother. My brother died six years ago..."

I let Gisborne's voice fade into the background and focused on Rob. "You're alive." Inappropriate as it was, I wanted to touch him, to make sure this wasn't a dream. "It was you, pretending to be Flemington." I *had* recognized his voice. If his hood hadn't been pulled so high, Gisborne would have recognized him, too.

"Yes." A smile creased his face but did nothing to mask the fear in his eyes. "You, my lady, look more beautiful than the early rays of the rising sun."

If he could pretend to hide his fear, I could too. I matched his smile. "You prefer me like this, rather than in a tunic and pants?"

"I have no preference so long as your face is smiling at me." He pushed the piece of hair away from his eyes, his smile wavering. "I'm sorry. For saying you were on Gisborne's side the last time we talked. And for making you think I would have handed you over to Gisborne to save one of the others. I would never have. I was just trying to upset you as much as you'd upset me."

I nodded. I knew. "I'm sorry for what I said, too." My bravado faltered and tears pricked my eyes. I shook my head. I couldn't do this. I could not shoot at him.

Rob took a step toward me. "It's okay. Tell them it was me who shot the deer, and this will all be over for you."

"But it wasn't you." I ran my hands down my face, trying to pull myself together. There were only two options here: don't shoot and let Rob hang; or shoot and hopefully save him. Put that way, there was only one option. "What are you doing here, Rob?"

He gave me a lopsided grin. "I heard there was a beautiful lady being kept here against her will, so I came to rescue her."

I glanced around. We could not walk out of here, we couldn't run. There was a ring of people at least ten thick the whole way around this field. There were soldiers with bows on their shoulders scattered around outside of that. And there was Gisborne, up in the gallery, currently speaking to the people, but soon to be watching whatever was about to happen. "I'm not sure you quite understand the concept of a rescue."

He tilted his head to the side. "I'm still hopeful for a happy ending."

"...imposter, preying on the tragedies which have befallen my family." Gisborne was leaning so far over the railing, he was in danger of toppling out of the gallery and onto the hard ground below.

"It's not right," said the Sheriff.

"It's not!" Gisborne started up again, denying Rob's place in their family and calling him every name under the sun.

The Sheriff leaned back in his seat, a smirk pulling at his lips. Today was about putting on a show for his guests. Gisborne's rant had everyone transfixed, and it was just the entrée to the meal Rob and I would deliver. The Sheriff was more than happy for Gisborne to continue a little longer.

Listening to Gisborne deny who Rob was, made me angry. I could only imagine how it made Rob feel. "Why didn't you ever try to get Gisborne out of your home? Tell someone who you were?"

He shrugged a shoulder. "I was going to. Had planned it for six years. I was even heading to Woodhurst Manor to kill Gisborne and take back my home. But I got interrupted." He watched me for a second. "At Edwinstowe." He let the words hang in the air, giving my brain a moment to catch up.

I thought back to the day we met. It seemed so long ago now, and more than slightly hazy. The realization hit me slowly. It wasn't Edwinstowe that had stopped him going back to his home. I covered my mouth with my hands, looking to Rob for confirmation. "You're saying you couldn't go back there because I shot that deer?"

This time he gave me a proper smile, all the tension falling from his face in an instant. I loved it when he smiled that way. "It wasn't that you shot it that was the problem."

"It was that you knew the soldier, Blackwood, would blame you, not me." I was unable to meet his eyes as everything fell into place: Tuck's anger about the outlaw poster, his anger at me, the hushed conversations. They all knew what Rob had been hoping to achieve, that he'd been biding his time, waiting to take his home back. Tuck might even have thought Rob could do it—until the moment he became an outlaw, that was. What I didn't say, what I couldn't say because he'd never believe me, was that things wouldn't have gone as planned that day if he'd made it to Woodhurst. According to Dad, Rob would have lit a fire in the manor house, leading to him becoming the merciless legend the people in my time knew. I might have stopped that from happening, but I'd also ensured he'd never get what was rightfully his. "I ruined your life. Now they won't allow you to have your land because you're an outlaw, even if it should belong to you."

Rob ducked so he was in my line of vision, those intense eyes staring up at me. Eyes I'd never expected to see again. "No. Let's get this straight right now. You did not in any way ruin my life. You did something I didn't think was possible. You gave me choices I've never had before. Every day you were with us, life was better. I felt lighter without that expectation on my shoulders. Without you, I'd have spent the rest of my life chasing after something I had very little chance of ever receiving, growing more and more bitter by the day. We'd never have been able to help the villages the soldiers ruined without you." He squeezed my hand. "I'm grateful every day, that I met you, Maryanne Warren."

I blinked back tears. Never had it sounded so good to hear my own name. "You called me Maryanne."

"It's your name, isn't it?"

Before I had a chance to think what the use of my name might mean, one of the soldiers marched up and took Rob roughly by the shoulder, and I realized Gisborne had finished his rant.

I met Rob's eyes, shaking my head. I was probably going to kill him. "I'm so sorry. For that day. And for this one, too."

The soldier dragged Rob toward the target. Rob went willingly, calling over his shoulder, "Let go of the guilt. I believe in you."

I watched his blond ponytail bob against his neck with each step he took. I would not let him die because I was too nervous to shoot properly.

I turned to the gallery where the Sheriff and Gisborne stood, calling to them in a loud voice that belied the nerves bubbling just below the surface. I had to make sure of the terms. "If I hit that target, you'll let him go. Right?" The Sheriff gave a single nod, but that wasn't enough. "Say it. Say you'll let him walk away from here and he won't be followed or chased. He'll be free to leave."

Looking slightly bemused, the Sheriff nodded again. "Very well. If you manage to hit the center of the target, he'll walk from here a free man today."

I turned back to Rob. He'd taken his target from the easel, his arrow from his earlier shot still lodged deeply in the straw. It covered his body from waist to mid-chest, a little larger than a modern dartboard. Unlike a dartboard, this target was stuffed until it was firm with only straw. Not only did I have to aim correctly, but I had to make sure there wasn't enough power in the shot that it pierced through the target and injured Rob.

I called over my shoulder. "Any chance of some practice shots?"

The Sheriff gave me an amused smile and shook his head. I hadn't expected him to say yes.

To my left, behind all the spectators, was a large birch tree heavy with leaves, the only tree in close distance. If I shot at those high branches, I'd learn about the bow, feel how it flexed, how it shot, how far the arrow flew, and no one would get hurt because it would fly over the spectator's heads. But it would be one of my five shots and Rob would have to move closer for the next one. And if I hit him from closer, I'd hurt him even more.

Slowly, I chose an arrow. I glanced once more at the target and made my decision. Picking out a place high on the trunk of the tree, I fired. The arrow flew straight, directly toward the place I'd aimed, but fell short. Good to know.

The crowd murmured in surprise and Gisborne called over top of them. "Take ten steps forward, sir. If that's how she aims at the target, it's not looking good for you."

Some of the crowd laughed. I bristled. How dare he be so callous about his own brother?

Rob seemed relaxed, more relaxed than me. I refused to so much as blink, refused to give my nightmares a chance to find me. My heart pounded loudly, and my hands were slick with sweat.

This was it. This was the shot I'd never expected to recreate. But this time was worse because I was doing it by choice.

I let my arm drop and closed my eyes, counting slowly as I took a breath in, then out. Then I imagined it happening: bringing my arm up, aiming, firing. This was the same thing I'd always done before I shot in competitions. But instead of clearing my mind, I saw the night of Josh's accident, the night I'd been so cocky, I hadn't bothered to keep him safe.

You're not to blame, Maryanne. For anything. Dad was suddenly standing in front of me, the Major Oak at his back, the way he had on the day he sent me away. Another memory I'd forgotten, brought back by my coin.

The weight I'd carried for two years lifted off my shoulders, and everything became clear. *I* wasn't the only one who felt guilty about what had happened. Dad did too. I'd heard him say a hundred times he wished he hadn't gone to that meeting at the archery club, or that he wished he'd made us kids stay in the meeting room with him. I'd always thought it was a dig at me and my lack of responsibility. It wasn't, and I'd never have understood that had I not been facing Rob with a bow in my hand, feeling the guilt of having to shoot an arrow at him.

Dad felt that same weight of guilt. He blamed himself, and he carried it in his heart, the same way I had—and would, if my shot went wrong. The reason he'd made me take archery lessons was because he knew I'd need them when he eventually forced me back in time. But in his effort to keep me safe, his lack of attention had injured one of his other children. Rather than tell me what he was feeling, he'd let me wallow in my own guilt. Until the day he sent me away.

No. Until today. Because those words weren't part of my memories until this very moment.

"Maryanne, you can do this." Rob's voice floated over the low murmur of the crowd. "I trust you."

Use the skills I've given you. Something else he'd told me as I left. Something else I hadn't realized until right now.

Dad *had* prepared me for this time. Or he'd tried to. With archery lessons, fencing lessons and self-defense lessons.

I didn't have much to thank my father for, but I could thank him for that.

I lifted the bow.

And fired.

Twenty-Four

I WATCHED Rob, rather than following the arrow's path. So long as he was still standing, everything was all right. The slight frown I'd come to know wrinkled his forehead. Then he smiled.

A huge roar came from the crowd, and I dragged my eyes from Rob to the target. My arrow had hit the center, splitting Rob's arrow in two.

I threw my hands into the air, grinning at Rob. Then I turned to Gisborne and the Sheriff.

Gisborne bared his teeth. He called for the two soldiers who were just five steps from Rob. "Take him away. He's an outlaw, and a lucky shot doesn't change that."

"No!" I screamed. I had nothing to lose now. Keeping quiet didn't protect anyone. "He's not an outlaw. *I* shot that deer. The only reason you want him gone is because he's your brother. For those who haven't recognized him, this man is Robin of Woodhurst, rightful heir of Woodhurst Manor." I turned to the Sheriff, prepared to get down on my knees and beg if it meant Rob would walk out of here, free. "Let him go, Sheriff. You promised you would."

Gisborne's mouth opened then shut.

I almost relaxed.

Then a man's voice rose over the hushed murmur of the crowd. I turned to see who was speaking, the voice coming from behind Rob.

"He might be Robin of Woodhurst," the man called to Gisborne. "But he is also Robin Hood."

I could have cried. We were so close. He was almost free, but here was Matthew—the coachman of Lady Sutherland's carriage—digging a deeper hole for us.

The crowd gasped and the air shifted subtly the same way it had in Eliza's room, like the cogs of a padlock slipping into place.

A flicker of hope lit Gisborne's eyes. "What proof do you have, sir?"

Matthew licked his lips. "I saw him, my lord. In the forest. I was driving Lady Sutherland's carriage when he robbed her of everything."

Gisborne nodded. His face was neutral, except the corners of his lips, which were trying not to turn up. "Are you quite certain this is the same man?"

Matthew nodded eagerly. Everyone was silent and straining to hear. "It was him all right. He removed his hood. He'd been attempting to woo Lady Sutherland and I think he was hoping to impress her with his looks. I could never forget those eyes."

Gisborne coughed into his hand, trying to hide his wide smile. *Bastard.* "It appears we *will* finish the day with a hanging, if only to make the forest a safe place once more." He indicated to the soldiers. "Take him away."

One of the soldiers grabbed Rob's arm and marched him to the side of the field.

No. This was not the way Rob's story ended.

I still had three arrows left, three shots to make my intentions clear. And now I'd hit the target I was plenty certain I could make the other shots I needed to make.

The soldier who'd taken hold of Rob had his back to me. I lined him up, firing before anyone thought to stop me. The arrow pierced his right buttock. The man screamed and let Rob go.

"Run!" I yelled.

"Lady Maud." The Sheriff's voice boomed over the shocked murmur of the crowd. "Put that bow down or you will find yourself in the very same place this criminal is destined."

I nocked my second-to-last arrow in the bow and turned toward Gisborne and the Sheriff. They ducked below the wooden railing. It seemed they now believed I could use a bow. Taking a long second to aim, I let the arrow fly. It cut through the air, hitting the rope holding the canopied awning above their heads. The awning fell, covering the entire gallery. The Sheriff, Gisborne and the nobles in their beautiful clothing would have to scramble out from under it.

I turned on the spot, searching for Rob, but he was already beside me. "Come on." He took my hand. "Let's go while we have the chance."

Gripping tightly to Rob with one hand and still holding the bow in the other, I followed him toward the crowd. They were tightly packed and I doubted we'd get far before Gisborne or the Sheriff recovered themselves, but at least we were trying.

We approached the wall of people, and the crowd parted. A narrow path appeared in front of us. People called to Rob, thanking him, trying to touch him, while we jogged between them. Behind us, the crowd closed again so no one could follow, and I let out a huge breath. We might get farther than I'd expected.

Rob dragged me across a field of long, dry grass, urging me to run faster. I couldn't in this beautiful dress. The excess material kept tripping me. But Rob's hand was strong, and each time I stumbled, he caught me. We reached the cover of the forest quicker than I thought possible, and without an arrow in either of our backs.

"Come on." He pulled at my hand as I started to slow. "We have to keep running. Not much farther."

I let him drag me along the rough and narrow trail, terrified I'd hear the surge of hoof beats gaining on us. Rob must have been worried about the same thing. Every few steps he looked over his shoulder. When I was certain I couldn't run another step, I spotted Miller, John and Tuck waiting ahead of us.

Miller and John each held the reins of a saddled horse, and the relief on their faces as we stopped in front of them was immeasurable.

"You did it." John shook his head in disbelief. "You actually got her out of there."

"It may have been the other way around, but if you want to give me the credit, I'll take it." Rob's tone was light through his puffing breath, and there was a smile on his face, but his shoulders were tight with tension. He turned to me. "Can you ride?"

I eyed the horses carefully. I *could* ride. I'd had lessons until I was eleven, when I'd fallen off my pony and broken my wrist. Did I enjoy riding? Not even a little bit. Although, I could see now that Dad had also made me take these lessons to prepare me for life in the twelfth century. I nodded.

He helped me onto the smaller of the horses, which was still far bigger than anything I'd ever ridden, and climbed on the other one as I arranged my dress around my legs. "Do I even want to know where you got these horses?"

John grinned. "Probably not. But after what you two have done today, I daresay stolen horses are the least of your worries." His face grew serious, eyebrows drawing together.

"Kings Cave." Rob looked between the three of them. "When it's safe."

They nodded, and Rob pulled on the reins of his horse, turning her away from Nottingham. I followed him along the trail.

"Stay safe. Both of you," Tuck called to our backs.

We rode fast. At least it seemed fast to someone who hadn't been on horseback for six years. I couldn't even look over my shoulder to see if we were being chased, I was so busy trying to hold on. But Rob did that for me, constantly checking behind us.

Finally, after what felt like hours, Rob slowed his horse and dismounted, leading her to a small stream to drink. Then he helped me down and did the same for my horse. His movements were steady, sure, and it was clear horses had been a big part of his old life, before Gisborne had tried to kill him.

"Did you get your coin back?" he asked, turning to face me.

I nodded, holding out my wrist and pulling back the wide sleeve to show him my coin hanging off the leather bracelet. He took it between his fingers, twisting it on the leather to look at both sides. "It's perfect for you," he said softly.

I raised my eyebrows. "Tarnished and with a hole in the middle?"

"Well, you do have a hole here." He touched the skin just above the bodice of my dress with the tips of his fingers. My entire body tingled. "You miss your brother."

I did. More than anything. "And my skin's a pale shade of green?" Better to joke than to think too much about the way his hand on my skin made my heart hammer.

He smiled and shook his head. "No. I just meant you have this protective layer around the outside of you, like your coin. Once you let people through it, what's underneath is more beautiful than anyone could imagine."

I looked at the ground as my cheeks flushed. Never in a million years could I be as eloquent as Rob. His words did as much to the speed of my heart as the touch of his hand had done.

"Thank you for saving me today," he said softly.

"Thank *you* for coming to get me."

"Told you I would." He glanced over my shoulder, back the way we'd come, still checking for Gisborne.

"In my experience, when people promise something, they usually don't mean it."

His eyes rested on me, sending tingles over my skin. "Not me. I don't break promises."

"Neither do I." I watched his horse move to a patch of bright green grass and begin to nibble. "I'm just surprised."

I felt rather than saw the impish grin that settled on Rob's lips, and my cheeks reddened again. I already knew where this was going. "Surprised I came for you, or surprised you like that I came for you?"

"I feel like we've had this conversation before," I mumbled.

He gave a quiet laugh and glanced over my shoulder again. "And still you haven't answered the question."

"Both." My voice was whisper-soft. I loved that he'd cared enough to come for me, but of course, I was surprised. Nothing in my old life had suggested I was worthy of such a dangerous gesture. "Do we...do you...have a plan?" Chances of us getting away from all the soldiers Gisborne had at his disposal were minimal, even if we weren't currently traveling on the main trail.

He threw me a grin that talked straight to my heart. "Always, Lady Maryanne."

My name, my actual name, on his lips was like rain against a tin roof after a hot day. He'd said it only a handful of times before, and never like that. "Do you..." I almost didn't dare to ask. "Do you believe I'm not her?"

Rob's voice was soft like mine. "I've spent a lot of time these past couple of days thinking about who you might be and why you're here."

"And?" I didn't want to know. But I wanted to hear his answer more than anything.

"None of it makes sense. But I realized I don't care. I like you. Probably more than I should." He looked at his feet, before meeting my eyes. "If I can trust you, nothing else matters. Anyway, Maryanne suits you better than Maud."

"Thank you," I whispered. Rob trusted me. And he wanted to call me Maryanne. It was a gift better than any Christmas present I'd ever received.

As he watched me, the edges of his lips curled into a teasing smile that lit my insides. He moved closer, eyes on my lips. I knew what he was going to do.

Before he could say anything, do anything, I stepped away. "We can't, Rob. I should go back to my own time." I indicated between us "This wouldn't be fair." I should go back to my little brother who needed me so much. Yet, a part of me knew I could stay here and be happy.

"Just so you know, I'm fine with this." Rob copied my hand movement then leaned in and spoke softly. "No matter how long it lasts."

The timbre of his voice sent a shiver down my spine and his lips brushing my ear made me draw a deep breath. Before he even spoke, I knew he was smiling. "See, your mouth says one thing. But the rest of you says something completely different."

I leaned forward to whisper in his ear while trying to ignore the sunlight and wood smoke smell of him. "It's my lips you should believe. The rest of me is entirely unreliable."

He barked out a rough laugh, his breath warm on my cheek. "Are you sure about that?"

"Completely."

"Mmmm. Because it doesn't seem that way." This time, when his lips touched my ear as he spoke, I sighed. Loudly.

Then, somehow, I was kissing him. One minute there was air between us, then he was there, his lips on mine, soft but firm. I forgot to breathe, winding my arms around his neck and into his hair, pulling him closer. His body was hard, muscular, and having it pressed against mine was heaven. I sighed. Since the moment he'd first shown his brother his face to save me, I'd wanted this. I'd just been too scared to admit it.

He tilted his head, deepening our kiss, his tongue sliding into my mouth. I scraped my teeth along his tongue and a tiny sound escaped from the back of his throat.

He kissed my neck, his hands sliding over my back. They skimmed up the material of my dress, over my stomach, higher. Every place he touched felt like it was coming alive for the first time.

Rob pulled away, his breath ragged. I opened my eyes to find him blinking at me. He gave a sheepish grin. "That was possibly the worst timing ever. Can we...finish this discussion later, when we're not running from a hundred soldiers?"

I took a deep breath, attempting to regain my senses. "Discussion? Is that what you call it?"

His grin grew, but it didn't meet his eyes. "We should...get going."

He helped me on my horse, then climbed on his own. We started down the track with barely another word. I wasn't sure what to think. He wasn't angry. He wasn't upset. And he wasn't pretending that kiss had been a joke. There was something else going on.

"Where are we going?" I called to Rob, trying to fill the silence.

He slowed his horse and fell into pace beside me. "Where do you want to go, Maryanne? If you could choose, where would you be right now?" He glanced behind, worry etched onto his face, half hidden behind something else.

"Home." I'd said it by reflex, because it was what I'd focused on for the past month. Because I wanted it so much my heart ached. But there was something else I wanted equally as much. Someone. I hadn't allowed myself to consider it because Josh needed me.

I believed in Rob's cause now. I wanted to stay and help them fight for the poor. With Rob, John, Miller and even Tuck, I had a home, a family, people who cared about me and who I cared about just as much. It didn't matter how dangerous it was here, not if I was with them. And it especially didn't matter so long as I was with Rob.

But I couldn't voice any of the uncertainties that were filling my mind, because staying wouldn't be fair to Josh. He needed me. Or perhaps it was me who needed him.

Rob glanced at his hands. When he looked up again there was no hint of a smile, or anything that resembled happiness. "Then, even though taking you there means I won't ever see you again, and that's the last thing I want, that's where I'll take you." He kicked his horse forward. "The Big Tree, right?"

Twenty-Five

"YOU can leave today, I think." Rob shrugged. "I felt it. When Lady Sutherland's coachman told everyone I was Robin Hood, something moved through the tournament field. It was like an invisible wind shifting through the trees and it stopped in front of you." He shrugged. "Don't ask me how I know, because I couldn't tell you, but I know it was something to do with you going back to your time." His voice was flat.

In the clearing beside the Big Tree, a cold blast of wind blew over me. The same chill had been in the air before I traveled to this time. He was right. The full moon that had just risen had opened the portal home.

"I think so, too." My task was complete. Everyone knew about Robin Hood now. Hundreds of people had seen him today. The legend was safe. "Thank you. For bringing me here." It seemed so inadequate. To thank him.

He nodded, staring at his hands and not moving to climb off his horse.

I wanted to say more. Explain how much his friendship meant. But the words wouldn't form, and the longer I sat on my horse watching him, the stronger the pull to stay became. When I cleared my throat and he refused to look at me, I slid silently down to the ground and pushed through the bracken toward the tree.

I was almost breathless with the anticipation of seeing Josh, of feeling his weight in my arms as I picked him up and swung him around, of kissing his cheek. But my heart was heavy as well. I'd never see Rob again.

I wanted to stay but needed to leave.

Tabitha wasn't here so I knocked on the tree trunk. She didn't appear. I glanced at Rob, feeling less certain than I had a moment ago. He watched me silently from the back of his horse, then ran one hand down his face. He was doing a good job of hiding it, but I thought perhaps he was sad, too.

I held his eyes and drank in his beautiful face for the final time.

Suddenly, Rob stiffened, jumped from his horse and unsheathed his sword. Before it was fully drawn, Gisborne was in front of him, his own sword flashing in the moonlight.

"No!" My scream ripped the forest apart.

As Gisborne's sword swung down toward Rob's neck, arms wrapped around me from behind pushing until I hit the ground, my face grinding into the mud.

Eliza Thatcher leaned over me, her mouth beside my ear, deep and unreasonably calm. "It seems you left something out when you told me about your memories returning, Lady Maud."

I'd never promised to share anything with her, other than the message from her sister. "Get off me!" I tried to push up on my hands. I needed to see Rob, make sure he was okay. She was tiny, I should be able to throw her off my back. But she was stronger than a man, and I could barely move.

"Oh, I will. Once Gisborne's dealt with his brother and I'm certain he can't do anything that will stop you bringing my sister here tonight."

My mind was still replaying the way Gisborne's sword glinted as it sliced through the air toward Rob's neck, still hearing the first clash as their blades met. I was going to call Tabitha anyway. Might as well make sure Rob was safe first. "Tell Gisborne to stop. Then I'll call Tabitha."

Her weight shifted as she looked at the two of them. The metallic clang of swords filled the forest. At least Rob was still fighting.

Eliza leaned forward again. "I don't think you're in any position to bargain, my lady," she whispered. The sharp point of her dagger touched my neck just hard enough to graze my skin.

I hissed in a breath, jerking back. "Fine. Kill me. But if I'm dead, you won't see her."

"Perhaps." She ran the tip lightly up my neck, laughing when I gasped. "Perhaps not." She rose, leaning down to keep the dagger near my throat. "Get up."

I threw Rob a quick glance. His and Gisborne's swords were locked together as they taunted each other with words I couldn't hear above the blood rushing in my ears.

Eliza stared pointedly between the tree and her dagger. Her meaning was clear. She'd kill me if I didn't call Tabitha.

With one eye on Rob, I knocked on the trunk in the same sequence Dad had used. *Tap, tap-tap, tap, tap.* Nothing.

Eliza moved a menacing step closer and I tried again. Still nothing.

I didn't understand. I thought I'd felt the magic fall into place when I got my coin back, and again today at the tournament. It was full moon and the air was icy. Everything felt right. Tabitha should come when I knocked.

"Do it." The blade of Eliza's dagger gleamed in the moonlight.

"I will. Just...don't rush me." Metal crashing against metal rang out behind us again. Rob blocked Gisborne's blow before swinging at him, only to have his own blade blocked.

Eliza cleared her throat, drawing my eyes away from the fight. I tapped on the tree again. Nothing. I moved and tapped again, trying to ignore the glinting blade so close to my throat.

"Tabitha!" I yelled her name, tapping the tree again and again, just like I had the day Rob brought me here. It didn't make sense. I was so close, but so, so far away.

Blades clashed again and someone roared. I turned to see Gisborne lying on his back, his eyes round in the moonlight as Rob stood over him, sword raised.

Eliza screamed and dropped the dagger. She sprinted toward Gisborne.

Kill him. Like a command I had no control over, the words rose inside me, but I swallowed them back like ash in my throat. I wouldn't tell Rob to end his brother's life. That was a decision for him, and him alone.

An icy wind blew over me, the magic of the tree showing me what I hadn't seen myself.

Avenge Avery Woodhurst's death for me, Maryanne. Take any opportunity you get. Two sentences that had disappeared from my memory until yesterday. And they hadn't made complete sense until right now. No wonder I hadn't been able to return home. Simply making Rob into Robin Hood was never enough to do it. Dad wasn't just looking out for the son of his friend, he also wanted to even the score. He couldn't kill Avery Woodhurst's killer; Jerimiah Woodhurst was already dead. Instead, he wanted the son of his friend's killer dead.

He wanted Gisborne dead.

For me to be released back to my own time, Rob must kill Gisborne.

But what would I be going back to? A father who didn't care enough about me to listen when I told him I didn't want to come here? A man who would ask for a person's life as the price to bring me home?

"Please," Gisborne's voice wobbled. "Would you kill your brother?"

Rob's mouth was twisted with hatred, his sword hovering above Gisborne's neck. But as Gisborne spoke, something loosened on Rob's face. The hate was still there, but perhaps he'd remembered there was a little piece of his mother at his feet. I could never ask him to kill his brother just so I could go home. I would never do it.

Rob pulled back his sword. "Go," he said, between gritted teeth. "Get out of here, brother, and don't come back. I won't spare your life a second time."

Gisborne clambered to his feet and scampered for the trees.

Rob watched him leave, then turned to me. "All right?" His face was pinched and drenched with sweat.

I nodded. I *was* all right. We both were. I placed my foot on Eliza's dagger. She'd stopped her run toward Gisborne and was now halfway between us both. "You should follow your cousin," I said softly. "I'm not calling Tabitha tonight." She hadn't come, and I didn't mind. I was staying, and I was fine with it.

Eliza's jaw jutted as if she was going to argue, then something on her face shifted. I followed her gaze over Rob's shoulder. And screamed.

Rob twisted around, his sword going up in time to block the blow Gisborne flung at him. The clashing of swords was so loud I could almost feel the jar of the impact reverberating through my body. Rob twisted, throwing Gisborne off balance. Then he drew back his sword and plunged it into Gisborne's gut.

Eliza screamed. And screamed again.

"Stop," Tabitha commanded, suddenly here. Her ebony hair was loose, flowing over her bare shoulders and down her back. The black dress she wore was short and strapless, paired with bare legs and a pair of black stiletto ankle boots. Today she looked like a woman from my own time.

I hadn't realized I was running. Running toward Gisborne, to Rob. But with Tabitha's command, I found myself turning to face her. Eliza turned, too.

"Tabitha," she whispered. "You're here."

Tabitha blinked, the effort of ignoring her sister weighing heavy on her face. She held her hand out to me. "Your tasks are complete."

I knew already. Rob had killed his brother and released me. Dad had his revenge. I had my ticket home.

"Tabitha?" Two fat tears slid down Eliza's cheeks. "Come on. Let's go."

Tabitha glanced from me to her sister. The likeness between them was stunning. If they hadn't been wearing different outfits, I couldn't have told them apart. "Go where, Liza?" Her voice was quiet, sad.

Eliza shook her head. "I don't know. Anywhere. Wherever you want. I'm not letting you out of my sight again."

Tabitha stepped toward Eliza, a slight frown lining her forehead. "Liza, you have to stop coming here."

Eliza scowled. "Well, yes. I won't need to come here if you're no longer here."

"Liza, listen to me. You must stop coming. Or it will be you stuck here as the Keeper of the Portal. Not me." Tabitha sounded stern.

"I just want you to be free." Her voice was small and sorrow filled.

Tabitha shook her head, her smile sad. "I know. And that's the problem. The Keeper can only be freed by one whose life is devoted to their biggest wish. Nessa, the witch before me wished for fame. I wished for a safer life for you."

Eliza's eyes lit. "Then I can save you. My biggest wish is that you're no longer trapped here. And I'd do anything to make that happen."

Tabitha sighed. "I know, Liza. But there must always be a Keeper."

"But—"

Tabitha was in front of Eliza in the blink of an eye. She gripped hold of her sister's shoulder's, shaking her. "Think about it, Liza. If you free me, who will be the Keeper? Who will send travelers through time?"

"Maybe there doesn't need to be one. I wasn't the Keeper, but I still sent Maud Fitzwalter away." She was pleading with Tabitha, her voice growing higher pitched with every word.

Tabitha shook her head. "You didn't send her away. I needed you to leave so you didn't free me and end up stuck here yourself. If you'd had enough gold in your pocket to pay the tithe that night, or tonight for that matter, you wouldn't have walked away from here. I wanted to scare you into never coming back. So, I sent Maud away and left you to deal with the fallout." A tear slid down Tabitha's face. I almost felt sorry for her. Except I blamed her for ripping me from my life almost as much as I blamed Dad. I wasn't quite ready to forgive her yet.

Tabitha straightened her back and wiped her face. "But don't worry. All I needed to ensure you lived a safe and secure life was gold. Every person that travels through time pays me gold as a tithe. When I get out of here, Liza, we'll be so rich. There'll be nothing we can't buy." Her voice shook. "But if you get stuck here, you won't receive a tithe. Because your greatest wish would already have been granted."

"You'd be free." Eliza's voice was flat and emotionless. She understood.

"It's not so bad, Liza. One day soon another will take my place. Until then, you can't come here." Tabitha closed her eyes and slowly turned to me. Shaking off her sorrow, she raised her eyebrows. Her voice slipped back to the measured almost regal tone I'd heard from her before. "Ready to go home?"

I shook my head. I'd changed my mind before she arrived.

If I left, this would all be a dream. I'd never again see Sherwood Forest so thick with flora and fauna. I'd never see John or Miller, or even Tuck again. And I'd never find out if I was part of Rob's legend. If I was his Marian.

Tabitha held a hand out to me. "Let's go."

I shook my head.

But.

Josh was just a few steps away. I could see his grinning face when I closed my eyes. Maybe Dad would be pleased enough with me to start talking to me again once I went back. But no matter what I'd done in the twelfth century, it couldn't erase what I'd done to my baby brother, so probably not.

A cold breeze settled around me, bringing Dad's voice and the words he'd said as I left. *Use the skills I've given you and make a legend.*

Eliza stepped toward her, and Tabitha stiffened. "Liza," she warned, holding up a hand for her to stop. Then she looked at me, no longer seeming content to draw this out. "Your family believes you have a different future to the one you see for yourself." She flicked her wrist and Dad's voice carried to me on the cold wind. *Make yourself a legend, too.*

She was toying with me. Dad hadn't said that.

Another flick of her wrist and I heard Josh. *Maryanne. Come home. I miss you.*

Make yourself a legend.

Come home.

I pushed their voices away. They were confusing me.

I'd already made a decision.

I just couldn't recall what it was.

I was supposed to go home, wasn't I? Or was I supposed to stay here? In Sherwood Forest. I couldn't remember. Didn't know what I'd decided.

"Maryanne." Rob's voice broke through the fog in my brain.

I turned to him, feeling like I was stepping out of a dream. He'd been…he'd been fighting with Gisborne, but it felt like so long ago, like I'd forgotten he was here. The open portal had been the only thing on my mind. Until I'd heard his voice. "You're okay." I could only breathe the words. I ran my eyes over him, searching for blood or anything that meant Gisborne had hurt him, but he seemed fine.

He grinned, but it didn't reach his eyes. I wished it had. "Of course. I'm the best swordsman in this forest."

"Modest, too."

His smile grew, then disappeared. He held out a hand. "I just want you to know you have options. If you need them."

Behind me, Tabitha cleared her throat.

In that moment, I felt the heartbreak Josh would feel if I didn't come home so keenly it brought tears to my eyes, and I doubled over. He'd miss me as much as I'd miss him. But Mom would comfort him. She'd wipe his tears away, build up his self-esteem. Love him.

If I went home, *I* wouldn't be all right. For years, I'd died a little more each day. I hadn't tried to make myself get over the accident, hadn't believed I was worth it, but then, neither had anyone else. Until Rob. To him, I was important. This was where I belonged. This was where I would stay. As for whether I was Rob's Lady Marian, well, time would tell.

A gust of icy wind kicked up the leaves around me as I started toward Rob. But each step took me farther from him, the open portal pulling me toward my old life.

"You called me here," Tabitha said. "You tapped on the tree. You must leave."

I had. But that was before I'd decided to stay. Now I'd made the choice, it was all I wanted. No one was going to force me into that portal a second time.

I dropped to my knees. If the gateway pulled at me when I was on my feet, then I'd sit on the ground and wait for the pull and the icy chill to disappear.

Rob took a tentative step in my direction, his eyes confused. Then he was gone, and Tabitha was directly in front of me, her forefinger raised as she reached out to me.

I screamed. "No!" She couldn't touch me. That had been the final thing she'd done before I came here. If her touch was the last thing required, then it would send me home. Forever.

"Please, Tabitha. No!" I shook my head, unsure if she even heard my screams. She gave no response. "Don't touch me. Please don't touch me." Tears streamed down my cheeks as I begged, the same way I'd begged her not to send me here.

I fumbled at my wrist until my fingers closed around the coin. My link to my family. My tether to my time. I just had to throw it away. Then Tabitha couldn't force me to leave.

I couldn't get it off, the tie was stuck.

Tabitha came at me, one finger outstretched.

"No! Please!"

She took another step. "Too late, Maryanne. Time to go."

I shook my head. I didn't want this. I'd made my decision.

She reached for me.

I couldn't move. The portal had trapped me.

I closed my eyes.

And Tabitha sent me home.

Get the Sherwood Outlaws Prequel Novella for Free

Thanks for reading Outlawed.

I really enjoy getting to know my readers, it's one of the best things about being a writer. I send a newsletter to my readers group once a month, and that group is the first to find out about new releases and special offers.

If you sign up to my readers group, I'll send you a copy of Outcast for free. Outcast is a novella narrated by Rob, set before he met Maryanne. And my readers group is the only place it's available.

Just use the link below, then complete your email address. I'm looking forward to meeting you.

www.hayleyosborn.com/outcast

Enjoy this Book?

You can make a difference.

Honest reviews are an important part of a book's success as they help new readers discover new stories to enjoy. They are the most powerful thing for getting attention for my books.

If you enjoyed this book, I'd be forever grateful if you could take five minutes to leave a review on the book's Amazon page—it can be as short as you like.

Thank you!

ALSO BY HAYLEY OSBORN

The Sherwood Outlaws story continues:

Outplayed
Outlasted

Go to www.hayleyosborn.com to find out more.

Acknowledgments

I've loved the Robin Hood legend since I was a child. I started writing this story back in 2016, and it's been through numerous changes since that first draft. I've really enjoyed bringing this story to life, and I hope you've enjoyed reading it just as much.

First up, thanks to Melissa for your editing insights. You were exactly what this book needed, and it's better because of your thoughts, suggestions and encouragement. And thanks to Patrick for doing the final proofread.

Thanks to Daqri for the covers you made for me. I love them—there's nothing more I can say.

I want to give a shout out to everyone on the OPWFT thread at AW. I've made some amazing friends there—Annette, Jill, Eva plus many others who've read some of the different drafts Outlawed has gone through. Your help has made this book better than it might have been.

Thanks always to Kat Seelig who has read Outlawed twice, and talked over changes with me too many times to count. Thanks especially for reading this series in such a short time frame, meaning you've had to put aside your own work to do it. I can't thank you enough—now get back to your writing!

Finally, thanks to my family. To Mum and Dad for always supporting what I do, and for being the best cheerleaders for my work. To Kelly, for always loving what I write. To Hayden for believing in me. And to Jacob, Ashleigh and Zach, for putting up with a Mum who has been permanently attached to a laptop these past few months. I love you all.

About the Author

Hayley Osborn lives in Christchurch, New Zealand, with her husband and three children, cat and dog.

Online, you can find her at: www.hayleyosborn.com.

To connect with her on social media, you can find her on Facebook at HayleyOsbornAuthor, or on Twitter at @Hayley_Osborn. Or if you prefer to make contact via email, you can contact her at hayley@hayleyosborn.com.

Made in the USA
Las Vegas, NV
09 December 2021